ELEPHANTS
IN BLOOM

Polestars

ELEPHANTS IN BLOOM

POLESTARS 5

Cécile Cristofari

NewCon Press
England

First edition, published in the UK January 2024
by NewCon Press
41 Wheatsheaf Road, Alconbury Weston, Cambs, PE28 4LF, UK

NCP318 (hardback)
NCP319 (softback)

10 9 8 7 6 5 4 3 2 1

Cover Art by Enrique Meseguer; cover design by Ian Whates
Editing and typesetting by Ian Whates

Contents

In memory of Marc Sarraud, who made music a part of my life, nurtured my love of stories, and sowed kindness in every place he could reach.

Introduction

Years ago, the peri-urban village where I grew up experienced a sudden invasion of poplar trees.

There was water in the ground, a thin stream that ran down from the hill and resurfaced here and there along its course. As a result, although pines would have been the first species to colonise an unsuspecting garden in most other places, poplars decided to try their luck in our neighbourhood, rich in water and loam.

Poplars live fast, and often die young. In a few years they can shoot for the stars, overshadowing houses and anchoring themselves with sturdy roots. Though my family had never invited them in, we received them gladly, and within a couple of years, the poplar tree at the back of the garden had become a favourite spot to play hide-and-seek.

The reception the trees got from our neighbour was not so warm. This particular garden was a tidy one, carefully planted with noble species, olive trees and oleanders and trimmed hedges. Weeds were not welcome, and as for a tree wandering there uninvited, with its shade and leaves and meandering roots – that simply would not do. In the time it took to take note of the intruder and fetch a saw, the poplar tree was gone.

I mourned a little and grumbled for a time. I didn't know what was to come. Neither did my neighbour.

Some stars burn so bright that after a few million years they exhaust themselves in a burst of energy, unimaginably potent. It is their end, a death so spectacular some have been recorded in astronomical annals as a new star shining bright in the sky.

It is, also, their unwitting way of dispersing spores of star-spawn. In the nebulae that emerge out of the remnants of supernovae, new stars are born, and the universe can go on.

*

The destruction of the poplar tree was a supernova all of its own.

The emptiness was glaring at first. Then the roots stirred, and got to work. In the years that followed, a new nebula of poplar saplings was born in our garden, right across the fence from our neighbour.

You can erase a tree, but not its presence in the ground. Right next to the place where a single tree was killed, there is even now a thriving coppice, home to birds and cats and tendrils of ivy. Its shade makes the house darker and its leaves moulder on the ground all winter long. It is messy. It came unasked for. It is very much loved.

There is nothing beautiful or romantic about the apocalypse. Grand statements about the end of the world only hide the fact that worlds end every day by the thousands, in every death, in every destroyed home of every living thing, human or not. Survivalist dreams of a barren land inhabited only by the bravest, nastiest and fittest specimens of humankind are a pitiful fantasy when confronted to the reality of what the end truly means: an accumulation of anonymous tragedies, many of them avoidable, most of them sinking into darkness as soon as they happen, because they lack the power to sear the universe with a last, dramatic flare. Dreams of rebirth are a necessity. They are also, sometimes, a lure, a lull to soothe the mind rather than mend the world.

Stories are dreams. Some of these stories will be sad, by necessity; there will be grief, and loss, and change too fast to understand. There will be joy, too; not to lure, not to lull, but simply, I hope, to *look*. To see how much is not lost yet. How much we could still pass on, if we ditch carelessness once and for all: life and love and the richness of an entire world, damaged treasures, but treasures nonetheless.

— Cécile Cristofari
April 2023

All We Ever Look For

When I opened the window this morning, three parrots were perched in a tree hanging over a deserted beach of pure white sand that stretched towards a dazzling horizon. I'd never seen anything so lovely. I leaned out, just enough to feel the caress of the breeze, the salty coolness of the surf that helped me brace myself for the day ahead. Not long after closing the window, I opened the front door and stepped out into the rumble of traffic and the dappled shadow of a maple, breathing in the damp heat of Québec summer.

The memory of that shore and gentle seaside wind stayed with me for the entire bus ride. It was gone now, I knew. What happened when I closed my window I could only guess; the wonders it let me glimpse vanished as soon as the latch clicked shut, and never came back. Now, watching my own world scroll past the bus, I wished I had left my window open a little longer.

When I reached the office, the two secretaries were talking about the latest missing person cases in town. I stared at them for longer than I should have. They waved, a little awkwardly.

My desk was in a corner of the office, out of sight, just under a mercifully powerful fan. I wiped my brow, and exchanged perfunctory greetings with my neighbours. I had never been good at making friends at the office. Neither was I cut out for the increasingly heavy heat waves these days, it seemed. I had another fleeting thought of how lovely and cool that beach had seemed.

From across the office, Marie-Ange interrupted my train of thought with a wave and a conspiratorial gesture, placing a folded piece of paper on the corner of her desk. I answered with an uncertain smile.

*

The heat had not abated when I returned home. I still held Marie-Ange's crumpled note in my fist. *Saturday?* it simply read. I had waited for her break to leave the office so I wouldn't have to respond.

I wondered if this was what guilt felt like.

I sat, or rather dropped, in the armchair facing the window, to scratch Toutou's ears as Tilou mewed in protest at being woken up. I stared at the maple billowing outside – when the window was closed it never showed anything but the maple outside the building, its branches stretched far and wide like a challenge to the concrete and cars and heat and fires and everything humans could throw at its kind. It was only when I opened it that the magic began.

I had never figured out how or why this treasure had fallen into my hands. I never heard reports of other portals opening elsewhere in the world, and the question of what I had done to deserve this one was never answered. One day I'd opened the window in my living room, hoping to get some fresh air while I read the news as usual with a cat peering over my shoulder – and instead of the customary drone of the street, I'd gazed over a cliff, snow-capped mountains dotting the horizon under an uncanny white sky. I'd banged the window shut in shock, only to open it again, seconds later. This time it was a desert, red sands stretching as far as I could see. The dance had begun then, opening and closing, never knowing what strangeness would lie beyond, only that it would be new, and odd, and marvellous – and that as soon as I closed the window, it would disappear forever.

At first I had sworn to myself that I would never let anyone else see it, but soon that had felt petty, and I'd begun to bring people in. The first few times, it had been simple, even made me a little proud for the first time in years. An act of sharing and compassion, inviting unhappy acquaintances to sit with me and gaze at the wonders beyond my window before walking back home with a lighter heart. They must have thought it was nothing more than a clever display; so had I, initially, and so did most people until the very last second. The truth was too extraordinary to entertain.

The first time someone asked to step through, I had only gaped. The possibility had never occurred to me. Her name was Angélique,

I recall, and she was a widow, just about my age, with an estranged son. Two days after I'd agreed to her request (it hadn't occurred to me that I might do otherwise), I'd watched her step over the window ledge and on the grassy slope of a mountain meadow. She'd secured her backpack and blown me a kiss, and only when the window pane clicked shut had I fully realised that the door to her world was now gone, and she would never be able to come out again.

After Angélique, there were others. I had a knack for light friendships, the seemingly shallow ones, acquaintances that would not disturb the quiet of my home. They almost always started in the same way: an exchange of glances on the bus or a café, a smile, a few minutes of conversation that usually led to a farewell, after a moment of companionship I'd enjoy but wouldn't miss. And then sometimes the conversation lasted longer, until I sensed that sadness, that longing I'd come to know so well, until I realised that I held the key to the one thing these people wanted.

It had been easy at first, watching them step through and waving farewell, sometimes wiping a little tear, telling myself I'd brought someone more happiness than anyone else ever could have. I only had to pretend that these people were just like me, lonely and stranded, with no one to miss them. It was only when the first missing person reports came up in the newspaper that I had to face the facts. There are many ways to be lonely, and not all of them are irreparable.

"How did you pick such a silly auntie?" I asked Tilou out loud. She rubbed her head against my cheek.

I petted her and stared ahead until, as always happened after sitting alone with my thoughts for too long, I felt compelled to get up. After some hesitation, I opened the window.

Outside, a deep rainforest was alive with whistles and fluted sounds, the songs of birds and beasts I had no name for. I leaned out and closed my eyes as the mist from a waterfall cooled my face, spraying scents of moss and orchids. My smile slowly returned, and for a very long time I stood there, trying to catch sight of monkeys or tree frogs behind every rustling leaf.

My cats, the only companions I had, would be just as happy with any other owner, I suddenly thought. I would miss them for a while, but it would be simple to make sure they spent the rest of their lives in a home that would be just as good as mine. There was nothing holding me here. The notion was unexpectedly comforting. My life was my own. Whatever I chose to do with it, however foolhardy, I would not hurt anyone else. One day, I decided, I would go too. But today was not the right time; I was out of cat food, and anyway, I was already too weary of the summer heat to enjoy a rainforest for long.

As always, eventually, I closed the window, and I could hear once again the endless drone of the cars in the street, as clouds gathered overhead for the evening storm.

Wednesday morning sailed by in its customary haze of boredom, until a shadow loomed at the edge of my desk.

"Got time for a sandwich?"

I jumped, startled from yet another reverie. Marie-Ange was standing in front of me, her bag already slung over her shoulder. "Come on. The falafel ones. You know you love those."

My eyes darted around my desk for an excuse not to go out. The blank file staring at me from the computer screen was enough of an answer. The prospect of going out was not that unappealing, come to think of it. I got up, groaned when my back protested, and stayed in place just long enough for Marie-Ange to drag me by the arm, waving to everybody who remained in the office.

The space outside the building was not a particularly scenic one: a large car park with a few maples and a couple of grassy banks on the side, where we sat in what shade we could find. Marie-Ange finished her salad in a couple of bites, then sprawled in the grass on her back, grinning.

"Look at how gorgeous that tree is," she said.

I smiled. In truth, it wasn't much of a tree, just a sapling they'd replanted as a token gesture after they'd razed the field to make way for cars. But Marie-Ange's enthusiasm never deserted her. No one else would have convinced me, for the third time this week, to take a break and breathe the outside air when I could instead have got rid of my work and ridden back home half an hour earlier. It still surprised me, sometimes, that she not only talked me into it, but made me *want* to do it. Now that I looked at the sunlight splintering through the maple leaves, I, too, began to see some beauty in that gracile, tenacious little tree.

Marie-Ange propped herself up on her elbow.

"So. About Saturday."

My heart sank at once.

"Saturday?"

"You promised you'd show me. Remember?"

I did, very well. It had happened at the start of summer, on a day when Marie-Ange had decided to drag me out of the city for ice cream after work. I'd grumbled and wondered why she would bother with me. But as we drove across the bridge to Orleans Island, she'd pointed to the waterfall on the other side of the channel and started gushing in the way she sometimes did about the most mundane little things, and I'd felt something unexpected – a flicker of girlish delight, the simple pleasure of feeling the damp heat on my face and the smells of the blooming forest stretching in front of us. It was a long time since I'd felt that way outside of my living room. And then I'd felt something even stronger: gratitude, pure joy at being with someone who would so casually offer this sense of wonder to me.

I'd wanted to offer something else in return. I had told her about the one thing I'd ever had that mattered. And now I wished I hadn't.

"All right,' I muttered. 'Just one look. Don't tell anyone about it, okay?"

She agreed, still grinning. It was time to go back to work. On the way back in, she changed the subject, and my mood lightened. If she thought I was only going to show her an amusing trick, so much the better.

On the bus ride back home, someone was reading the headlines out loud, and the lady behind her burst into tears. Her friend comforted her, saying something about the uplifting notes all these people had left, that they couldn't have been taken by force or ended up in a bad place. I swallowed and moved to the back of the bus.

Québec City officials overwhelmed by missing persons epidemic, I read on my phone later in the night. Three more in a month. A secret cult, underground experiments, theories were blooming all over the place. I shoved the device back in my pocket.

Missing persons epidemic, indeed, I thought to myself, as if facing a crowd of haunted relatives demanding justice. What if I told you that they wanted to go? That they made this decision by themselves, knowing fully well what it would do to you? Would you blame me?

I stopped as I realised that I was starting to mouth the words out loud. From their place on the sofa, Toutou and Tilou were gazing at me, green eyes and yellow eyes indolently blinking in a pool of sunlight. I had been living on my own for too long.

I leaned out of the window one last time before going to bed, to breathe in the smell of salty wind. Tilou had jumped off the sofa and, with a soft thud, landed on the sill; she didn't complain when I gently picked her off and held her against my chest so she could watch safely. A marble balcony hung over a rocky coast with pines and aloes tumbling into the sea. Underneath, the waters shimmered, light and deep blue interlocking towards the horizon. A fish leapt up below me, sending a flash of silver over the water. When a seagull dove, missed and flew back up with a cry of frustration, Tilou tensed, and at last wriggled free and strolled back to the sofa, all interest in other universes gone. I watched the bird until it disappeared over a clump of dark green trees, knowing that I could follow it if I wanted to. I thought once more of all those who had gone through, of the felicity they had seized for themselves, the mourning they had left behind.

Then I thought of Marie-Ange. It had been an imprudent idea to invite her. But it would turn out fine, I hoped. She would understand that this absolutely needed to remain a secret. And she would only take a look. She, at least, was perfectly happy with the world she lived in. Perhaps she could even come back, I mused, and we could stand in front of the window together, bet on what we would see that day, count to three, open it…

Maybe that was what friendship felt like. I smiled, closed the window, and went to bed next to a comfortably snoring cat.

On Friday, Marie-Ange dragged me out for lunch again. We chatted (or she did, while I smiled and nodded) all through the way to the fast food joint. When we sat down in the grass, however, her expression suddenly changed.

"I'm going to ask you something really outlandish. You can laugh at me if you want, but promise me you'll tell me the truth. All right?"

There was nothing I could do but swallow my dismay and acquiesce.

"I saw those missing persons report on the news," she went on. "This is absurd. Québec City is as safe as it's always been. These… other worlds you said your window opened to. People haven't actually *gone in* there, have they?"

"Please don't tell anyone," I blurted out.

She opened her mouth. Covered it with her hand. For a few moments, she seemed halfway between laughter and tears, long enough for me to hope that it would be the former. I could handle being dismissed as a cat lady with one too many quirks. But if she started to accuse, threatened to denounce me…

"I need to see it," she said.

I breathed deeply.

"Yes. Of course. Just see it. Swear to me you won't tell anyone?"

"Not a chance. Don't worry."

"Thank you.' I realised that I held my hands balled tight against my stomach. I unclenched them and spread them on my knees. 'These people wanted to go, you know. It's not a decision they rushed into. I wouldn't have let them if they hadn't wanted it so badly."

"I know."

"I suppose it can't look good when you read the papers. But it won't happen again. I've been thinking about it lately. I'm going to quit. The only ones who knew about my portal are gone, and I'll keep it to myself now. And you, of course. Nobody's going to disappear again."

Marie-Ange made a strange face and touched my arm.

"I want to go," she said.

That evening, for the first time, I opened my living-room window with no anticipatory thrill, only through the force of habit.

Through the entire day Marie-Ange's words had bounced around in my head, as if trapped in a vertiginous echo chamber – *I want to go* – along with my next, foolish question – *Why?* – as if asking her to explain herself would make her realise that there was no good reason for such a wish after all. Her explanations, however, had left me no space to argue.

The world was too small a place, more so with every passing day. I'd admired her ability to light up at every little joy life could throw her way, so much that I hadn't noticed how tired she was that small blessings were all our world had to offer her.

Or perhaps it was simply that I was incapable of imagining how she felt. I could not recall the last time I had felt genuine delight outside of my living-room. How the person who had communicated that wonder to me could be unsatisfied with the world she lived in was unfathomable.

My thoughts ebbed as the landscape before me came into focus. Pillars of crystal in a translucent sea reflected the light of the setting sun into my living room. I stood there for long minutes, unable to take my eyes off the twin moons overhead.

How could the universe have decided that I would be the best person to entrust this portal to, of all the places it could have appeared? There was no answer but the gentle song of the water lapping, flowing towards a horizon that seemed to curve more sharply than the one at the end of an earthly sea. I rested my hand on the sill. If I leaned out, only a little, perhaps I could touch the closest pillar. What would greet me out there – the thin air and cold of a mountain pass, or inviting warmth like the tropics at the dawn of time? I stood on tiptoe, reached forward. The breeze of another world stroked my fingers, like a hand, urging me forward with infinite gentleness. If I left now, there would be no more guilt, no more worry. One step out was all it would take...

I pulled my arm back, closed the window, my heart beating faster than it should have. Tomorrow, I would call Marie-Ange and tell her I couldn't let her through. She would understand, I was certain of it. And then I'd never open that window again.

I came home late the next day, exhausted by my Saturday chores and the constant drone of the city, but with renewed resolve to make the phone call I needed to end this.

The day had slipped by so frantically I'd forgotten to check the time.

As soon as I took out my phone, the bell rang. When I opened the door, a flustered Marie-Ange dropped her huge backpack on my feet. After a second of shock, I swore in silence. As usual, I had let time carry me along, not taking action until the last moment.

I made her sit down and have a glass of water.

"I drank on my way. Can I go now?" she said. Then with a nervous giggle, "If I don't I'm going to have second thoughts!"

I pushed the glass in front of her.

"We're not doing this, Marie-Ange," I blurted out.

She opened her eyes wide. My voice shook, but for once I could find the words, and didn't let her speak.

"Maybe it sounds like this is what you need, but it's wrong. I can't keep this up. You'll end up who knows where, in a parallel universe where you could die tomorrow, and no one would ever know. Ever. My window has never opened twice on the same place. Your family will be shattered, and if I meet them face to face, I won't even be able to tell them you're all right. Because I won't know that. I'm sorry. And your family won't be the only ones. I..."

The cascading words dried up then. How I felt about her departure was my own concern. I couldn't expect her to alter her decision on my account, shouldn't even think of asking. I stood, silent, expecting her to make a fuss. But she nodded as if she understood.

"No matter what I tell them, people will be upset," she said. "They'll have to understand. This is what I need."

"Why?"

But I realised that I knew already. Loneliness was not the only force that drove people to seek what lay beyond my window. Her yearning for a new world matched my own, almost exactly. She only had one thing I lacked: enough courage to plunge into the unknown, while I remained trapped here, between marvellous worlds I would never know and one I still had to figure out.

Out of kindness, perhaps, Marie-Ange only smiled, and if she had guessed what I was thinking, she kept it quiet.

"Can I ask you something?" she said as if I hadn't spoken.

I leaned back. Not everyone asked *that* question, but I'd got it often enough, with varying degrees of awe, condescension or repulsion. Marie-Ange merely sounded curious.

"Why do this so far? Why help so many people?"

"*Help* truly isn't the word you want," I replied.

Thoughts of the weeping lady on the bus – someone's mother? Or friend? I'd never know – came unbidden. It had felt like the right thing to do at the time. Yet all I could witness now was people hurting; I would never know how the people I had 'helped' had fared, nor even if they were still alive.

"It seemed wrong to have a magic portal in your home and not use it for something..." I wanted to say 'good', but the word sank in my throat. "...special," I said.

But that was not all it had been. All these times I had let someone through, a little piece of me had gone with them as well. At times, when I gazed aimlessly out of the office window, the cityscape blurred into their faces, disbelieving, then ecstatic as soon as they stepped into another world. If I was so pleased to have given them a new life, it was also, perhaps, because I'd never been brave enough to seize that opportunity for myself, and had made do with vicarious glimpses instead.

And after each glimpse I would drop into the deep crease at the centre of my sofa and scratch my cats behind the ears as I'd done every day for the last couple of decades. I shook my head. Suddenly I was finding it hard to breathe.

"It was the only thing I had to offer, on some days the one thing that made me want to get out of bed. Sometimes I think that might be why it was given to me. Without it, I might as well stop pretending I even exist."

I laughed: a silly, croaking sound. How human of me, to balk at facing my own selfishness and instead look for explanations, a message to me from the universe, while standing right next to the proof that the universe was even bigger and more incomprehensible than anyone suspected. I expected Marie-Ange to stare at me with that uncomfortable pity people sometimes exhibited when they realised how long I had been living on my own. Instead she smiled and squeezed my arm.

"Maybe we don't know why you have it, but it's yours all the same," she said. "It's your decision." She bit her lips. "Could you open the window now? Just let me take a look. I promise that's all I want."

I almost refused her. I already knew how this would end. But the yearning in her voice was so strong that I gave in. Just the view – I couldn't deny her that.

"One look and I'll close it," I said, pulling the latch.

A meadow teeming with butterflies came in full view. Reds, gold and blues flashed in swaying grass under a gentle breeze, a ballet of breathtaking beauty. Far ahead, a few hills swelled, soft purple against the cloudless sky. I'd seen many wonders through this window. A tear still warmed up my eye, with the familiar thought... why shouldn't I step through this time, and leave this world at last?

I glanced at Marie-Ange. Her hand was still on her backpack, bursting, I knew, with everything one would need to fight the direst odds in the wilderness. She was more than ready, perfectly confident. Yet right now she only stood still, staring with the longing of a starved woman.

"Let me go," she pleaded. "Then you can quit. Please."

"What if there's no food out there? No clean water, no..."

"And what is there for me here? Work overtime, buy a bigger car and wait until global warming gets me while I pretend to be happy? I'll take my chances. Please."

I closed my eyes. I couldn't hurt another family. I couldn't read Marie-Ange's name in the news and pretend to know nothing. I couldn't risk letting her throw her life away in a universe she had only ever watched from afar, through the window in her friend's living-room.

I didn't want her to go. But this was not – had never been – my decision to make.

"I can't stop you, can I?" I muttered. I turned away, leaving the window open.

Marie-Ange squealed and kissed me on the cheek.

"I'll never forget what you did for me," she said.

She squeezed my hands one last time. For a moment I entertained the wild, terrifying hope that she would ask me to go with her. But she didn't, and once a brief pang of mingled relief and disappointment had erupted and withered in me, I knew better than to ask. I had been her friend, for a while, but I'd needed her more than she'd ever needed me. I was grateful that I hadn't been invisible to her, but couldn't delude myself about the place I truly held in her life, even more so now that she was claiming that life back, seizing her chance to chase dreams of freedom that were hers and hers alone. This was her world now, not mine. She was strong, and ready, and I felt with absolute certainty that she would survive, and be happier than she could ever have been in this universe. All I could do for her was to let her go.

And then she stepped outside. I watched her as she took more and more confident steps in the tall grass, waved one last time, and I closed the window.

Later, there would be another missing person report. A family would be in shock, and it would be my fault, again. I had no idea what I would say to my colleagues in a few days, when word of Marie-Ange's disappearance reached us. This had to be the last time. I'd make a promise and stick to it.

And then, after a while, my eyes would meet the eyes of a stranger on the bus, catch on a hollowness mirroring the one within me – though I buried it as deeply as I could – and I would start thinking again of Marie-Ange dancing with butterflies. And Damien treading in the snow near a mighty river. And Christine swimming with catfish in the ruins of an ancient city. Then I would look outside at the droning cars and thick air and concrete roads stretching as far as I could see, and remember what they had fled from, and it would dawn on me again that just because I happened to live next to a magic portal did not make me arbiter of what anyone else chose to do with their life. And I would open my window again.

Someday, I would be unable to take my eyes off the wonders there, and a middle-aged cat lady living an eventless life near the Saint-Lawrence River would be reported missing, too.

But not today. I made tea and sat down to read the news on my phone, with a cat in my lap and my back to the window, listening for the wind from other worlds that whispered through the cracks in our own.

If you listen to Kate Bush's song "All We Ever Look For", you will first notice that the lyrics don't bear any relation to the story you've just read. Towards the end, however, you will hear the sound of a person walking across the floor, opening doors and windows, and listening to sounds from the outside, so different every time it seems that all the windows open on different universes. This is the seed this story grew from, just as several others in this book grew from music. Or in part, at least.

Once upon a time, there was a young woman whose favourite thing in the world was to write stories. Somehow, she ended up pursuing an academic career, which led her to a post-doctoral job in Québec City, where she filled her days with work and stopped writing altogether. It was a wonderful time, forming friendships she treasures to this day; it was also a miserable time, mired in homesickness and the sense that nothing had meaning any more, and on some nights the young woman dreamed of wings, ships, portals... any means of escape she could imagine.

So, come on in. Climb through, or take a peek and save it for future dreams. And may there always be a home waiting for you, wherever you are.

The Fishery

1.

The fishing boats crowded the jetty, nets overflowing with dead things from across the cosmos. The fishery opened at dawn, its great maw ready and ever-hungry. The cranes were ready to drop the day's load on the conveyor belts, food already, regardless of its origins. Their world rarely fussed any more, as long as it could eat.

Orna hadn't bothered to be inconspicuous. Showing up unannounced was usually enough; incognito inspections were rarely received well, and she did not want to deal with more aggression than she had to. She was only doing her job, like everybody else here.

It had been more than a job, once. The thought of entire solar systems ripped apart, plundered for food that was more pleasure than necessity, like theirs had been, had filled her with anguish. She had become an environmental inspector because she was passionate about making sure that protected areas would thrive again, and because she deeply believed about doing this as law dictated. But there were scant supplies of anguish, belief or passion left now. They had been plucked, like everything else, emotions and sounds and light and dreams and *life*; harvested in increasingly industrial proportions, fed into industrial fisheries and packaged for easy consumption in supermarkets. Genuine feelings now had to be sought off-world, fished from increasingly remote areas of the universe and as often as not poached from protected areas, and she had long ago decided that if she could not source them ethically, she would not source them at all.

At least she still had her job.

The overseer of the factory was arguing with a boat captain about something. She walked in on her own. The conveyor belts droned, a sound that was no longer really sound to her ears, and she passed by workers in drab grey, some of whom nodded to her, while others went about their business as if she wasn't there. Nothing was out of the ordinary, which was a good sign. On days where there was anything exciting to process, she ended up either investigating where the catch had come from for the next few days, or confiscating it. Someone had to keep watch before the fisheries bled the universe dry.

She raised herself on the tip of her toes behind a line of workers. Nothing out of the ordinary, indeed. The boats had been combing the same areas of space they were allowed to sail in, and brought in the usual fare: debris, fragments of asteroids that had been roaming the void for aeons, a few anaemic rays of light here and there, some lithium that smelled like it had been projected into space in the explosion of a star too long ago to even remember if it had been near an inhabited world. A bit of primordial soup stranded on a drifting fragment was the closest the catch of the day had come to actual life. It was tiny, and she hoped that the workers wouldn't miss it, or deem it impossible to package and throw it away. She didn't point it out, however. They could do their job and she could do hers.

The overseer stormed in at last, mumbling. When his eyes fell on her, he scowled.

'This day keeps getting better,' he said.

'Good morning to you too,' she replied.

Without asking for his permission, she began to walk with him. He threw up his hands.

'Go right ahead,' he said, with something that could have sounded like anger. Probably synthetic, but supplements were getting popular these days. 'Who knows, maybe we're about to make a tiny bit of money? That would fuck your day right up, wouldn't it?'

She shook her head.

'You know I don't blame you,' she said. 'But I have a job to do. Last time someone checked here, you were processing a whole *summer*, Ary. A whole summer! You have to realise why that's wrong, don't you? That's an entire planet, dead of hunger so that people here could eat a single season. A few summer days would have been fine, but an entire –'

'Spare me the lecture. I know.'

Orna suspected that he didn't, not really. But at least he remembered how much they'd fined him, and that would have to suffice.

'Had to lay ten more people off last month,' he suddenly said.

She spread her hands.

'I'm sorry to hear it. But you know they would have been without a job not so long after that anyway, don't you? When the stocks run out, they run out.'

'And I hear those new protected areas are doing their job so well. Just let life recover for some time and it will leak out in the rest of the universe before you know it, they said.'

He waved at the conveyor belts. *See anything leaking here?* his gesture seemed to say. Orna didn't answer. She'd had this conversation with so many people, so many times.

Her inspection revealed nothing untoward. The factory made do with what it got, and as the overseer had pointed out, the stocks clearly weren't recovering as well as had been announced, and there was no way out in sight, either for the workers or for their depleted world.

She wondered if this was the sort of realisation one ought to feel something about. She wondered if she would have, once; and if she should start thinking about taking synthetic supplements, anger, maybe, or at least dedication. She shrugged the thought off.

This was only a job, after all.

2.

The fishing boats rounded the jetty, trawling their nets behind them like overgrown dead limbs. The fishery opened at dawn, or what still passed for dawn now that most of the light had been consumed. Cranes hauled the nets and poured their contents on conveyor belts, prized finds and by-catch alike. Their world could not afford to be choosy.

Jana put on her gloves and sorted the mess into vats. Bits of sunlight here, tainted after travelling unprotected through the galaxy. Meteors there. Today it was mostly asteroids, bits of tough rock that had never sailed close to a real planet; only sometimes, a glint showed through the dust, a fantasised meteor, or even the memory of a meteor, of the kind that still terrified worlds. These she carefully set aside. When she was young, many such pieces landed in the nets. They were packaged in individual boxes and sent to gourmet markets. Nowadays the boats had to fish far from uninhabited worlds, and the stones they brought were emotionless and dry on the tongue.

Jana used to fish, herself. When the demand for bits of alien worlds had soared, her little boat had been unable to compete and she had to sell it. Now she lived in a flat on the coast. There was no sunlight and the walls were concrete, so empty it hardly looked real, although through the back window you could glimpse the memory of the place where the sea used to be.

She pried out a tiny beam of red light from under a tangle of cosmic radiations. This was a good catch. You could almost smell summer on it. When you looked closely, you could make out the reflection of clouds, and a distinctive sense of reverence. This came from a world with no weather control, but with creatures advanced enough to have deified their sun. A chef in one of the gourmet restaurants of the port would turn it into a meal to remember, one that she would never be able to afford.

'Oi, send that vat over here!' Ary, her overseer, shouted. She pushed the vat of meteor dust towards the sorting line.

The beam was very small. Back when she was a fisherwoman, she would have had to release it into space. In large fisheries, you didn't fuss over such details. It would be far too expensive to release all the by-catch and, by the time they did, it would have withered away already. Selling it to chefs skilled enough to shave it into thin slices and make it look like part of a big, healthy chunk from a world of abundance was far more profitable. Jana despised those chefs. They decorated their restaurants with real preserved storm clouds and boasted that they served only the most natural, pristine bits of the universe, but they worked in dry concrete towers like everybody else, charging fifty times the price Jana earned to sort through the belly of the fishing boats. And they served illegal catch at that.

Jana shot a glance at Ary. He was rummaging elbow-deep in the vat of meteors, swearing at the poor quality of the stuff and ranting about fishermen and government alike. She wrapped the beam in a bit of wet cloth that would keep it alive for a little while, and tucked it into the front of her overalls.

As usual, it was a long, unrewarding day. Jana clocked out of the factory not a minute later than required. Outside, people milled through the grey mist, projecting two-dimensional holograms around them and laughing and pointing at the crude colours. She stopped at the supermarket and bought a bottle of rust soup, with artificial sleep flavouring.

Back in her flat, as the soup was reinvigorated in the microwave, she unfolded the cloth. The beam of sunlight still shone, but weakly. That didn't worry her. Light was sturdier than people gave it credit for, although few still knew how to take care of it. She brought the beam to her living-room and laid it carefully between a tiny scrap of moonstone and a piece of precious driftwood, close to the window with the memory of the sea.

In her neighbourhood she was known as something of a miracle worker. She sat in her armchair and allowed herself a moment to relax. On the walls around her, her own private world thrived in the indoor garden: blots of natural colour, pieces of stone, feathers and metal, a couple of sunrays from various stars, a little water, even a real flower, yellow with bitter-tasting leaves. The key, she liked to explain when friends admired her work, was to stay away from artificial fertilisers, and to know how to pair her finds so that they worked together instead of competing with each other. If you left a bit of sunlight next to a shiny stone, for instance, they would grow a reflection between them after a while, and you wouldn't have to lift a finger. No, not even trim off excess light. It was all a matter of trust, refraining from eating everything at once, and letting the universe do what it did best: balance things out.

It had been a long day. She deserved a little pick-me-up while the microwave did its work. Carefully, parsimoniously, she helped herself to a tiny serving of the choicest food from her living-room: a little organic home-grown emotion, peace and quiet with a hint of spring.

3.

The fishing boats arrived at last, trawling a rotting bounty of worlds in nets behind them. The fishery opened at dawn; no one could afford to waste time. Cranes lifted the nets with rusty efficiency, pouring the stock of the day on conveyor belts. Their world was forever hungry.

Ary walked around the factory, shouting directions and sorting through the vats along with the workers. This was not a good day. The fishing boats had roamed the least alive corners of the universe and brought nothing but dust, radiations and cold. Impure cold, at that. A nice absolute zero might have fetched a good price in an exotic food store, but those limp pulsating particles would barely interest supermarket customers.

'What happened?' he shouted over the noise of the cranes. 'Solar wind pushed you out? Couldn't you go anywhere near uninhabited worlds?'

'Surprise inspection,' the fisherman shouted back. 'We're not supposed to go closer than a light-year to life-bearing planets. I got fined last time I went past the legal limit. I can't afford that again.'

Ary frowned. Some captains were less circumspect, and most inspectors took bribes anyway. The truth was, their world needed food. What good would it do to make sure the next generations had food if the present one starved? All the factory workers, every single hand on the fishing boats, everyone depended on catching precious bits from faraway worlds, now there was so little left on their own.

The last inspector to have been assigned to the factory did not take bribes, sadly. He'd learned his lesson. That hadn't changed anything for his factory, however, or made the situation all right.

In the dim artificial light, brighter than the half-eaten light of their sun, he went back to work, sorting through vats of anonymous cosmic dust for little bits of rocks that might actually have terrified a world, or burst into flame in a remote atmosphere and made children squeal. The day's offering was dismal. Another few weeks like this and the management would call him in to ask for his opinion on who to lay off. Again.

The new girl sorting bits of cold by grade would be first to go, he decided. She spoke better but worked slower than anyone else, and she wasn't even here on a permanent contract. If she thought that this was just a summer job, a holiday among the working class, then she could just ask her parents for money. Better get rid of someone who wouldn't be here for long anyway than face the heart-breaking task of telling one of the regular workers that they were no longer needed.

'You, over there!' What was her name again? Lara? Lira? *Mira.* 'Mira! Stick that thermometer at the core or you won't get the right temperature!'

'All right, Ary!' she replied with a smile. He felt a pang of guilt. Mira was nice enough, she had called everyone by name on her second day on the factory and she was always willing to lend a hand. Who was he to assume she didn't need the money? Rotten times, when you had to rate the men and women working with you by expendability.

From the corner of his eye, he saw Mira tuck something into her jacket and fumble with the thermometer.

He strode towards her. Pinching from the line was not tolerated. He might look the other way when old-timers did it – they'd earned it, after all, and he was not the kind of man who yelled at old ladies for going home with a measly bit of sunlight – but a new girl who slowed the whole line down when she fumbled with her tools? Not a chance. He grabbed Mira's arm. She gasped and straightened, but not before he could see the camera disappearing inside her pocket.

Ary's arm fell. This was worse than stealing. This was betrayal, pure and simple. He marched Mira towards a quiet corner.

'You're filming us,' he said through clenched teeth, still careful that no one saw them although it would have served her right. 'What are you trying to do? Prove that we process illegal by-catch? All right, we do. Everybody knows. It's the only way we can keep this factory running.'

Mira opened her mouth. Ary didn't let her speak.

29

'What are you trying to achieve? Fine, so our boats are destroying other worlds bit by bit, we know that too! Are you going to tell me you don't eat any of it? What do you do, survive on home-grown hope alone? Don't expect me to believe that!'

'Actually, I do,' Mira said. 'I'm not a hypocrite. These worlds you're destroying...'

'We're *feeding* off them! If we stop, what good will it do? You won't even get to see them!'

'Relax, Ary.'

She looked right and left.

'No one is going to close your factory. As you said, everybody knows. We just want to shift mentalities. We don't have to keep feeding off other worlds. We can make our own...'

'Fine. I've heard that rubbish a thousand times. Give me the camera.'

'Can't we work this out?'

Before he told her off, she produced something from her pocket. It was lacy and light, earth-brown, and it smelled crisp and delicate. Ary gasped.

'Is that... *a real leaf?*'

Mira nodded. Ary bent forward. There were only brown veins left, but the scent of the memory behind it was unmistakable: winter, falling down in the snow, and the simple delight of a child.

'My parents took me to that world when I was little,' Mira said. 'There were still plenty of these over there. And snow, too. It's yours, if you want it.'

A real leaf, oozing with memories.

'It must be worth at least...'

'It's not a bribe, okay? It's for you. If you look at it often, it won't wither. It may be a bit silent for a while, until it adjusts to you. Then it will start producing again.'

'Producing?'

'Joy. Just a sip, every two weeks or so. If you nurture it, it will last forever.'

Ary took the leaf in his hand. The cold pricked his fingers. It had been so long since there had been any winter left on this world. He blinked.

'We've never worked together,' he said. 'I don't know who you are and you've never seen me. Now be more careful with that camera.'

Mira smiled and ran back to work. Ary went back to his corner of the factory, waiting to go home and revel in a child's memory of winter.

4.

The fishing boats advanced on the jetty, trawling their nets behind them after relentlessly combing the universe. In the artificial dawn, the fishery looked unbelievably gloomy. The nets burst open over conveyor belts as if they were being gutted in turn. The whole world survived on evisceration.

Mira watched as the workers lined up to start their shifts. Journalists were not allowed into the fishery, but new workers were welcome. Officially, her job consisted in sorting through the catch of the day. Her camera was hidden in her jacket, ready for her other assignment.

It had been her idea, although she had several journalist friends waiting for her recordings. She had no idea how much of a scandal it would make. Most people knew how the fishery plundered worlds across the universe, robbing them of substance, purpose and emotion so that their world could feed. However, having that fact rubbed in their faces was another matter. She had shown videos of fishing lines wrenching an entire spring from a world, leaving it bare and shivering. She had seen people avert their eyes and wipe tears then. There was hope yet.

And that was precisely what she needed before going in. She ran her fingers over her chest until she found a little strand of hope, pulled gently and pried it free, careful not to disturb the rest of the growth. She nibbled at it and let it melt on her tongue. The flavour was warm, full-bodied, spicy. Hope was a rare delicacy, incredibly tricky to grow and difficult to maintain, and locally-sourced varieties were almost impossible to find these days. She hid the root under her clothes, so as not to appear suspicious.

Inside the factory, the spectacle was heart-breaking. Pieces of dismembered worlds were poured on belts and shelves, sorted into vats, manhandled, thrown around, treated without care or respect. So much was wasted in this way. You couldn't hack trust apart on a conveyor belt and expect it to retain its strength, or store light in boxes and be surprised when it turned into darkness. No wonder their world had to rely on artificial flavourings so much. Worst of all, what was being sent to the conditioning wing often consisted of illegal catches: warmth plucked in excess from too-young suns, emerging languages, newly-deified comets. Who would not be moved by such absurdity?

At midday she joined the other workers for lunch. Jana passed around a box of home-made nibbles: tiny reflections in drops of freshwater that tasted like morning. For a moment there was no sound to be heard but delighted groans. Grinning, Jana explained how she grew reflections in her living-room, using real sunlight and home-made dew. Mira liked Jana. She was a quiet old lady who made no fuss about her skills and often looked a little sad, but she reminded Mira of something her grandmother used to say: when some people became very good at growing things, they started developing seeds inside them, and once scattered around, those seeds could take root in anyone careful enough to nurture them. Seeds of joy, of pride, of hope. Too bad no one knew how to recognise them any more.

It was a stressful day, but Mira managed to get through it despite her overseer coming close to throwing her out. After he left her alone, she discovered a little sprout at the back of her mind. Thrill, or fear, she didn't have time to figure it out. She rearranged her hair to hide it. Fear was a popular spice, but most of it came from artificial flavourings now. She would have to be careful before tasting the real thing. It was rumoured to be extremely addictive.

When she turned on her digital device at home, the first thing it did was project an automated picture of a crude wide-eyed animal on the wall. 'PUPPY!' the electronic voice squealed. She started and turned around, before realising that there was no one in the room with her. Under her hair, the little sprout of fear stirred.

She loaded her recordings online. As the process bar unfolded, she ran her finger through her hair and thought about what was coming next. She was going to lose her job. There would be other ways to earn a living, but her online records would bear the dreaded 'untrustworthy' stamp. She could be unemployed for some time. She would have to ask her friends for money. That would be easier to do if the recordings reached a wide audience through the press; otherwise she would go back to becoming what she had been most of her life – a burden, full of wild dreams but not focused enough to let them grow and bear fruit before she consumed them.

Then again, the recordings might go viral. They might even start a public debate about how the fishing boats abused the galaxy, rendering other worlds as grey and sterile as their own had become. Then the other side would grow vocal. She would be called a hypocrite, a bourgeois idealist with no regard for her former co-workers at the fishery, a hysteric with no sense of reality. Her parents would pretend to support her, acting like fatalists while eating through slices of imported rainbows and sandy beaches, and her aunt would say, 'Better not think too much about where it comes from', while digging through a platter of northern lights. It was going to be a very dark time for her.

Mira closed her eyes and smiled, as her racing heart sent nutrients in spades towards the scion of fear taking root in her brain. Over her heart, a blossom emerged from her sapling of hope.

5.

The fishing boats reached the jetty, nets bulging, competing for space on the docks. Most were already in place when the dawn bell rang and the fishery opened. Cranes unfolded, sailors secured nets overflowing with cosmic dust to their hooks, over the conveyor belts. Their world was ready to swallow it all.

Julius greeted the grumpy overseer from his deck, bracing himself for another string of recriminations. Not enough of this, too much of that, the fishery was going bankrupt and everyone would starve including the fishermen. The truth was, he wouldn't have sold his stock to the fishery if he could have helped it. Their rates were shamefully low, and they all but pressured him into fishing in illegal areas. One of these days he would have to think about direct-to-consumer sales. One of these days.

When the speaker announced how much he was getting today for the contents of his net, he jumped on the dock. There was barely enough to pay his crew, but when he found the manager, the man only shrugged.

'People don't want asteroid dust, you know that. I'm sorry, old man.'

'Of course you are. What do you want me to do? We can't get close to life-bearing worlds. Dust is all we get out there. I can't afford those fancy fishing lines. I'm doing what I can.'

The manager had already started talking to someone else. Julius went back to his ship. There was nothing he could do except rant a bit and go back to work.

His father had been a fisherman, and his grandfather too. Back then, life had been so much less complicated. In his grandfather's time, there had still been a sea in their world. You could find everything you needed there: brine, wind, seasons, smells aplenty, sounds of crashing waves, even fish, sea birds and whales. Food for an entire world, back when the world was smaller and less greedy. Dip your net into the sea and it would come up brimming with life, his grandfather said. Of course, that must have been an illusion, even then. His grandfather was still alive when the fish disappeared for good. When his father was still working, it was the turn of the winds and seasons, and now even sunlight was scarce. All of those things were still plentiful in other worlds, but now lawmakers had to meddle. Now there were endless talks of regulations, sustainability, conservation areas. Not that Julius had anything against that. But he still had to pay for his boat.

'Finish cleaning the nets and we're going back,' he announced to his crew.

As it turned out, there was nothing much to clean. They had hardly managed to catch any filth, not even a little damage. Not that damage sold for much these days. Halfway through the afternoon, they fired up the motor again. It would have to be better this time.

The sailors talked among themselves. Some items were in high demand at the moment. Music could fetch very high prices. One of the chefs who worked in the hidden dens of the ports, the ones only initiates had access to, was rumoured to have found the perfect way of turning music into heavenly, melt-on-the tongue sashimi, and now raw music was all the rage in town. Julius rolled his eyes. He could almost hear his grandfather talking about the golden days when you only had to cut the motor and you would have heard music echo all over the galaxy, ripe for the picking. These days virtuoso music was incredibly hard to find. Unless, of course, one sailed a bit too close to conservation areas, where strange tunes blossomed from planets yet unconsumed.

This wasn't a good idea, but one more week like this and the boat was as good as bankrupt. Besides, they had been inspected the day before. It was unlikely the authorities would have their sights on them two days in a row. Just this once, and they would be very careful. They wouldn't use the tighter net, only the one loose one that would let clumsy children's tunes slip away. After that they would have time to put up with a little paperwork. Direct-to-consumer might become more than a dream.

He set the course under the questioning looks of the sailors.

'There will be no inspection today. I'll pay from my own pocket if there is one. Onward!'

Many hours later, they arrived in view of a yellow sun with tiny planets dancing around it. A quick inspection revealed that only two of them bore life, one cold and hidden under ice, the other spread between oceans and stretches of rocky ground. Julius ordered the sailors to cut the motor. They would make a quiet approach.

The familiar rush of exhilaration greeted them as they came in view of the world they had found. Worlds with colours were becoming rarer and rarer. They caught a little sunlight on the way, and a little starlight, too, reflected in the minds of poets and local sailors. How long had it been since anyone had fished near this world? It seemed that they could cast their net anywhere and bring a bounty of life, beauty, colours and sounds to the ship. It was pristine. It was wonderful.

'Only music,' Julius said, breaking the awed silence of the sailors.

They were close enough to see the details of the surface, when a long, loud sound reached their ears.

It could have been a horn, or a sort of deep trumpet. Slowly it rose, and called, and crashed down again. Julius had never heard anything like it. And, strangest of all, when most intelligent life seemed to live on the rocky part of that world, the song came from out at sea.

'Here, captain!' a sailor called, getting the net ready. The song rose again. Julius raised a hand to stop the sailor, and listened.

Down in the sea, a massive creature rose. It broke the crest of the waves and sank again, its black tail whipping the water once. Another creature answered in low bellowing tones. On and on they sang, and played, breaching through the water and breathing out plumes of mist. Then they disappeared under the sea.

It was a long while before Julius remembered what they had come here to do. His hand was on the crank, poised to release the net.

He let it go.

'Let's go home,' he said. None of the sailors objected. Their eyes were still trained on that foreign ocean, in a world so bountiful even the sea had its song.

Catch a beam of light in a box and you will kill it. This is true of many other things, though perhaps in less obvious ways. Pack away and eat too much of the sea itself, and... well, we can all see what is happening in this world of ours now.

I cannot picture the dreary hopelessness of living in a world without a living sea. I hope I never will have to.

A Kingdom of
Seagrass and Silk

The boat swayed, drawing nearer the island with the inexorable slowness of a spider climbing its gossamer lifeline. In normal times (if I could still remember such a thing), it would have taken us less than twenty minutes to reach the lighthouse. It had been nearly an hour today and the pebbles on the beach were just coming into focus. My son strained on the oars while the motor sat idle. Petrol had become too rare to hurry.

My breath caught when I shifted on the plywood floor, but I did not groan. I could not allow Maël to believe that he was leaving me in pain, or worse, that I was attempting to saddle him with the parting gift of guilt. From across the boat, Laurent glanced at me sympathetically. After all this time, I didn't need to make a sound for him to know when arthritis was gnawing at my bones. Instead, I leaned forward and brushed long strands of brown hair away from my son's face, as he turned his head to find a good spot to land. He smiled, lips tight. His cheeks were wet with brine.

At last we stopped, swaying softly. For a while I did not move, only watched, as that man of almost forty reviewed the packages piled on the floor of the boat. His long curls were still thick, tossing around his face where a pair of large brown eyes were all that remained of the baby I had once worn on my chest all day long.

'This one's fuel and matches. You should have enough for a couple of months, if you're careful. You'll be careful, right? Here, this one's pasta and rice. Make sure you keep them in their wrappings. If you get moths, there won't be any way to find more. The keys are here...'

I touched his back.

'I know, dear. We'll be careful with everything.'

Maël, my grown son, my little one, bit his lips and screwed his eyes shut.

'I have to do this,' he whispered. 'You understand, don't you? If you catch the disease they won't even let you through the hospital door. You're safer here. Almost safe.'

'I know,' I repeated.

You can never know when a grown child will, for once, tolerate a hug from his mother, the way he would have when he was no taller than my hip. But when I touched Maël's arm, he leaned towards me and let me hold him. His breath was calm, forced.

'We'll be perfectly happy here,' I told him.

He hugged me more fiercely in response. For a little while I did nothing but enjoy the moments we had left, pushing away everything we had left unsaid. There would be no coming back for us before the tide of the epidemic had ebbed again. Promises to save every life, at whatever cost, had rung loud and clear, once. It had not been long before no one had dared use that refrain any more, in the face of what was really happening. This would not be the first place in history where old lives were forfeited to give the young a chance. On the island, deserted after the ferries had been shut down and its inhabitants had left for places where food could still be bought, we could at least hope to make it.

I tried not to think that Maël would be going back in a matter of minutes, to work at the hospital where he was desperately needed. Where he would brush elbows with the virus every day, and have to hope masks would be enough to keep it away.

I watched Laurent and Maël unload the boxes and sat in the cold water, letting the sea soothe my sore joints. The island was not large, and we knew every stone and tree by heart. The only thing that was new about it was the silence.

The click of the switch under my finger echoed a couple of times in the empty house, before I remembered that the power had been cut. Laurent was already forcing the shutters open, producing a long series of creaks. Little by little, the scent of eucalyptus and pine from the garden crept back and dispelled the cool musty smell of the closed rooms.

Afterwards, I walked to the end of the garden, where a short path led to the sea. Maël's boat was long gone, and the bay enclosed between the islands and the mainland had reverted to its mirror smoothness, unbroken by human presence.

Laurent walked towards me and put his hands on my shoulders.

'Do you think we could see his house from here?' he said.

We peered together, in silence. From here, all the houses on the mainland looked like tiny dots, his neighbourhood a maze of trees and fences.

'Too bad we didn't think of getting one of those solar chargers before they ran out,' Laurent said after a while. I took his hand and he squeezed my fingers, gently enough not to hurt.

'He'll come back when this is over," I said. "Now we just have to stop worrying or we won't last a week.'

'I hope he'll be able to stop worrying for us,' Laurent replied.

I nodded. He had been over the stocks of beans and pasta three times before I'd stopped him. There would never be enough to make sure we could stay on the island forever without starving. We could not afford to think of this as waiting time. However long this took, we were here for good, to make this island either our grave or our own little kingdom in the middle of the sea.

'How long since you last went fishing?' I said.

Every joint in my body shrieked when I sat down. The first few days on the island had been gruelling. Finding food on our own was much easier in theory than it proved to be in practice.

Grinning, Laurent clinked his glass against mine. The water from the well tasted of dust and old age, and was the most satisfying drink I'd ever dipped my lips into.

'Who knew we'd manage to lift that huge stone?' he said.

He skewered a piece of sea lettuce on his fork, examined it for a while, then shrugged and bit into it. 'My eternal thanks to whoever planted that lemon tree,' he added.

I nodded. The raw flesh of sea bass drizzled in lemon tasted perfect. It had taken us time, but the lace curtains in our borrowed house had proven sturdy enough for our purpose after all. After countless tries, we'd dropped them on a school of bass, catching five in our makeshift net. We'd saved the bigger two for dinner.

As the sun set, lights began to dot the town on the other side of the bay, like fireflies coming to life. I was so absorbed in the rising lights, trying to make out one that might belong to my son, that I did not notice that Laurent had moved away from me and down to the beach. He had stepped into the water and was staring down, frowning.

'What do you think that could be?' he said.

I could see nothing but the trail of the setting sun in the milky opal of the sea. I rose, inch by inch, and then, when all my bones were aligned in a standing position and I was able to focus on something else once more, the sun dipped behind the horizon and all the sea came to life.

Around his feet the water had started to glow, blue-white spirals forming and dispersing like smoke. When I stepped in, the water stirred and bloomed with light in the dusk. I stared, too, for a very long time.

'Algae,' I remembered to say at last. 'Plankton. Something like that.'

'That's what makes this light?'

'Yes. Like tiny fireflies.'

We looked at one another. Smiled. Started at the same time towards the diving suits and snorkels we had left to dry on the beach after gathering sea lettuce.

The cold stung, but the suit kept the worst of it off, and I let myself relax into the water. I started moving, slowly at first, then more confidently, with renewed wonder at how much lighter my limbs felt, the pain in my joints soothing until it felt like a faint heat glowing in the background like the swirls around us.

There was hardly any light left from the sun. The reefs that festooned the shallows sank into darkness, and came alive again in blue-gold waves as we swam above and disturbed the bloom of plankton. Night did not dull the extraordinary clarity of the water. Five or six metres of sea might as well have been air, and we might have been flying there, carried by a soft, cold, glowing wind.

We were far out already. The bluffs where we had gathered seaweed earlier fell into a prairie of seagrass, dark lambent gold instead of brownish green. I waved to Laurent and, without waiting for a sign from him, dove, pushing the air from my lungs so I would sink faster.

A couple of fish started at my approach, uncovering a large, dark mouth near the sea floor. I swam a little closer. In the last push, a cloud of plankton illuminated the long, spiny body of a gigantic mussel, swaying along with the seagrass.

I hadn't dived in a long time. I was already out of oxygen, and I pushed hard on my diving fins to swim back to the surface.

Laurent watched me emerge with slightly pursed lips.

'Give me a word of warning before you do that,' he said. 'What did you want to see?'

Brine splattered my teeth when I spat out my snorkel.

'Giant mussels,' I said. 'I thought they were extinct around here.'

We swam back to shore. It was much darker now, and cold. We splattered a parsimonious measure of water from the well on our diving suits before entering the house. After days of use, the living-room still had the coolness of dormant stone. We had taken to sleeping with doors and windows open, letting the chill of the night caress our faces as we huddled together in our sleeping bags.

That night, with the full moon glinting through the French windows, Laurent said: 'They used to make cloth from giant mussels. You know, those threads they use to attach themselves to the bedrock? You can dry them and spin them. Sea silk, they called it. They ravaged mussels for sea silk in ancient times. And they still didn't manage to damage them as much as global warming did.'

I pondered that for a while.

'Let's take good care of those we have left,' I said.

I drifted quietly into sleep, as I had every night of our life on the island. When I woke up the next morning, I was still swathed in the shreds of a dream, one where I had sailed on the sea in a golden cloak, shimmering and shifting like the waves.

The sun was setting again. Laurent and I stared at one another in silence for a second, then burst out laughing and spitting out pieces of acorn bread.

'This tastes… completely foul,' Laurent hiccuped.

'Completely. Why couldn't they grow chestnuts here?'

I tossed the rest of the bread on the compost heap. We would still have a way to go before we managed to process acorns into something edible.

'Let's see if there's any couscous left instead,' I said.

Munching on the dry grains, we watched for the first lights to come alive on the shore. We had not discussed how there seemed to be fewer as time passed, but it was becoming too obvious to pretend that it was only an impression. Every night, the constellation of windows and headlights grew sparser, darker.

'Do you think he's still at the hospital?' I said.

Laurent didn't answer.

It was this, I think, the way he kept his mouth closed as if the only other option was to scream, that cracked the wall I had spent days carefully building against the darkness. I covered my mouth, strangled back a sob, then couldn't strangle the rest. Laurent drew me against him and hugged me, fiercely. I don't know if he cried as well. I was so absorbed in my own tears that nothing else existed.

After that I got up, squeezed my husband's hand, and walked towards the sea. The sun was almost gone. But when I looked down, there it was again, blinking and falling in rhythm with the waves, the bloom of light of the plancton cloud.

'I'll just go for a swim. I'll be back.'

I slipped on the diving suit and the mask, and walked into the sea, cold pricking my ankles, then fading as water welcomed me, constricting my breathing in that gentle way that forced me to quiet. And I drifted forward.

I could never orient myself well while swimming. I followed the shore, every kick sending ripples of blue gold through the seagrass below. After only a few minutes, I was surprised to recognise the underwater bluffs and prairie. Scattered here and there were the thin dark mouths of the giant mussels.

After days of gathering sea lettuce, I had grown better at diving. I breathed out, just enough to sink, careful not to exhaust my lungs too soon. This time I could stay long enough to run my hand along the prickly side of the shell, feel the place where woolly strands connected it to the bedrock. I was out of air then. I swam up, took in the growing darkness, briefly wondered how cross Maël would be with me if he saw me dive alone at nightfall. I thought of his face when I told him the story, and smiled. And I dived again.

This time I snagged my fingers in the clam's filaments, and pulled, gently. The shell swayed, but did not react when I pried a pinch of threads loose. They billowed in a golden cloud, tangling around my thumb. I kicked my fins and swam up.

Up there, there was nothing impressive about them, a few fine brownish hairs scattered across my palm. I hesitated. Then I dived back down.

There were more of the great upright shells dotting the seabed. I had no trouble reaching the next one, loosening a few more filaments and swimming up. It was completely dark now, the only light coming from the plankton. Underneath, the prairie was growing deeper. I wondered how far it would be before I had to give up and swim back to the shore. As far as I could see, the shells were only becoming more plentiful. A whole world waited below. Drifting there, limbs as light as clouds and pain almost forgotten, was intoxicating. I looked up to the stars, the Milky Way that, for a few days, had started to glow strongly again. One last dive. Then I would swim back.

I swam to the bottom, as far down as I could reach. When I looked up, everything had gone black.

I had a moment of panic. Then the darkness floated away. An undersea current ripped me from the shell and I tumbled even farther down, and before I even thought of how little air I had left in my lungs, I stared in astonishment, as the whale above me circled along the shore and disappeared into the depths.

I was out of oxygen and very cold. Heart pounding, I swam up, and back to the shore.

Laurent was standing there with a torch. He cried out and waved when he saw me. I kicked the fins faster, until pain jolted my knees.

I was back in reality once more, with a handful of unnaturally thin hairs sweeping my palm.

'Are you all right? Put this on. God, Alice. Did you get lost? What happened?'

The thing he tossed on my shoulders was one of the dozen first aid blankets Maël had stuffed our emergency kit with. He had a hot mug ready. I didn't even think of the waste of our resources this represented. I grinned and kissed my husband, basking in the silly sweetness of the gesture, and a giddiness I couldn't quite explain.

'It wasn't cold,' I said. 'I just took a swim to the place where we found the giant mussels. Oh, and I saw a sperm whale.'

Laurent stopped.

'What do you mean?' he said, slowly, carefully, transparently attempting to hide his growing dread.

'Over there. Must have been deeper than I thought. It swam right past me and left.'

'That can't have been a *sperm whale*,' he said, wrapping the blanket more firmly around me.

'I think it was. Its belly was dark. It was too oblong for a right whale.'

This was not the answer he expected. He gently pulled me towards the house.

'Don't do that again, please,' he said.

I nodded, but promised nothing, and before I went to sleep, I laid the filaments to dry on a windowsill.

It took Laurent a few days to accept that I was not going to stop my nightly dives. By this time, a thick handful of filaments were already drying on the windowsill.

Harvesting them was slow, careful work. I swam back home exhausted and aching, sometimes with coloured spots dancing in front of my eyes, when I had dived deeper than might have been safe. There were a hundred more productive ways I could have spent that energy, I knew. There were acorns to harvest and driftwood to collect and water to filter through layers of cloth. There was a house to clean and diving gear to carefully rinse and dry every day. There was no time for futility.

Perhaps I needed a purpose, something to carry me beyond our daily survival, beyond the dreaded hour when the sun set and we counted the lights on the shore, at first a galaxy, then constellations, dwindling to a handful of dots. Or perhaps I could not tire of watching seagrass billowing in the eerie lights of beings so tiny I could not glimpse them individually. I kept diving, mapping the seafloor so I wouldn't inadvertently hurt the molluscs by harvesting too often from the same ones.

It was late on one of these outings that I saw the sperm whale again.

Its massive black form occulted the prairie and drifted towards me. I swam to the bottom, out of the way, as fast as I could. I looked up to see the narrow jaw, the scars dotting its throat and fins, the small beady eyes that did not seem to notice me. Even if I hadn't been underwater, I would not have remembered to breathe.

Then the whale swam away. I was too deep, too far, running out of oxygen, and I did the single most unreasonable thing I could have. I followed.

Deep down, the plankton still bloomed in the wake of the whale, gathering in swirls of light behind its massive black shape. The sperm whale sank behind underwater buffs, my lungs burned, and just as I was about to swim back, I saw another shape.

It was long, uncannily so, slender and swift, with a light belly and a dark back. A fin whale, rising to breathe and floating just below the surface, then rising again before sounding the deep. I almost breathed in water. I kicked up, up, up, much farther than I thought I'd dived, and finally broke the surface, gulping in oxygen and darkness before looking down again.

Below, the sea stretched for thirty or forty metres, crystalline and unbroken, alive with the lambent swirls of the plankton. I had no idea where I was. My right hand was still balled tight around a handful of brown hairs, shining like strands from some golden fleece. A school of silver fish as long as my arms glided past. Deep down against the seafloor something brown glided, tentacles caressing the bedrock. It would be a gorgeous place to drown.

I didn't want to drown. I kicked my fins, trying not to let panic submerge me. My joints ached and I felt as if my lungs had shrunk underwater. When I saw the beach at last, with Laurent's torch going back and forth, I raised a hand and slowed down. He was waiting for me with a towel. He smiled, grudgingly.

'Nice swim?' he said.

I reeled when I stepped on the beach. My fingers were still tight around their bounty.

'I... I think I need to sleep. Let's go.'

I hugged the towel around my shoulders. The night was cool, but that was not why I was shaking.

I went to sleep as soon as I'd wrapped the covers around my body. Before dawn, I dreamed that I sailed over a shimmering sea where dark unreal shapes swam like angels, holding Laurent's hand, and that both of us had long cloaks of gleaming gold trailing from our shoulders, like emperors returning.

The filaments had dried. Following Laurent's instructions – I had no idea how he could remember so many things – I'd washed them in lemon juice, and in clear water, until they shone a very soft golden-brown.

Making a spindle was a bigger conundrum than I'd expected, until, as I roamed the house racking my head for ideas, I happened upon a large, rusty screwdriver. The heft was just enough to gather momentum without breaking the delicate fibre. This was not my first attempt at spinning, though I hadn't tried it in a long time, and had never felt the awe of such precious material slipping between my fingers, inch by inch. After an hour or so, I had a tiny spool of thread coiled around the handle of the screwdriver, and the final fur-like strands ran at last, just as the sun went down. I hurried outside.

Laurent sat in silence on the small outcropping where we'd shared so many evenings. I clutched the screwdriver, and looked ahead.

A greenish-grey band of light lingered on the horizon. Overhead, we could already see as many stars as we would have during the darkest nights, centuries ago. On the other side of the bay, however, the mainland was completely dark.

My head swam. I sat, made myself breathe.

'The power must have gone out,' I said. 'They must have saved the last of it for the hospital. It makes no sense to keep lighting houses when there's a shortage going on. This means nothing. He's fine. Laurent, he's fine.'

I took his hand. He stared ahead, expressionless, and didn't respond when I squeezed his fingers, as hard as if I was drowning. I brought a hand to my chest. The ache was so strong that I felt it as if I'd gone back in time, the phantom weight of a small body cradled against my breast as he sank into sleep in my arms.

The lights did not come back.

It would have been easy to sit there and do nothing, just wait for the horizon to send us a sign that the world out there was still going, still fighting. We had not been sent to this island to wait until life got back to normal. We had been sent because dying in the sun, bathed in water the colour of aquamarine, would always be preferable to seizing to death at the hospital doors. If Maël did not come back, when we died would matter to no one except ourselves.

But we did not give up. We ground acorns into meal and washed it in brine, then clear water, until we were able to eat it without wincing. We devised new ways to season seaweed. We burned driftwood and smiled when blue-green flames flickered, as if the sea was clinging to it to the last. I kept diving, though I stayed close to the beach, only going as far as I needed for one more handful of the sea's miraculous fleece.

The spool grew and grew, brighter and more regular as my fingers learned their way around the makeshift spindle. In the evenings I showed it to Laurent, who smiled as if we were sitting at home and I'd just discovered a new hobby in a wholly unchanged life. We sat and talked until there was nothing left to say, then enjoyed the silence before going to bed together. Little by little, our beings turned into the island, flowing and as serene as the sea.

One night I stayed up longer. I'd stopped trying to will the lights to go back on. Up above, the Milky Way was already waxing brighter.

'It's a bit late to go diving, don't you think?' Laurent said, yawning.

'Perhaps. I'll just take a walk along the beach.'

We parted with a light kiss. My knees and hips groaned, and I recalled the frustration and bleak helplessness I'd felt, when I'd first realised that my body would simply no longer cooperate the way it used to. After these weeks on the island, my body was still quite enough for what my life required. The pain had not faded, but it no longer drove me to distraction the way it used to. Perhaps I had learned to look old age in the face, at last.

My eye was suddenly drawn to an oblong yellow shape at the end of the beach. A couple of kayaks had been left in the sand, tethered near an abandoned house. I'd noticed them before, but had not seen how they could be useful. Now I walked closer, and realised that they were in perfect condition, two paddles arranged neatly on top.

It was too cold this late at night to get into the water, but the bay was smooth like a mirror. There would be no danger if I paddled close to the beach. With a grunt, I pulled one of the kayaks into the water, straddled it when it wobbled, and paddled, hesitantly at first, then effortlessly gliding away.

I would never cease to wonder at how perfectly clear the bay was. I decided that I would turn back as soon as I stopped seeing straight to the seafloor. Swirls of blue-gold light emerged in my wake, tangled in the lazy, swaying fingers of seagrass.

I didn't know how long it was before I realised that there were over twenty metres of crystal-clear water underneath. Schools of fish still swam close to the bottom, buoyed on a lambent wind. I looked back in alarm. I had gone farther than I'd intended, but the shore was still visible. I stopped paddling and watched the reefs drift underneath.

Just when I stopped telling myself to be rational, the large shape of the sperm whale loomed and almost brushed the bottom of my boat, dispersing clouds of plankton in its wake. My breath caught. I had never been a fast swimmer, but kayaks in calm weather were fast enough. I braced myself and followed, pushing my arms and back as fast as they would go, and followed the giant towards the open sea.

I was not fast enough. It broke the surface once, took a deep, shuddering breath, then sounded and disappeared. What came in full view then was enough to make me forget about the whale.

The sea was bottomless. Seagrass, aquamarine cutting on turquoise, still swayed on the bluffs, sixty or eighty metres below. The space between was churning. A pod of dolphins crossed, broke the surface as if I hadn't been there. Schools of fish, larger than anything I'd seen here before, weaved in and out of the reefs. The tremendous mottled shadow of a humpback cut across the waters to disappear into the bay. All around them, the glow of the plankton suffused the night in the quiet sea.

I turned around in a panic. Amazingly, the shore was still within reach. I paddled as fast as I could, clumsily, hitting the water flat and sending it spraying with every other stroke. At last I reached the beach. The kayak nearly capsized when I rose too fast, and I stumbled into the water, waded and ran to the house.

Laurent was already asleep. I shook him awake.

'I'm not crazy,' I said.

He groaned and stared, blinking.

'Come on. There's another kayak. Tell me you see it too.'

It felt like an eternity, but at last he got out of bed, grumbling, and followed me out to the water.

'It was this way. I think.'

'What do you mean, you *think*?'

I didn't answer. I knew there would be nothing. As soon as somebody else would be there to see it, there would only be the seafloor, and it would be proof that I had lost my mind. I simply wanted to know it for certain.

Plankton still glowed, that eerie blue-gold I knew now was nothing natural. The floor dipped. Laurent glanced over the side of his kayak.

'All right. I forgive you. This *is* pretty.'

He paddled faster, let his momentum carry him to my side, and took my hand.

'We're here. You're here. No matter what happens elsewhere… you have no idea how terrified I was to not have you any more. At least we're safe from that.'

His voice was croaky from sleep.

'Remember the first time we brought Maël here? We thought it would be the most gorgeous place he'd ever seen. Instead he just had so much fun making bubbles in the water.'

'You taught him how to do that.'

'True. But it made you laugh the most.'

He squeezed my hand. I swallowed.

'Just a little farther out,' I said. 'If we don't see it, we can go home.'

Laurent nodded and followed me.

Underneath there came the dark face of the bluffs. We were flying, again, above fifteen metres of perfectly clear water. Then thirty. Then fifty. I paddled faster, pulled myself forward, as fast as I could, until the soreness was too difficult to bear and I stopped, gliding away above an infinity of light and salt.

And in the bottomless sea, they appeared again. First the long, tapered body of a blue whale, parting the waters miles underneath. Then a white pod of belugas. Then the familiar sight of a school of sea bass, incongruous in its mundaneness. Then it was an entire pod of bowhead whales, sending us reeling in their wake, and scaring away a giant squid that pumped its tentacles back towards the depth.

I looked at Laurent, expecting to see a blank, questioning face. Instead he was staring at the sea, with both hands on his mouth.

'What *is* this? Why didn't you tell me?'

'I told you,' I said.

'Yes. Well, don't brag. Oh my.'

Protected only by the flimsy shells of the kayaks, we ought to have been terrified. Any one of the giants cavorting in the depth could have sent us drowning without even noticing. Instead we felt as if the world had been suspended. There was nothing but the wonder of having been allowed to see the sea for what it really was, away from the years of destruction humans had visited upon it.

At last we paddled back to the shore. I dropped myself on the sand and vowed not to move for the next decade. Laurent sat next to me. Neither of us spoke for a long time. I looked at the kayaks, at the dark, quiet sea. I thought of what we had been allowed to glimpse, what could be ours for the rest of our lives if we stayed here, away from whatever was left of civilisation.

I thought of my dreams, Laurent and I sailing, cloaked in glorious gold from the sea.

'We have to go back,' I said.

He froze.

'I know he wanted to bring us here,' I went on. 'We shouldn't have accepted. For all we know, he's out there, and he's alone. He needs help. We should never have left him.'

'We can't go back now,' Laurent said. 'He said he would come back for us. If he doesn't...' If he didn't, there would truly be nothing to leave the island for, I thought he would say. I was wrong. 'If he doesn't, it's because he thinks we will be a burden. We can't act as if what he wants of us doesn't matter.'

'But what will happen when everyone decides that the best way out of this is to find a nice desert island and quietly wait until everybody else dies?' He shook his head, pursing his lips. 'We'll be careful," I continued. "We're not daft. We've been hiding for too long. It's time we went back and did our part.'

Laurent didn't answer. When I turned to him to argue some more, he was gaping.

Over there, the mainland was as dark as it had been for days. But on the edge of the shore, a glow flickered behind a clump of trees. Laurent ran home, and came back with a pair of binoculars. After a couple of seconds, he dropped them, shaking.

'I can't see which house it is,' he said.

He looked down at his hand. I had been squeezing it so hard the pain in my knuckles had alerted me before I realised what I was doing. I couldn't speak. I pleaded with my eyes instead.

'Yes,' he finally said. 'It's a lamp. It could be...'

Maël. We looked at one another for a while, unable to know if we ought to dance in joy, or cry, or yell.

'We *are* coming back, aren't we?' I said.

The thought was much scarier than paddling above an entire court of whales. We had no idea of the state the world was in now. We might as well have spent a couple of centuries on our own. But we had no other option. We were not young. We were not strong.

51

Yet if we had managed to endure on our own, to befriend both the island and the sea in a way even our son could never have imagined, we certainly were not useless.

'How are we going to do it?' Laurent said. 'He's gone with the boat.'

'We have the kayaks.'

'And your arthritis. It's at least an hour to the other side.'

'I'll just have to try.'

I thought of my dream again, and then of the small uneven spool of silk wrapped around the handle of a screwdriver, which was all that weeks of diving had earned me. There would be no saviours landing in a shroud of gold on a shore ravaged by disease. Just two old folk who loved one another very much and would go look after their son, whatever it cost them.

Laurent smiled and pulled me close.

'Promise me you'll let me drag your kayak if you're in too much pain.'

'I promise.'

'Then we'll go. Tomorrow morning. Before the wind rises.'

I hugged him back. Hand in hand, we walked back to the house, and began packing. On top of the bag, I laid my spool of sea-silk, and I hoped that the world would be beautiful again.

It is said that, in difficult times, Japanese villagers would practise *obasute*: send elderly relatives to die in the wilderness, so that there would be enough resources to feed the rest of the community. It is difficult to assess how much this story draws from reality; but it is difficult to think of this legend without remembering some discussions that took place in recent years, speculating about whether it was truly worth bringing society to a halt in order to save the lives of the elderly.

In another Japanese legend, a fisherman, Urashima Tarô, discovers a marvellous kingdom under the sea and is forever transformed, to the point that he is unable to go back to the world he left. Urashima's tale is a tragic one, and not one I was ever inclined to think about when enjoying summers by the seaside, or kayaking in the crystal-clear waters of the Mediterranean.

But the *obasute* legend has a less well-known side. In a popular version, a son hides his mother instead of abandoning her, until, through her wits and perseverance, his mother saves the entire village. And here is the hidden side of the story: the elderly may be unable to work, but their love and wisdom is to be treasured. Some of us will never fully fathom the depth of our grandparents' cunning. Perhaps, if Urashima Tarô had been a grandmother readying herself to be abandoned on a mountaintop, she would have devised a way to come back.

A Stray Cat in the Mountain of the Dead

Time dilates in the summer heat, or maybe I can't get used to how slow I have been lately. As I rush around the corner, panting, the bus stop in sight at last, a new message from Anthony pops on my phone. 'Hey sexy. Just wanted to know how things are going in Narayama...'

He *knows* I'm tired of this stupid quip and it didn't even make him sound edgy the first time. Classy film reference, my foot. I mutter – 'Fuck you,' before shoving the phone in my pocket.

The world is full of jerks who believe a retirement home is a purgatory for old people with uncaring children, and that the people working there are torturers in the making. You get used to it. Of course it's more complicated when the jerk in question is your boyfriend.

I shouldn't have paused to read the message. Two missed buses later, when I arrive at the Olive Tree Residence, my heart feels like a wasp trapped inside my chest and the outside of my vision disappears in a smudging of yellow and green. The wind sears the pines and oak trees, and everything looks asleep except me, as I rush to start my shift.

Corinne is waiting on the threshold, Madame Tozzi's son and daughter walking behind her. I'm so busy trying to breathe I don't notice the gloom on their face, and I wave hello, while the blur at the edges of my vision recedes. It takes a blank look and a nervous frown from Corinne to drive home my blunder. I stop in my tracks, face falling.

Poor Madame Tozzi. Of course the news shouldn't come as a surprise. But working among near-centenarians, you don't expect people to go so soon. She was eighty-three, poor thing. I think of Anthony's message, wince inwardly and try to find something nice to say, when something mews and rubs against my leg.

'Gaspard, where have you *been*?' I say.

The stray cat of the retirement home looks up at me and props himself on his hind legs, front paw reaching for my hand in a strangely human gesture. He looks splendid, with his grey coat and silky white paws. Silly thing to think right now…

Madame Tozzi's daughter smiles and wipes the corner of her eye.

'At least she had a companion to the end,' she says, kneeling next to him. 'Purring in her lap as if they'd always known one another.'

I don't think I've ever seen Gaspard show that much affection to anyone, and I've never seen him around Madame Tozzi, but I keep quiet. When the lady tries to touch his head, he recoils, bolts and disappears into a thicket of oaks. She shrugs, still smiling sadly, and we all shake hands. Another day starting with condolences – another familiar face, morning greetings and weekly laundry, gone forever.

Corinne is still staring at the lean shapes of the oak trees when they leave. She's paler than usual. I give her shoulder a squeeze.

'Are you all right?' I say.

'Yes. We shouldn't let that cat in, though. It's unsanitary.'

My first impulse is to argue, before I realise the incongruity of the situation. We walk inside together, not saying anything. Silence is our best refuge, as usual. The people we take care of are just patients to us, or should be. Tears indulged once never seem to dry.

The day I started working at the Olive Tree Residence, I was convinced I was entering Hell. It was not so bad after all. Of course you have to see people die more often than you'd like, and not all our patients are lucky enough to get regular visits from their families. Take Madame Darmon – I've only met her son once. She's a lovely little old lady with a flimsy memory, who loves to tell you as much as you're prepared to hear about her childhood, because it's the only part of her life that hasn't entirely slipped from her brain yet. Sometimes I think she's lucky. When her son tells her he will visit and cancels at the last moment, she never remembers.

My heart still hums when I arrive in her bedroom. She's leafing through an old album of black-and-white photographs.

'Good afternoon, Fethia,' she says without looking, a smile on her lips.

'Good afternoon, Madame Darmon,' I say as warmly as I can.

She forgets a lot, but she doesn't forget my name, and that's something I don't want to take lightly. With other patients, I do my job. Distance is key if you don't want to break down one day and never come back. With Madame Darmon, I look for little kindnesses, small things to make her smile. It's a big responsibility, being one of the last names an old lady remembers. Anthony says that's why I'll never last in this job. It annoys me, but deep down I know he's just terrified. When an old lady's memory frays at the edges and you're the only face she can cling to, it's like standing in the eye of a storm: the one calm, safe spot where nothing can happen to you, although everywhere around is a bottomless well of oblivion waiting to swallow you whole.

Madame Darmon knows I like her stories, poked full of holes as they are. Pages rustle as I make her bed. Her album is full of photographs from Switzerland, nearly eighty years ago. That's where she spent the war and a couple more decades, waiting for a family that was taken to the police station one day and never came back. She's told me a thousand times about that day when she reached the other side of the border, a twelve-year-old bewildered thing, clinging to the hand of a student in medicine who risked his life for years passing children across to safety. Our young doctor, she calls him, dreamy-eyed.

A meow interrupts us. Gaspard has come back to rub against my legs.

'Kitty,' Madame Darmon croons, tapping her lap. 'Come sit here!'

I squint at him. How this cat manages to sneak past closed doors even when we try out best to keep the heat locked out is a complete mystery to me.

'Get out of here, Gaspard,' I say.

I kick him out and close the door, before wondering why I've done that. But Madame Darmon is staring at her pictures again and, tired or not, I should really get back to work.

'My son is coming tomorrow,' she says. 'You'll see him.'

I force a smile out. Her son hasn't announced a visit in weeks. But for Madame Darmon, he's always coming tomorrow.

'I'd love that,' I say.

That's all I can do for her, unfortunately.

In the dining room the blinds are closed and the noise from the electric fans covers the sound of the TV. Better this way: they're going on again about the heat that's already killed scores of grannies in Paris. Monsieur Melchior dozes; only his fingers are moving, mindlessly stroking Gaspard who's sprawled in his lap. Gaspard himself doesn't look very lively. He scratches at the air once or twice and settles back. Corinne clears the last tables, glancing sideways at the old man and the cat falling asleep together. I sit by the window, catching my breath.

'Fethia, are you all right?' she says.

Not really. I feel like I've swallowed a stone. Anthony must be right; I should exercise more.

'You should see a doctor,' Corinne says.

'I should get some exercise. As soon as it gets cooler.'

'This weather will kill us,' she sighs.

Monsieur Melchior snorts when I walk near him. He nods once or twice, begins to snore. It sounds like the two of them are purring.

With Corinne gone, I sit at a table on my own for a while, basking in the waning afternoon light. Such a shame to keep the blinds lowered all the time, with that lovely view on the mountain. When they're open, you'd believe you're inside one of Cézanne's landscapes, except that if Cézanne did paint our mountain, he never painted the breeze or the smells of rosemary. But that's not something tourists can know, how different the truth is from the blotches of colour they've admired in museums. I draw the blind and the sky unfolds over the limestone cliffs, right in the middle of the window.

'I've hung your painting, Monsieur Melchior,' I say. 'Look!'

It's time for him to wake up. Even Gaspard has disappeared. He doesn't answer. He sleeps with his mouth open and his head on one side. He'll get a stiff neck if he doesn't wake up, I think as I come closer. I have time to call him in a low voice, to touch his shoulder. Of course it's useless. He's not breathing any more.

After the doctors take Monsieur Melchior's body away, a wave of consternation hits us. It's one of those summers, again. I can almost hear Anthony's voice smugly declaring that *he* would never send his parents to die in a place like this. In my head, I cannot find anything to answer.

I soon stop thinking about it, however, because other concerns loom in my mind. I know I should have gone to the doctor's long ago. I'm not even sure why I put this off, what I'm afraid of. Hearing that something is wrong? Or rather, hearing that everything is fine with my heart, that Anthony was right after all, and knowing that he'd say he told me so and maybe sneer a little?

Whatever I might have hoped for then, as I leave the cardiologist's office I wish for nothing more than for him to call me back in, say he's taken another look at my file and he was wrong, nothing out of the ordinary after all. But there's no sound aside from my feet echoing on the stone steps that circle the stairwell. In these old city centre mansions it's never too hot, nor too cold, nor too noisy or bright. A cool stone cocoon where sickly bodies wait to be restored to health... when something can be done for them.

I get ready to go out, a hand on the door handle. One more second of quiet and cool; I've earned it. Outside, it's a market day, bright enough to make your eyes water, a crowd packed so tight it's impossible to cross at normal speed. One more second in the stairwell where my heart is not going to race. Then I open the door, the heat seizes me by the throat and I walk very slowly, telling myself that it's not such a big deal. The doctor said so.

I walk into the crowd, the glare, the din around the marketplace, where are so many tourists congregate that you hardly hear a word of French. The square smells of ripe peaches, cheese and olives, limestone and shade. Here, when a heat wave strikes, people think of selling melons instead of wondering who's going to die first. For the first time, I wonder if I already have my name written on fate's long, inexorable list.

As I crawl through the marketplace, I stop to buy a slice of ham for Madame Darmon. I'm not supposed to do this, but the ham they serve at the retirement home looks like congealed wax, and she likes to tell how she developed a taste for ham after her parents were put on that train to Poland never to return. On second thoughts, I buy another one for myself. Since the doctor gave me a good excuse to skip Ramadan, I might as well go all the way.

Madame Darmon leafs through her album while I make her bed. My heart buzzes in my chest. I try to silence that little voice that tells me I'm only twenty-three. I remember all the residents I met since I started working here. Those who survived cancer for twenty years. Those who reached a hundred in spite of tobacco and alcohol. And I can't help thinking of all the others: those who didn't see it coming – Madame Tozzi who was so particular about her healthy food and exercise, right until that aneurysm hit. I know it's stupid. My chest hurts…

A small hand lands on my arm. I hadn't realised I'd just been standing there for the last minute. I sit on the bed, facing Madame Darmon, who looks at me with big milky eyes.

'What's wrong, Fethia?'

Nothing. Need more exercise.

'I have a weak heart,' I say. And then I don't manage to stop. 'Chronic fibrillation or something. It's congenital. The doctor told me this morning.'

'But you'll be fine,' Madame Darmon says as if it was obvious.

'That's what he said.'

I feel I can't breathe. I touch my throat.

'I'm stupid, right?' I say. 'He said it was nothing to worry about for now, but I looked it up on the internet anyway. I'll be okay, until the blood clots in my heart. I'll have a heart attack. And I'm twenty-three. And my boyfriend keeps telling me I should keep fit as if it's all my fault, and I don't want to tell him…'

'There, Fethia. You should trust doctors with these things instead of working yourself up, shouldn't you? Come sit here.'

60

I sit on the windowsill, facing her. She looks like she's going to impart me a great piece of wisdom about living your life to the fullest before you need someone to wipe your backside for you. She opens her mouth, tilts her head to one side, then shakes it as if she had forgotten what she was about to say.

'You'll be fine,' she says. 'You're a good girl.'

I smile back. So strange that she can live so peacefully, with only shreds of her memory to call upon. She is looking at her album again. I should write her stories down one of these days. In fact I would stay here all day to ask for more, if there wasn't so much work to do. There are so many things I'll never know, all because I didn't think of asking until it was too late. What Algeria, the *bled*, was really like; if it should mean anything to me beyond the crescent-stamped flags people wear around their shoulders on football game nights. But I only have one living grandmother who could tell me about that now, and her French is as bad as my Arabic.

It would be a good time to ask for stories, to take my mind off death and hearts that don't work as they should. And then I think of everything she's forgotten, how sad she would be if she couldn't answer. I let her look at her old memories, the wispy, imperfect ones she's managed to fit on the two dimensions of a page, watching her in silence.

And then noises interrupt us. I hear 'Get that cat out of the way!' through the open door. I wipe my forehead, while the doctor's short hurried steps reach the next room in the corridor. I know those muffled sounds, when nobody wants to speak too loud for fear of triggering a panic. When I leave Madame Darmon's room, Doctor Tardieu is there with two nurses. Sitting on his haunches with his back to me, Gaspard watches them. He watches me walk past without asking to be petted.

Doctor Tardieu sighs. Her small blue eyes, usually so youthful in her wrinkled face, are clouded with worry.

'We must fix the air conditioning as soon as we can,' she says. 'Three deaths this month... What will people think of us?'

'Monsieur Esposito...?' I say.

I glance into the room. It's the first time in a while. Monsieur Esposito didn't want an Arab girl to take care of him. His eyes are closed, his mouth open, as if he were thirsty. I hope no one forgot to give him water.

'He wasn't allergic to cats, Monsieur Esposito?' a nurse asks.

I lean back against the wall. When my heart stops buzzing, I force myself to smile until I feel better. It should be easier when it's a racist old fart, but instead I only feel like a jerk for remembering his unkindness. He was from another time, I tell myself. *A time when people thought nothing of denouncing their neighbours to people who forced them onto death trains*, a little voice answers unbidden. Why do we have to feel anything more complex than sorrow when old people die? I go back to Madame Darmon, who hasn't realised anything is going on.

'I wondered where you had gone,' she says, smiling.

Her album is open on a picture of a medical student – early twenties, tall and decided, with a shock of dark hair. How she obtained it I can only wonder. She doesn't know any more.

'That's him. My young doctor,' she says. 'I have to visit him one of these days. I think he went to live in Marseilles after the war. You should come with me, Fethia.'

I smile back. I doubt the doctor can do any miracles, even if he did one for her. My brain calculates in spite of myself. He'd be over one hundred now. I try not to change my expression. She lays a hand on mine.

'Don't worry, dear. Angels have amazingly long lives.'

Corinne and Fabien stand around glumly, coffee in hand. I lean on a nearby window, panting, and decline the cup they offer me. Corinne opens and shuts her mouth several times.

'We have to get rid of that cat,' she finally says.

I pretend I don't understand what she's talking about.

'That's seven now,' she says.

'Seven what?'

'Don't tell me you haven't noticed anything! He never sits in anybody's lap. Fethia, did he ever come to sit on you?'

'Seriously, Corinne,' I say. 'Do *you* have time to sit down?'

'He never comes when I do. He doesn't even stay in one place, most of the time. And every single time I've seen him in someone's lap... Madame Tozzi, Monsieur Melchior, Monsieur Esposito, and they were not the first ones… Two hours later, at most. I'm positive. We've never had this many deaths in one summer. There's something wrong about that cat. He scares me.'

Fabien finishes his coffee. The smell alone makes my chest ache.

'You know, between global warming and Gaspard, I'm not sure we should blame the cat,' he says.

He tosses the cup into the bin.

'He knows,' Corinne says. 'He just shows up from nowhere and he *knows*.'

'Maybe he does. Animals sense things we don't. So what?'

'It's creepy, that's what. And where does he come from anyway? How come we've never seen his owners?'

'He's a stray,' I say. 'He comes and goes. That's what strays do.'

'Then how can he be so well-fed? Nobody gives him anything to eat around here!'

We say nothing for a while.

'We won't make our residents immortal just by driving the cat out,' I say. 'Besides, why bother? He'd come back.'

Corinne and Fabien both nod and fall silent, as if I've just said something extremely profound. Suddenly I'm the one who's a little scared.

I have to get back to work. As soon as I'm alone in the corridor I lean against the wall, a hand on my chest. I don't feel the beat at once. It hurts. My heart, I think first. And then I think of Anthony, of my long-gone grandmother, of our patients in their small vanishing worlds – incongruously, Gaspard's pure white paws flash in my mind, as if it took nothing less than pristine gloves to touch the dying – and suddenly the pain seems to be coming from all directions at once.

The sun is setting. I have a few minutes to myself, so I lean out of the window, wide open now the day is cooler. Before me looms the white cliff, rosemary smells wafting up to us. I've never climbed to the top. I wonder if I'll ever be able to.

Once, Anthony showed me a movie about Narayama, the mountain of the dead, the place where they say Japanese villagers took old people to die when they could no longer afford to feed them. I still remember his smirk – the first time I was angry at him. And yet I stayed. If we left every time we were angry, we couldn't even stay in this country, and look how nice it is for us when everything is fine, my grandmother used to say. She, too, was from another time. Me, I'm a modern girl who should know better. I'm still staying, though if verbal jabs were needle pricks I'd have more blood than skin on the surface of my body.

In spite of myself, I often think about his tasteless joke when I gaze at the mountain looming over us. Here, sons and daughters only carry their parents as far as the foot of the mountain, to a home where they'll be taken care of, in as much as we can. But every day, when we open the windows, a few eyes turn towards the cliff, and their souls climb up to the top, try their luck at travelling alone, now that their legs can't carry them any more.

Madame Darmon is asleep. Her son has called to say he'd come, and she's dozed off waiting. I used to believe all Jewish men worshipped their mothers. Funny how you let silly ideas live in your head as long as they sit there quietly and don't make a fuss, and then one day you realise they've been here for far too long and you feel like a complete fool.

They've cleaned Monsieur Esposito's bedroom. A new resident should arrive tomorrow. I decorate her new room with her things: a painting of the Virgin Mary in a golden frame, dried flowers in a vase, family pictures. If she's lucky, she'll see more of them than just pictures.

There's noise in the next room. Madame Darmon has woken up, and is staring at two turtledoves bickering in the pines. She's so pale, so small. Her son has called to say he wouldn't be able to make it today after all, but she doesn't think about it.

'You look so happy,' she says. 'What a lovely sight. Come sit here. How are you feeling?' she adds, pointing at my chest.

This leaves me speechless for a moment. I carry on smiling, since she seems to like it. She remembered. Everything is gone, except for her photographs, the war, an old god she still likes to defy even though she doesn't believe in him any more, and our daily routine. But now a tiny new memory flickers in the storm. And she's concerned about my heart.

'I've asked Doctor Tardieu if I could go to Marseilles next week,' Madame Darmon says, 'and she said yes, but she wants someone to come with me. Will you?'

'Of course!'

She beams at me, transparent.

'Then we only need to look up my not-so-young-any-more doctor,' she says. 'Will you please do it? I can't read those tiny letters. I've never thanked him properly. And you know, I'm sure he can do something for you.'

She's already got the name written on a slip of paper, a very commonplace Jewish one. There must be dozens of them in Marseilles. I squeeze Madame Darmon's hand and go out, unsure about what I should do.

In the end there are only two of them with the same first name. I stare at the phone for a little while, preparing to make myself sound like a fool calling a complete stranger. I dial the number. Nobody answers, until a kindly, ageless, masculine voice tells me to leave a message and he will be in touch soon. I hang up, a bit relieved, and go back to Madame Darmon.

'I may have found him,' I say. 'I'll try to call again as soon...'

My heart whistles in my ears and I clutch the door. Madame Darmon looks serenely at me. On her lap sits a big grey cat, purring under her hand.

I dash into the bedroom.

'Gaspard! You bloody fucking beast, get out of here! My God...'

'There, Fethia, what's going on?'

I kick Gaspard out. Madame Darmon sit up, pallid. I take her hands, touch her forehead. Her skin is cold...

'Madame Darmon, are you all right? Are you feeling well?'

'Of course I feel well. He's just a nice kitty, Fethia! You haven't been listening to this talk of allergies, have you?'

I can't breathe. I run to the reception.

'You have to call Madame Darmon's son at once! He has to come now. Just tell him he has to come!'

I listen to the call, as the receptionist's features harden. The son doesn't sound too pleased. I go back to the room, with a big glass of water.

'Drink this,' I tell Madame Darmon. 'You'll get dehydrated.'

I sit by her side. Where is Gaspard, now? She puts her hand on mine as if I was the one who was unwell. I try not to faint.

Half an hour goes by, a whole hour. Still no sign of Madame Darmon's son. I walk out, come back to check her temperature. She seems perfectly well. She's just so thin, with her buoyant smile. And then they call me into the corridor. I hear a man's voice I haven't heard very often, irritated inflexions. Irritated that we reminded him to visit his mother! I reach the entrance hall. Doctor Tardieu is there with a well-dressed man, balding on top.

'The doctor and I haven't quite been able to grasp the nature of the emergency, Miss,' he says.

Everyone is looking at me. I haven't felt so stupid in my entire life.

'Your mother…'

They're waiting for the rest, and I really don't know what to say.

'You haven't come to see her in six months! Every time you call, you cancel at the last minute! Is that manners for you?'

I run away into the corridor, without waiting for an answer. Not very far. I stop, wheezing, next to a window, I hear sighs behind me as they walk up to Madame Darmon's room, and as I double over to catch my breath I hear their 'My God' and 'What happened' and 'How did she…?' and as I close my eyes and bite my lips something vibrates against my leg and purrs, and there is Gaspard, facing me, his yellow eyes innocently planted in mine.

September took its time. I've just changed the bed sheets for the new resident who took Madame Darmon's place, and now I'm sitting on a bench outside the building, taking what little rest I can to catch my breath and still my heart. The new lady frowned a bit the first time she saw me. I don't think she expected me to smile at her and ask how she would like her room arranged. After that she was much more pleasant, and she spends ten minutes chatting to me every morning, as much as I can spare from my schedule. I know I shouldn't get involved, but I don't care. I'd rather hurt than keep pretending people don't exist as soon as I know they won't be around for long.

There's a seventh message from Anthony on my phone; more pleading, I suppose, but I ignore it. Too late for him. Some parts of our past we can choose to discard at least, instead of waiting for them to slap us in the face or die just when we've realised we didn't want them to. I delete without listening and instead start fiddling with my caller history. I still have the number of that old man in Marseilles. Did he carry on, one life saved after the other, never hearing from them again? Every day my finger hovers around the number before I put the phone back in my pocket. I don't know what I would tell him if he was not the right man after all, even less if he was. Or maybe I would tell him about the old lady who never thanked him but still kept his picture to the end, and I'd hang up after a few pleasantries exchanged, without mentioning my heart. That's the saner option, I suppose, though every time I tell myself that, an image comes back, unbidden – Madame Darmon's confident smile and her words about angels.

I take a few minutes to listen to the silence outside, after months of cicadas, and follow the line of the cliff, up to the top. There's a cross on the summit, barely visible from here. You can't see it in Cézanne's paintings. But my eyes always stop on it, whenever I look at the mountain.

The bench vibrates with a very slight thud. Gaspard has climbed up and strolls towards me. He lays a paw on my thigh and stares at me with big yellow eyes. For the briefest moment I'm very, very scared.

Then Gaspard withdraw his paw and darts away into the pines.

**

For Dr Georges Meyer, 1919-2022

Even angels have to leave, eventually.

Dr Georges Meyer passed away in late 2022. As a student, he had spent part of the war smuggling Jewish children across the Swiss border, carrying them on his shoulders sometimes. Though Jewish himself, he never followed them. After the war, he settled near the Mediterranean sea and became a doctor, a father, then a patriarch of a growing tribe; he kept saving lives and making others happier. He was also a wonderful great-uncle.

Everything else in the story is made up. Except the cat, of course.

Que la Grenade Est Touchante

My dream is a hall of grey and green where they drink and laugh, crimped hair, slicked-back hair catching the golden light. Music blooms from pianos and trumpets, twirling and creeping around the drum's beat. In their glasses, drinks gleam like garnets, like emeralds. Women's dresses are dewed with sequins. They tap their feet to foreign music, short hair tossing, short dresses swirling.

In my dream they have flowers and vines sprouting from their hands and from their mouths and ears. Sometimes their laughter is silent, and there are tears flowing from their eyes even as they dance and embrace and rejoice.

My bedroom is small, with curtains of colourful printed cloth, red tiles on the floor, and two cots. One of them is rumpled, with a doll's head emerging from the covers. There, I'm tucked safely away from the cold, until my mother's voice cracks the silence. Slowly, I untangle myself from the blossoms and twisted vines of my sleep.

I splash water on my face and make my bed, though it's never as neat as the other one, the bed that's never been slept in. I get dressed and walk down the stairs for my morning bowl of soup before I go to the chicken coop.

I scatter a bucket of kitchen refuse, stare down the rooster, gather a couple of eggs, pluck the lovely purple flowers that have grown back during the night and now threaten to crowd the hens out of their shelter. They smell of honey and green melon. Back in the kitchen I shove them in the vase. Mother glances over her shoulder and frowns.

"Don't bring those in here. Next thing we know, they might grow roots in the table."

"But they smell so nice!"

Mother sighs. She doesn't start a discussion. Between scrubbing, cooking and walking to the market to sell her eggs and the odd chicken, she doesn't even have time to talk on most days. She, too, sleeps next to an empty bed. My father, forever sleepless, watches over her from a black picture frame on the wall.

My one bright memory of my father is as silent as a dream. I am sitting in my mother's lap, in the colourful folds of her Indian cotton skirt, trying to keep still. My father stands behind us in his blue uniform, his dark moustache drooping over unsmiling lips, tall and proud as he was before the trenches in the North swallowed him for good.

Sometimes I wonder if I remember at all, or if it's only the photograph on the mantelpiece brought to life in my head. But the next moment I keep the memory like a treasure, never mentioning it in case words snuff it out. That's the moment when my father's face blossomed into a smile as he met my mother's happy gaze, and she touched her stomach, lightly, before brushing a stray lock from my face.

Large brown mushrooms overflow from the sink. Mother sighs, shakes her head, then starts chopping.

"Jeanne? Take one of these to the doctor, will you? We might as well know if they're edible."

She wraps the mushroom in a towel and tosses it on the table. Amédée props himself on tiptoe.

"Smells nice," he says in his high little voice.

"Yes, but don't touch it before we've asked about it," I say.

Mother glances at me.

"What was that?"

"Nothing," I say, and put the mushroom in my basket.

"Good. Hurry up or you'll be late for school. Oh, and grab a couple of eggs for the doctor. I hear his wife is pregnant again."

"Yes, Mother. Come on, Amédée."

I grab my little brother's hand and saunter out of the house.

This morning when I woke up, a little boy was asleep in the bed next to mine, thumb stuck in his mouth, brown wispy hair falling over his eyes. His presence seemed so natural that I just shook him awake and helped him into his clothes. He still fumbles with his buttons, my little brother, and we don't want to be late for school.

"Why do we have to see the doctor?" Amédée asks as we climb up towards the village.

"Because he knows all these new plants that keep growing all over the place. He will know if these are poisonous mushrooms. It's very dangerous to eat mushrooms you don't know," I add for his edification. That's what big sisters are for.

Amédée gazes at me with big, awestruck eyes.

"But why do we have mushrooms growing in our sink?"

"Same reason we have purple flowers in the chicken coop," I say, loftily, and pick up the pace so I won't have to tell him I don't know.

The doctor's house is right at the edge of the village. I've never met him before. Mother is shy around people who don't speak Provençal. I stand very straight in front of the door, neat brown in a garland of yellow blooms, and knock.

It's a woman who answers. Her face is pale, hair cut elegantly short. She has deep blue circles under her green eyes. The baby she holds whimpers against her chest, above the swell of her belly.

"Good morning, madam," I say in my most precise French. "Is the doctor home? I need help with a mushroom my mother found." Amédée nudges me. I remember the basket. "Oh, and she sends these," I add. "Fresh from this morning. For the new baby."

She smiles and says something I don't understand, then in flawless, needle-sharp French – "Aren't you sweet. I'll call him."

Amédée stares at the baby. Such a tiny thing, cradled against her mother's breast.

"What's her name?" he asks. She doesn't hear. So I repeat, louder, and this draws a bright, sun-warm smile.

"Ghenrieta Lievovna," she says. I gape and she laughs. "Little Henriette. Wait here. I will call my husband. Léon!"

She retreats back into the house. Then the doctor comes out and my mouth falls open again.

The few times I saw the doctor from afar, he was wearing a dark suit and hat, as serious and proper as any gentleman visiting from the town. Now, he is wearing a long loose robe that covers his feet, and an oblong cap of curly black wool over his dark hair. People said he has come all the way from Tunisia when fantastical weeds started blossoming uninvited around the village. Now I can believe it.

"Yes?" he says, without smiling. He is very young, for a doctor.

"Good... good morning," I answer. "Mother asks if you can please tell us if we can eat these."

He turns the mushroom around in his hand for a moment, then puts it back into the basket. "Where does that come from?" he says.

"Our kitchen sink."

"Kitchen sink. Good." He frowns and peers at me. I try not to retreat. "And on you? Anything growing?"

"No, Sir."

"Are you certain? Let me have a look."

He lifts my hair, makes an impatient noise when I start backward. He looks inside my ears, my hands, my mouth. Eventually, he nods and stands straight.

"Good," he says. "If you feel a tingle somewhere, or something scratchy at the back of your throat, come at once, will you?"

I nod, vigorously. "I was very ill, once," I say.

"Were you?"

"Yes. So was Mother. And the neighbour. She died, you know."

The doctor makes a sound, as if he's just understood.

"That flu won't come back, hopefully," he says. "Run along, now, or school will start without you."

"And the mushroom?"

"Ah, yes. *Suillus collinitus.* You can eat it if you want. Don't expect it to taste very good."

I thank him and walk away, hastily, holding Amédée by the hand. Around the doctor's house, dry heat already rises from the ground. I steer my brother in the direction of the school when he tugs on my hand.

"Don't we say hello to Father first?"

I stop, look into his large, thoughtful dark eyes. And we turn right instead of left.

The cemetery gates are always open now. A shrub has grown overnight, pushing the stone post aside. Round fruits hang from its

72

branches, with thick skin the colour of ochre. Right behind, the monument looms, with its solemn angel gazing upwards.

Father is not here, of course. He has stayed North, buried in a land they say will never bear fruit again, not with all the bombs and the poison gases they poured over it. But the angel bears his name all the same, with all those others who never came back, and no epitaph.

1892-1918. It's 1922 now, I'm eight and the angel and I stare at each other in silence, while my little brother tries not to fidget.

After a while, it just seems right to leave. I run to the school gates, leaving Amédée at the door.

"Wait for me here, all right?"

He nods, and I get a last glimpse of his lonely form gazing at me, as the door closes and he remains still in the silent playground.

In a hall where vines twist and music clangs, someone pours their drink on the floor. A strip of orange peel falls like a feather into carnelian-red liquid.

A soldier shambles through and his footprints bleed for a while before vanishing. The woman only stares at the mess. Wide purple flowers grow out of her eyes, new leaves sprouting with every tear.

I've just helped Amédée button up his shirt when I hear the voices, and Mother calls me, with a hint of panic.

When I tumble down the stairs, I come face to face with two smiling gentlemen, who hold their hats in front of their bodies, faintly embarrassed. Mother takes my hand and smiles.

"Our new neighbours, Jeanne," she says in Provençal. Then lower, still smiling, "I have no idea what language they're speaking. Please manage them, will you?"

I come forward with my hands clasped. Amédée's face peeks out from the bottom of the stairs, but nobody pays him any mind.

"Good morning," I say in French.

One of them says something. I gape. He coughs a little and repeats, slower – "Good morning, Jeanne. I'm Édouard. This here is Guillaume."

It's French they're speaking indeed. But it has nothing to do with our schoolmaster's French, or the sharp, high-born accent of the doctor's wife. In fact, I've never heard anyone speak like that.

The newcomer kneels down in front of me. He's young, and he looks very kind. "We were friends of your father's, Jeanne," Édouard says. "Could you tell that to your mother?"

"My father," I repeat, not knowing what else to say. Then I repeat again, in Provençal, for Mother.

She makes a little noise and covers her mouth with her hands.

Édouard speaks again, then Guillaume, finishing his sentences. At some point Mother remembers to offer coffee, and her hand circles the grinder, again and again, while I keep translating. They talk about Father, about befriending him in the trenches, somewhere up north where Canadian troops had joined the French regiments. I can't show my excitement at the mention of Canada, not just yet. I'll ask them about it later.

"It took us months to find out where he had come from," Guillaume eventually says. "We would have been sorry not to meet you. César Lesnel was a great man. I mean it."

Mother swallows, and pours the coffee.

"It's… kind of them," she says, looking at me. Then she changes her mind and says, in slow French, "It is kind of you. Will you stay here? You not have wife at home?"

They exchange a glance and a brief smile.

"Nothing better in Canada than what we have here," Édouard says.

They're silent for a while. Guillaume glances at a stalk of clematis hanging from the rafter. "César loved plants so much more than he loved wars," he says.

I translate. Mother pinches her lips.

Guillaume goes on – "Whenever he found something growing near the trenches, he wouldn't stop until he'd learned its name. He got so excited. That's how he met that German sergeant, by the way. Did he write about it?"

"German sergeant?"

"The one he befriended, yes." Guillaume shrugs. "I suppose they intercepted his letters. They did that. Anyway, that German was a botanist. They became friends. One thing led to another and they got us a truce that lasted almost a week. Good folks, those Germans. A whole week without a single bomb."

Both their faces light up at the same time.

"César would never have done such a thing," Mother gasps. "He loved his country."

"Oh yes, he did. He was the greatest man we met on the front. If they hadn't disbanded the regiment, when they found out about the truce..." Guillaume swallows. Édouard touches his arm, lightly. "If we'd stayed together, we wouldn't have let him fall."

Something tugs my sleeve.

"What is Canada?" Amédée says.

"It's a place where people wear fur hats and it snows all the time. Hush now."

Édouard grins. "Not all the time," he says. "Come visit us one of these days. We'll tell you about Canada. There may even be hot chocolate."

"Hot chocolate!" I squeal, before Mother silences me.

When they take their leave, parting the curtain of vines hanging from the door, I've already forgotten about the war and only think of a vast, white country, sparkling under the winter sun.

Mother tastes the stew she's just made for the doctor's wife. Two babies within a year – the lady needs strength. The smell of wine, bay leaves and orange peel permeates the kitchen. My mouth waters, but I know better than to ask Mother for a taste when she's in that brisk mood.

Helpful as the doctor has been, excising flowers from wailing children and scraping seeds from their parents' mouths, only reluctant help comes that couple's way. They haven't gone to church yet, not even to baptise the new girl.

"Jews don't baptise their children," Mother says, when I ask her about it.

I ponder that for a while.

"Are we Jews?" I ask.

Unexpectedly, it makes her smile. "No, we're not. But Jew or Christian, we're all honest workers greasing the wheels of capitalism with our blood, and God's never done a thing about it," she replies.

"That's what Father always says," Amédée whispers beside me.

I wonder how he knows this. But before I can ask, Mother has wrapped the pot in a big towel and thrust it, still steaming, in my hands.

"Tell her to come for help whenever she needs," she says.

I've been to the doctor's house several times now, giving a hand with the cleaning, tearing the weeds from their window-sills. His wife is just back from the hospital in the city. When I step in, the doctor nods, and I hear her voice blooming in the back, to a child's soft whimper.

"*Spi mladiéniéts, moi priékrasny, baiouchki, baiou…*"

"Mother made this," I say. "Because the lady needs to get stronger."

"So kind of her. Come. You haven't met Élisabeth."

I step in, gingerly. Little Henriette is sitting on the floor, tugging her mother's skirt. Even exhausted, the doctor's wife is so elegant. She motions me to the armchair next to her. I squeeze my body to one side so that Amédée can sit next to me.

"And here she is," she says. "Elizavieta Lievovna." The way the syllables fall from her mouth is mesmerizing. There are whispers, in the village, asking how on Earth a Russian princess ended up marrying a Jewish doctor from Africa, but all I think about when I hear her voice is a dizzying expanse of white forests, as mysterious as the Canadian wilderness.

She motions towards the box of sweets. "Help yourself. Will you bring some to your mother? I can't thank her enough."

"You don't have to. We all grease capitalism with our blood and we just have to help each other," I say, as solemnly as I can.

She opens her eyes wide and stiffens, as if in sudden pain. From the door, the doctor sighs.

"Don't speak nonsense," he tells me.

He stops me before I go, for the customary examination.

"Healthy as a horse," he pronounces. "The weeds must love you. Thank your mother kindly."

He lets us go without looking at Amédée. I seem to have reassured him about the health of the entire family.

A woman dances with a tree, its bark broken, shards of copper jutting from the wood, a blue uniform hanging from its branches. They leap to the frantic music and step around a bed.

An empty bed.

I jerk awake with a cry. Then I hear soft breathing coming from Amédée's still form in the moonlight. I sigh and go back to sleep.

On the way back from school, we stop to see Guillaume and Édouard.

"Our company!" Édouard exclaims. "Come on in, clever girl. What did you learn today?"

Two bowls are already laid on the table. Amédée is too shy to ask for hot chocolate, but after I once asked Édouard for another bowl, he never forgot again. His hot chocolate tastes like heaven.

"We learned about rivers today," I say. And I proceed to enumerate the rivers of France, with every tributary I know of. Édouard and Guillaume exchange a look when I mention the Somme.

This is a little ritual they enjoy, asking me about school before I get to ask them for stories. They have a lot of them. They tell me about the war, sometimes, about the trenches, Verdun and Ypres and a place called Vimy Ridge, about friendship and bravery. But the stories I most love are the ones from before, back when they were two farm boys in a remote corner of Canada, and the only thing they knew of France was its language.

Today they tell me about encountering a bear on a fishing trip. I gape and clutch the bowl of hot chocolate; Amédée listens with big grave eyes, his own bowl lying untouched, forgotten. I already know how the story ends. They became such good friends afterward that when Édouard was drafted, Guillaume faked his age to enlist at once.

Amédée turns towards me. "If they ask you to go to war, I'll enlist too," he says.

I ruffle his hair. "There won't be any more wars now, silly," I say. "The government promised."

"If all men had been like your father, there wouldn't have been a war in the first place," Guillaume says, brushing a bright orange flower from the back of his chair.

I nod. I still don't know what to make of that story. Father gave his life to save us from the Germans, or so the teacher says whenever he congratulates me for remembering my lessons. It used to make me proud, before I knew he had made friends with them. Édouard and Guillaume showed me a drawing he made, once. It was a shrub with big rounded fruit, like those that grow at the cemetery gates. A *Punica granatum*, the writing said – a pomegranate tree. It was so beautiful that I spent the rest of the day trying to picture my father, with his blue uniform and neatly trimmed moustache, carefully drawing seeds and leaves while crouching at the bottom of his trench.

We all sit silently, me with my bowl of chocolate cooling in my hands, Édouard and Guillaume looking at me gravely.

"There were many officers in that war who never set foot on the battlefield," Édouard says. "And then there were men like your father, who were told to kill other poor sods but made friends with them instead. We're supposed to honour the officers, because it's a stupid world we live in. But let me tell you, Jeanne. In a hundred years, people will thank men like your father. I'm proud to live near his wife and daughter."

Something grips my throat then, and I grab Amédée's hand. "And his son!" I say.

Amédée bites his lips. His hand squeezes mine, trembling.

"And his son, of course," Édouard says, smiling at the chair where my brother sits. "Little Amédée."

But his gaze is trained above Amédée's face, as if there was someone taller there, and Amédée's mouth trembles more and more violently.

"It's all right," I say, gathering him into my arms, though I don't know what it is that's choking me, too, and I bite my lips and hug him as hard as I can.

"I want Daddy," Amédée whimpers.

And then he slithers out of my arms and hops off the chair and runs out.

I cry out his name, but he's already gone. Guillaume calls my name in turn, but I run out of the house, run after my brother who's nowhere to be seen.

I pause, looking around. I'm alone. *I want Daddy.*

I start running again, towards the cemetery.

The Angel of Victory stands there, alone in its tangle of vines. I call my brother's name. I try to run through the gate, but my jacket snags on a twig from the shrub. It's much taller than I am, its fruit so ripe they're bursting open, bright red, sweet, jewel-like.

I stare at the lovely fruit from my father's drawing, and instead of seeds I see a weapon, ready to burst the battlefield open. I see the exposed brains of a fallen soldier, and that's when I burst into tears and run away across the village.

I don't know why the place I run to is the doctor's house. I bang on the door, sobbing. He opens at last, with a look of alarm.

"Well now, Jeanne! What's the matter with you?"

I open my mouth but no word comes out. Frowning, the doctor bends, a hand on my chin, peering inside my mouth in a gesture I've come to know well.

"You're perfectly fine. What's going on?"

The question that comes is not the one I thought I'd ask. "Is it because of my dad? The weeds everywhere? Is it his fault?"

For a long while, the doctor says nothing. Then he ushers me in. "Let's get you something warm," he says.

His wife comes out, makes a little sound of pity when she sees me, and walks into the kitchen. The doctor sits at the table in front of me.

"Not your father's fault, no," he says at last. "Who can say? There has never been anything like this war. Isn't that what happens, when you destroy everything? On fallow land, anything can sprout. Cripples. Immigrants. Communists. Ghosts."

I swallow.

He shakes his head and smiles, very slightly. "These weeds are not a bad thing. They're just confused. How could they not be, after everything?"

He pats my hand. There seems to be such wisdom to his words that I don't mind if I only half-understand what he's trying to say.

Years later, however, my most vivid memory of that moment was of how young he looked, and lost, just as lost as I was – tossed in that brand-new world that already was half a ruin.

When I finally arrive home, Mother cries out, anger mingling with relief.

"Where have you been? I've been asking all around!"

"It's Amédée," I say. "He…"

Mother puts a hand to her mouth and I can't go on. I don't want to face her incredulity, or be chided for being foolish. I run up the stairs and crumple on my bed, and cry until there's nothing but darkness.

It's very dark when I drift awake, disoriented, somehow tucked under the covers in my nightgown, with my doll beside my face. Moonlight floats around the other bed. I think I glimpse convoluted leaves resting on it, but it is only the prone form of my little brother, sleeping tight with his thumb in his mouth… and someone else.

The shock is such that I stop breathing. Mother sits next to Amédée, smoothing out his hair, looking at him with a sad, loving smile. Then she kisses his head, very, very gently, and I screw my eyes shut.

I don't make a move, but I feel her sit on my bed, afterwards.

"Jeanne?" she whispers.

I pretend to keep sleeping and she sighs, a hand on my back.

"I've never told you about the baby," she says. I don't move. If I do, the world will crumble. "That last time your father came home, I got pregnant. We were so happy, both of us. We bought a little bed, swore we would be the happiest family, once he came back for good. Then he left again, and…" She squeezes my arm, gently. "That was when the flu came. You were so ill, my darling. So was I. I lost the baby."

She pauses. Colours pulse before my eyes, so tightly I keep them shut.

"I lost everything. The man I loved, the son I thought I'd have. My perfect family." Her voice becomes soft, like the blossoms of almond trees in winter. "But not you. I still have you, my darling Jeanne."

And now she kisses me, and I want to cry and hug her, but exhaustion carries me back and when my eyes open again, she's not here any more.

I sit up. Flowers hang overhead. There is music playing, a foreign beat, lively and panicked and blasting with trumpets, and people dancing, drinks sparkling, dresses rustling. And in the middle, there's a little bed, with a little boy sitting, eyes wide open, two tears staining his cheeks.

I walk towards him, and a few eyes turn when I sit down and take him in my arms. "It's all right," I whisper. "Don't be afraid. Everything will be fine."

I don't know that. But it has to be, and so I make myself believe, because my voice is the only thing keeping the fear away from him.

"Where are we?" he says. "What's going on?"

So many possible answers. Desperate joy, never-ending frenzy, the dead, the forgotten and the ones the war erased even before they existed, bouncing in their whirlwind of leaves. Through curtains of flowers I see the world the war left in its wake – life exploding after death, pain and joy and grief mingled too tightly to tease apart. Life sprouting in the tiniest cracks, on fallow, battle-scarred earth. And the drifting soul of a scared little boy.

I squeeze Amédée's hand. "Listen," I say.

And then the music pauses.

I take a long, deep breath. The dancers have stopped, and they're looking at us, stranded on a bed in an ocean of green.

"A few years from now…" I begin. I want to tell him how I'll never forget him. How I'll give his name to my son, so he'll be remembered forever. But I can't do that. I can't talk about my own children, not just now.

"The doctor, and the Russian princess," I say. And I know it is right this time, because my voice is steady, and words come to life like flowers. "They will go back to Tunisia, soon. But their two little girls will grow up, and one day they will come back here. They will find husbands. They will marry…" No. If I am to tell a story, let it be the best one I can tell. "One of them will marry a doctor. The other will *become* one." I hear sounds of awe around me, and I know I told it right. Amédée's eyes are rapt and he doesn't let go of my hand.

"There won't be another war, will there?" he says.

I let out a breath. No, I want to say. But it cannot be true, and this is not a time for lies.

"Yes," I say. "There will be. But nothing will happen to them. They will spend all their lives near one another, love each other until the end. They will have children one day. And grandchildren. And a hundred years from now…" I look around. The dancers have gathered around us. A young woman sits on the floor, her arms wrapped around her knees, flowers tangling in her fingers. Another stretches out her hand towards Amédée, without daring to touch him. "A hundred years from now," I go on, "one of her granddaughters will write our story. She will write about here, about us. We will never be forgotten."

And this time I swallow hard, because I've told a lie after all. I'll be forgotten, and no one will remember Amédée, my little brother who was never born. But I keep speaking, because my story is the one thing that can make it true, the only thing that can save us.

"She will write. And she will travel. She will have her own children…"

"Will she go to Canada?" Amédée asks, in a wispy little voice.

"Yes. And it will be every bit as beautiful as we've imagined."

All is silent around us. The musicians sit on the floor, listening, instruments forgotten. A girl smiles through her tears and the vines in her eyes. I hold Amédée in my arms and rock him gently, and I begin to sing half-remembered syllables, the beauty of a world I know so little of.

"*Pi madiénés, moy piékasti, baioutchi, bayou…*"

Amédée holds me and his slowing breath seeps through me, like sap rising in spring. I sing on and on until the brightness fades, and the moonlit walls grow real again as I wake up, silent, alone, grieving, loved, with the taste of words on my tongue, lost and confused on the eve of a world blossoming from ashes.

**

In loving memory of Henriette Cristofari and Élisabeth Meyer, nées Debbasch.

History has its lights and shadows. There are those today in France who would paint over ours, swap some of its more surprising colours for uncomplicated ones, White and Christian and staunchly monolingual. I want to tell these people that if they travelled to a remote, quiet Provençal village a hundred years ago, they would indeed find none of the uniformity they treasure so much, but instead there would be a Jewish doctor from Tunisia married to an exiled Russian princess, and their two young daughters who would later grow up on a Tunisian farm, learn Arabic and Russian and English, weather another war and become a beloved grandmother and great-aunt in a very French family.

Our country is a mosaic, shattered and remade a thousand times, in a thousand places. It grew out of seeds blown there by many winds. And this reality is more beautiful than any national myth will ever be.

When You Meet
the Wild Hunt

It will be broad daylight, and you won't be anywhere near a forest path, only driving up a narrow road up a steep seaside hill, momentarily lost on the way to who knows where. You will have slowed down, to watch out for falling stones as much as for the view; perhaps you'll have noted a storm cloud towering over the sea, lightning coursing through it, ready to burst.

You will not be ready.

The Wild Hunt rides in a cloud of light and overwhelming noise. They careen down mountain roads in gleaming machinery, sleek cars painted in eerie colours, launched along the road as if precipices had no meaning, as if the curves underneath the wheels were only manifestations of the Hunt's own sinuous momentum. They wear hoods and goggles that don't hide their exalted, predatory faces. The years have not slowed them down, only focused them, like a beam of light scattered away from its peers in the explosion of a star and stubbornly carrying on, until it stabs the eye of a telescope, thousands of light-years away.

The bodies of their cars glimmer, forever new, in changing, terrifyingly unnatural colours. Their windscreens are clear enough to see their faces, though you will not meet their eyes.

To stand up without fear when the Wild Hunt rides by takes the strength of one who knows with the certainty of the new-born that life does not have enough calamities in stock to hurt them – or of one who has gone through too much pain to fear it again. A plain life, with small griefs etched along the way, lives and love and dreams lost – that life isn't nearly enough of an armour. When you meet the Wild Hunt, there will be pain. There will be terror.

However it unfolds – when you meet the Wild Hunt, your life will end.

When you meet the Wild Hunt, your hands are tense on the wheel. The poorly-maintained road jolts you left and right, you have been wondering what would happen if you met another car driving in the opposite direction; the path is too steep either way to back up safely. You wonder if your new boss will forgive you for being late.

The roar reaches your heart before it reaches your ears. The first car, a screaming red and yellow, surprises you just after the curve. The driver opens a deep, dark mouth to scream something while waving at you to get out of their way. Then you notice the second one, blue and orange, fire and electricity. Then the third. Your breath catches; you panic. You try to back up and your wheel bites on the air.

You lose control. You turn back, just as they race by, an absurd, endless number of them. Your eyes fall on the children's seats, and for a heartbeat you lose yourself in the purest terror, before you remember that the seats are empty, the children safe at their mother's home. The wheels skid, fail to find purchase again. You slide down, and the terror is back; one mistake, one wrong turn, one fraction of a second when you failed to see how close the drop was, and this is all it took to sentence you to your doom, to never see your children again – risking your life to go to work, as if that was what truly mattered, a ridiculous ending to a mostly wasted life –

The Wild Hunt rides by like lightning. You fall, the car thumps against a clump of trees. Your head hits the wheel. You stop feeling anything.

Or perhaps –

When you meet the Wild Hunt, you come to a screeching halt just before the curve. Your right wheels are centimetres away from the drop.

You watch in disbelief, then mounting awe, as they ride by, furiously waving their hands, saying something you cannot understand. You clutch the wheel as if this could tether you to the ground. They are predators on the prowl, lightning-fast, too deadly for prey to hope or beg for their lives. You wonder if that prey is you.

The first car drives by and you realise that it isn't. They see you, in the same way they see the trees by the road: something living but insignificant, something small and still when their lives are power and speed. They drive by, too bright for this world, lightning and bursting stars and everything that crackles and burns and is gone in the time it takes to sear the eye. It has been a long time since you have last genuinely felt this awed admiration for something. Or someone.

The Wild Hunt drives by and the road is silent. Not long after, you will take another turn to a safer roadway. Your life after that will be an endless echo of *What ifs* unanswered.

Or even –

When you meet the Wild Hunt, you freeze. There is no way you can get out of their path, and you stare at the impending crash, the dark, open mouth of the first driver, yelling something you should hear, but don't.

This is where it ends. This is where your life flashes in front of your eyes, the wreckage of it. Love you didn't know or didn't care to keep. Years you cannot remember, invested in a better future, an investment that kept growing, a future that kept shrinking. Small concessions getting larger, small joys getting smaller.

You've never brought yourself to remove the children's seats from your car. If you closed your eyes now, you could hear them sing off-key, you singing with them, along a road you don't remember.

You don't close your eyes. For the first time, there is no future to come nagging, no present to flee from. You stare the driver in the face. You smile.

You think you see the driver smile back.

The crash sends you flying in flaming shreds. Fire pulls you apart, etches itself into your body, over the nondescript blue of your car, into your hands that clutch the wheel with renewed ferocity, into your heart that turns into an exploding star, powering you through eternity.

There is an empty space in the Wild Hunt, right in the place where you fall back down on the road, and you hit the ground speeding, screaming, with joy, power, speed, life.

The Wild Hunt rides on around you and you step on the accelerator, and you let out a long yell of victory.

On this side of endings, everything begins.

Picture yourself on a narrow potholed road, snaking through the lower reaches of the Italian Alps. You have an encounter there, specifically with a vintage car race that no sign or poster had announced anywhere. As they careen down the road towards you, you suddenly realise that there are many of them, that the road is not nearly large enough for them to drive by you safely, that there's no safety railing between you and a thirty-metre drop and that they're going very, very fast.

You genuinely fear for your life then, the kind of fear that pokes at your brain so sharply you don't actually feel it; it just brings all of you into focus, until you and the other occupants of the car find a solution that will allow you all to escape unscathed.

Later, you will be able to have a good laugh about it. The encounter is seared into your brain, however, and, as absurdly funny as it turned out to be, there's also the knowledge that your life and your family's could have come to an equally absurd but far less funny ending – an intuition that locals will later confirm, when they tell you of the accidents that have indeed happened on those races.

You'll sit down then. And you'll write a story.

The Hangman's Legacy

Crowds were as eager to forget about public hangings as they were to watch them. Their cruelty was a blessing, at least where I was concerned. On the night following an execution, I always dreaded what would happen if someone grew inquisitive about the fate of the body. I also knew that I had no choice but to wait for the fateful knock on my door.

I could always tell if it was the hangman coming by the cold draught he brought even in summer. The way from the castle walls to my hovel crossed pastures, lush with new greenery blooming between oaks trees where flocks of sheep had crossed, but he didn't take time to scrape the mud off his boots before entering. The only stool I owned groaned when he sat down without waiting for an invitation. Without seeing him, I could feel the darkness from the gibbet hanging around him, like a veil fluttering over his blood-red cape – and in its wake, my usual turmoil of dread and resignation.

'Evening,' he said.

I looked up from the embers, where a couple of turnips simmered with my last spoonful of stale lard. Queasy as I felt, I did not want him to think that I was afraid to meet his gaze.

'I have something for you,' he said.

'Don't you always,' I replied.

He smirked. I crouched to lift the flat stone by the hearth, where I kept a few silver coins in a pouch. As I grunted to dislodge it, he helped himself to a cup of wine.

'You ought to find a less obvious cache for your money,' he said. 'If I was a thief, this is the first place I'd look.'

'So what? You hang thieves.'

'Gladly. But I'd hate the thought of all that good flesh going to waste. Who will buy it if you run out of coin?'

I pressed my jaws together. The worst part about the hangman's visits was how genial he sounded, as if he truly believed that he was making conversation, not taunting me.

'Let's go,' I said, eager to get it over with.

'After you, my dear.'

The hangman opened the door for me – *my* door – and let it thud shut. To an outside observer he might have seemed every bit the handsome gentleman, though there would be no outside observers, anyway. The sun was low; the hangman and I agreed on discretion. I didn't want to burn at the stake and, if I did, he wanted to remain at a safe distance from the flames.

The body was waiting on a wheelbarrow, half-concealed behind a midden outside the castle wall. I recognised him. He was a vagrant, who sometimes stopped by to beg for a bit of gruel, or to spend the night under my eaves. Incongruously, his eyes and mouth were closed, though the brutal purple of his skin was as violent a reminder of his fate as could be. Dirty grey hair lay tangled on his brow. The rope that had killed him lay coiled by his side. I had stopped trying to understand what the hangman meant by those little attentions. Perhaps he did construe them as acts of kindness, an honour of some sort for the people he dumped on the midden, to be pulled apart like carcasses before he threw their remains into the common grave.

The dark depths of the hangman's mind were a mystery to me.

I took out an array of knives, clean towels and a candle, and set to work. Leaning against the wall, the hangman started whistling.

I cut off the hair first. The locks felt rough on my hand, like unspun flax, smelling of misery and death. I'd comb and clean it later, before threading it on a needle and working it into intricate embroideries on squares of linen.

Then I cut through the clothes and ran a knife along the skin, cutting where it held to the flesh, parting it from the limbs in one brisk motion elsewhere. Dried, tanned and beaten, it would turn into the finest parchment, to write verses on in tinctures of poisonous weeds.

I severed the muscle holding the jaws stiffly together, so I could retrieve the teeth one by one. Once I'd sanded down the brown outer layer, I'd have tiny ivory beads, just large enough to carve into figures of humans and demons.

It was completely dark when I cut through the muscles, now exposed and glistening by the light of the candle, and stripped the bones as bare as I could make them. Ants in the forest would finish the work, devouring scraps of flesh my knife had not been able to get. I'd fashion them into flutes, their sound as thin and faint as a reedy wind.

When my work was done, little of what remained was recognisable as having been human once.

I turned to the hangman, who still whistled serenely.

'Hair's decent. Three usable teeth. Couldn't get all the skin, though. Too many rashes on the back. Round it to three sols?'

'Hm.' He peered into the man's mouth. I had not touched the skull; it was the only part of the body that was not mangled beyond recognition. 'You could have taken the other two as well. That's two liards.'

I nodded. That was unfair and he knew it, but I did not haggle over broken bodies. Besides, he did not really mean me to argue. Whatever he asked for I would pay, in the end.

'Three sols and two liards. Here.'

'Thank you kindly,' he said, pocketing the coins.

He helped me arrange my harvest into a bundle, still dripping, though not much. After years in the craft, I had learned how to take a body apart without touching the main arteries. On top of it, he folded the rope, a tidy coil. I took it in my arms, delicately, and nodded.

'It will take me some time to work through all this. I won't need more for a while.'

'What a shame. Don't take too long. There has been talk of highwaymen on the road to Narbonne. I have no doubt they'll be brought in soon.'

'Try to delay the execution, then. You know what will happen to us both if someone finds a stash of human parts in my house.'

I let my voice weigh on 'both'. This time, he did not pretend to take it lightly. I took most of the risks in our business, and if anyone discovered the nature of our dealings, I would thank fate weeping when they finally burned me at the stake – but I would make certain that the judges knew, long before the interrogation was over, who had been supplying me with corpses.

This was the only bit of sweetness in the hangman's bitter hold. He might threaten to denounce me if I put an end to our arrangement, but a word from me could kill him just as surely. Had he been anyone else, I would have used that knowledge to put an end to our dealings once and for all. I would have been certain that he had no more wish to die than I did.

But one did not bargain with the hangman, nor try to understand him. I walked back home alone, and pilfered a little sleep from the remnants of the night.

I stopped being a witch when the sun rose.

It did not bother people that I lived on my own, on the edges of the village, where the rocky side of a hill hid the castle. Widows failed to remarry all the time. Sometimes women patted my belly, with a doleful shake of the head; but they knew I was poor, unprepossessing, and not very young any more. I sold remedies, poultices, lucky charms of all sorts: figures carved out of hard bead-like seeds I found in the forest, embroideries of the finest wool (young wives could cajole me all they liked, I always refused to give them the trick to spinning such even, shiny thread), rolls of very fine vellum with poems calligraphed in brown ink. On occasion, women dropped baskets of eggs at my door, with joyful thanks and a conspiratorial gesture towards their rounding belly; or a mother would drag a child by the hand to where I sat on the market, and made him thank me for the decoction that had saved him from winter fevers. Smiling, they would joke about the pretty trinket I had given them with their potion. They'd call it miraculous, then apologise with a laugh. You didn't publicly credit a woman with magic powers, not unless you wanted her to burn.

I was not a witch. I was safe. I kept what money I made in a pouch hidden under a flat stone right by the hearth, in such an obvious place only a fool would have kept anything precious there. It wasn't folly on my part, whatever the hangman pretended to think. Should thieves visit my house, I prayed that they would take the silver and run, and would not trouble themselves to look for a better hiding place – becoming destitute would be a thousand times better than having someone stumble on the cache in the garden.

On the day after the hangman's visit, I cleared a patch of earth, safely hidden under cabbages I'd let go to seed, and took out a chest that reeked of meat and dirt and darkness.

I spread out a sheet of skin, spreading it with salts and ground acorns. I washed a tangle of grey hair in a basin. I rubbed teeth with sand, slowly wearing the brown enamel away. I laid bones near an anthill under oak trees, where they could be mistaken for the bones of a boar.

As I cured and combed and polished, I kept my fingers stretched out for strands of magic spilling out of the remains. I pulled and pulled, winding them around my hands, until there was nothing left but crumbs I could not dislodge. I stored it all in a jar and buried it deep under the foundations of the house, in a hollow in the rock where so many other jars slept with their bounty of ghosts.

There is potent magic in a hanged man's body. My mother taught me how to braid a belt with the hair of the dead, so I could fly on the wind like a bird; she showed me how to write wishes on the skin of the dead and burn them on consecrated nights so they would be granted by benevolent spirits; she taught me ways to string the teeth of the dead like beads to bind the wills of animals to my will. She showed me other arts, too, secrets so terrible even she cautioned me against using them. She was not a cautious woman. She died on a pyre after a villager spotted her flying over the hills, on a clear morning when she wanted to watch the sun rise far, far away over the sea.

She might have escaped, if she had taken her charms with her. Or if she hadn't pretended not to see me when I reached out through the crowd to hand her the bone lyre, her most potent one. She saved me. Sometimes I wished she'd asked me about it first.

I would have stopped making charms altogether, if the hangman had not knocked on my door. He knew my mother had taught me some tricks, he said. It would be such a shame if I were to die over old wives' stories of witchcraft and other nonsense. Besides, he missed the fine wine and cushy blankets the extra income from my mother's trade had afforded him. He left me no choice but to agree, though I now ripped as much magic as I could from the remains he provided me, so I could sell them again as safe, harmless charms. Every time the strands of power tangled around my fingers, however, I thought I smelled charred wood and flesh, my mother's last screams echoing in my ears.

Just as I spread the sheet of human leather in the shed to dry, someone knocked on my door.

'Good morning, Madeleine!' a bright young voice called.

There was a puff of sunlight and warm breeze, and a girl (sixteen, bright-eyed and slender as an egret) entered the house. Her name was Lisa, I knew. I often saw her behind a market stall with poultry and eggs. We'd never had any reason to talk, but I liked watching her, always smiling, always with a pleasant word for anyone who came near. For the past couple of years, I'd noticed eyes turning more frequently in her direction, and some of those glances she seemed happy enough to return. I'd expected her to show up here, one day or another.

'Good morning,' I answered. 'Kind of you to visit a lonely old woman.'

'I've brought a chicken,' she said. 'And wine my cousin makes.'

She put the limp, sad-looking bird on the table, along with a little wooden cask. I smiled and thanked her. She didn't need to know that I only accepted gifts of meat because I didn't want to arouse suspicion. I couldn't stand the sight of exposed flesh.

'My cousin Julie says you can work wonders with herbs and remedies,' she said. 'She'll never thank you enough for the fertility brew. She says you're really, really good.'

I nodded. I remembered Julie, desperate at twenty-nine that she'd never be able to bear children. I'd given her a fertility charm, which I doubted had helped much, though what power was left in the skin could have given fate the slight nudge it needed to grant her wish. A little magic, just enough to keep villagers happy, was always useful.

Lisa leaned forward, all anticipation, and a little embarrassment.

'Could you... have you ever... I mean, there's a man I really, really like...'

'I can't make love potions, girl. These are just fairy tales.'

Five dewdrops on a piece of hangman's rope at midnight under the full moon, my mother's voice rang in my head. I pushed it back. The girl shook her head, apologising.

'I didn't mean it like that. I would never... But could you, perhaps... make me prettier? So he'll notice me?'

I grinned. She had no idea how pretty she was already. To make a girl like her even lovelier, I wouldn't need magic at all.

I went to the cupboard and took out a jar of honey, and some dried mallow flowers I pounded in the mortar. I handed the mixture to her.

'A spoonful on your face every morning. Wash it off well,' I said. 'You'll be radiant as an orchid.'

Orchids were sad things compared to this girl who made spring bloom around her from her humble market stall. With a little more confidence, she would be irresistible.

'Let him talk to your parents before you do anything foolish, though?' I added, though I knew she wouldn't. Even I had fallen backwards in the hay a couple of times before kneeling in front of the altar, and I had never enjoyed it that much, nor looked at anyone with the dreamy restlessness I could sense in Lisa's manner.

'Thank you, Madeleine. Thank you so much!' She kissed me on the cheek and left.

I'd never had children, to kiss me like this. They tell stories about mothers succumbing in childbirth and leaving orphaned heroes to seek their destiny, but the truth is, most of the time the children are the ones who die. And sometimes their fathers follow them, and widows are all that remain, eking out a living around the village and trying not to be noticed.

Winter had come, but the chill that invaded the house when the door opened caught around my neck like a rope. I was putting the finishing touch to a figure of a woman with closed eyes, carved in the ivory of a tooth. I didn't look up until the polish was perfect.

'Prime material for you today, my dear,' the hangman said.

Liquid sloshed, as he helped himself to the last of Julie's wine. I grunted.

'You'll have to make do with broken bones, though,' he added. 'The Wheel, you see. The baron insisted on it. You can't afford leniency when you catch a highwayman, or your roads will never be safe again.'

'How thoughtful. Will the baron make sure everyone has enough to eat this winter? If he wants to keep brigands off the road, that would be a good start.'

The hangman shrugged.

'God provides, God takes away,' he said. 'It's not the baron's fault. Shall we?'

We made our way to the midden in silence. As used as I was to handling corpses, I winced when I saw the highwayman. Blood had pooled under every bit of skin, shards of bone jutting out in places. I sat down, quiet, for a while. This had been a man once, a child. I wondered if his mother was still alive.

'Speaking about useless mouths starving in winter,' the hangman suddenly said. I raised my eyebrows. 'Do you suppose, if a man came to you about a young lady friend who might be, ah, in an embarrassing situation...'

'Don't even think about it,' I said. 'I'd burn for that and you know it. If you'd come to me before it was too late, I could have given you some herbs.' The charm I'd just finished was, in fact, meant for that exact sort of situation. Men or women would ask quietly, and pay a handsome price for that sort of thing. But to be even suspected of ending unborn lives...

'Don't be so gloomy. You'd hang, for certain, but that's a far preferable fate.' I turned around in disgust. 'Anyway, you understand me wrong. It's not too late. I just want to make sure that she won't find herself in troublesome circumstances. Such a delightful girl. If she came from an executioners' bloodline, I could even have considered marriage.'

My knife slipped on broken bone and sank into a bruise. Blood oozed and dripped on my skirt.

'You're a beast, you know that?' I said.

He started as if I had slapped him.

'My dear! You would be begging for food if not for me,' he said. And added, with a pleased smirk, 'I didn't seek her out, you know. She was the one who came to me.'

I stared at him. If horns had sprouted from his forehead, I would have been less aghast.

'I'll give you something,' I said. 'You'll pay the same price as everybody else, mind you. Talk to this girl's parents if you're half a man. I don't want to hear about it.'

I resumed my work, salvaging what I could from the mess of flesh and bones in front of me. My hands were trembling. It was almost as if the magic was already squirming out, hissing and writhing with ghostly pain and fury.

The hangman walked me back. I gave him a bag of herbs, and the charm. He paid what I asked, and didn't argue when I refused to pay for the broken bones.

'Always a pleasure, dear Madam,' he said. 'I should have Lisa call on you one of these days. You would see what a prize she is.'

I watched Lisa on the market for another month. Sometimes she greeted me joyously, and left me little gifts – a couple of eggs, some wine from her cousin, who expected another child. When she came to my house again, it was a warm day, and she left the door ajar so that a ray of light played with dancing dust.

'I've never thanked you properly, Madeleine. I'm going to get married,' she blurted out, and she clasped her hands and grinned.

All I could feel was cold tightening around my throat.

'Did he propose?' I said.

'Not yet. But he will. He'll have to.' She took my hand, and laid it on her stomach, with an eager little squeeze.

I froze.

'Lisa. Lisa, what did you do?'

She released my hand, grinning.

'It's all right. It's the best thing that could happen. He was afraid to speak to my parents, you see, because of what he does. Now they'll see who he truly is. A man who does the right thing by their daughter.'

I stared at her stomach in horrified confusion.

'I gave him a charm for you,' I said.

'You did. Thank you. I didn't keep it. I knew we wouldn't be together until something *brought* us together. Also… I wanted this. When I held Julie's little one, I couldn't wait to have one of my own. It's all right, isn't it?' I couldn't speak. She went on, 'You should get to know him. He's a wonderful man. And he has money, enough for the three of us. This is what I want. He is. They, I mean.' She stroked her stomach again.

I thought of them, this walking springtime of a girl, the demon of a man who would torment me until one of us died.

'Don't,' I said. 'Lisa, please don't do this. Have your baby if you must, but stay away from him. He's a monster.'

'Somebody has to do what he does to keep us safe,' she replied, gently. 'Besides, he has no choice. The baron would never let him stop. His father was an executioner before him. This is the way life works, for all of us.'

This gave me pause, though only for a moment.

'This isn't…' I began.

He will stand by a corpse he tortured to death, and talk about his new paramour as if we were walking out of church. I could tell her that, yes. And sign my own death warrant if she believed it.

I stood up. From the chest by my bed, I took out a thin, misshapen bone whistle.

'Here,' I said. 'No, I don't want payment. If he still doesn't ask for your hand after you break the news, play this at night by the brook. Then speak his name and spit into the water.'

Her smile vanished. She stared at the magic flute, then at me, its maker. This was it, I thought – the moment of foolishness that would land me in front of a judge. But she took the instrument and folded it into her apron.

'Thank you, Madeleine,' she said, graver than before.

I didn't answer. I wished I'd left more magic in the bone, enough to be certain that she could move what passed for a heart in the beast she had fallen in love with. It was too late now, and I prayed that the nudge would be enough, that he'd take her and her child and would save his evil for those sentenced to death.

It would have taken a stronger kind of magic to move the hangman's heart.

Months passed by and Lisa stopped coming to the market. Her parents' desperate insistence that she was ill did nothing to stop the sneers. Such a beauty – she had half of the young men in the village pining, and she had to give herself away to the one man who wouldn't take her to church, and humiliate her whole family, to boot!

'He should do the right thing and marry her,' I blurted out once, unable to stand the conversation that was happening right in front of me.

One of the matrons whipped around, scandalised.

'What a suggestion! Using a baby to coax an honest man into marriage? For shame, Madeleine!'

Their talking resumed, and I withdrew, cowed. I hated to admit it, but Lisa's predicament had made some villagers better disposed towards me. They had seen her in and out of my house. If she had suddenly come back to the market with a flat belly, my doom would have been signed.

They couldn't know that I would have helped her without a second thought, whatever the risk, if this had been what she wanted. They couldn't know that I woke up drenched in sweat, from dreams where I watched the hangman's genial smile as he bent to take Lisa's child in blood-stained hands.

That horror was spared us, at least.

I embroidered a handkerchief with a dead woman's hair and tied it around Lisa's wrist three days before she gave birth. She screamed and wept and begged for release, but in the end she lived, and so did little Sophie.

I visited her the next day. Her eyes were puffy, but she gazed at the child latched to her breast as if she had never known happiness until that day.

My arms ached, suddenly, remembering the only time they had held a creature like this, a purple thing that had never breathed the air of this world. It would have taken stronger magic to untangle the cord from around my baby's neck before it was too late. My breasts had ached for days afterwards.

I stroked the baby's head. People should have been feasting in this house. Instead the curtains were drawn, and Lisa's parents moaned downstairs.

'I'll help you,' I said. 'I'll come around, look after her while you work.'

'Thank you. But we'll be fine soon. He's going to marry me, you'll see. After all,' she giggled, 'he can't deny it. Sophie looks so much like him!'

Afterwards I would tell myself that it had all been my fault. Someone must have heard her play a bone flute and speak the hangman's name, taken fright and accused her. Young women who shamed themselves were easily suspected of the worst.

Hard as the guilt was to bear, it was still better than considering other possibilities. That the only mistake she had ever made was to be too trusting; that the monsters are invisible to those who have no evil in themselves. That she'd told the hangman that the world would soon see how much his daughter looked like him, and failed to understand that he really, really did not want to marry her.

They found my trinkets on her during the trial, the flute she had used to converse with the devil and ensnare an innocent man, the sculpted likeness of Astarte she had sought to use to murder the innocent life within her, or so the Inquisitor bellowed over her screamed denials. She named me during her interrogation, of course. More witnesses were summoned and cleared me. Madeleine? A simple widow who sells trinkets she carves to pass the time. Superstitious women buy them for good luck. If there had been any real magic in them, she would have been stricken dead as soon as she set foot in church, every good Christian knows this.

This could have been the end of the trial. But the herbs in Lisa's house were another matter. The inquisitor had seen countless of these cases. She had obviously tried to commit the unthinkable and send an unborn life straight to the torment of Limbo, and the fact that she had failed made her crime no less great. God had punished her with shame, then with justice. On the market, the matrons nodded and declared that they'd known all along. No iniquity was too low for a girl who had forfeited virtue. The fact that she'd denied the crime to the end, desperately wailing innocence in the face of the inquisitor who demanded her confession, was more proof of her guilt, they said. How black did her heart have to be that she refused to repent when her immortal soul was at stake?

I had no magic bone left, nothing that could help her escape. I locked myself in my home on the day of the execution.

I was watching the door, unblinking, when the hangman came in.

He started. I rose and walked past him, leading the way to the castle walls. By the midden, Lisa's body was as pale as the moon.

'It's almost dark,' he said. 'You'll want to be quick.'

I turned to look at him. He was not looking at Lisa. He paced to and fro, his eyes darting around.

'I defended you when she denounced you, you know,' he said. 'Wouldn't want you to come to harm. After all, you're not a real witch.'

I scoffed. He recoiled.

'How generous. Why would you bother to do that, I wonder?' I said.

His eyes opened wide.

'You're my friend,' he said. 'Why else?'

I stared at him for a while.

'It's getting cold,' I said. 'I'll just take her home. I'll work better there.'

'Yes. Yes, that's a good idea. Take her away.'

I lifted the body, grunting. He didn't offer to help and didn't ask for payment, either.

I reached home in the dead of the night and laid her on my bed. Bruises darkened her neck and lips. Her eyes and her mouth had been closed, gently, respectfully.

I went out and dug under the back wall of the house. There were more jars stacked there than I'd bothered to count. They pulsed with life, the anguish of highwaymen, the stupefied misery of beggars, the terror of the wrongly accused.

I brought them home and took a lyre from the chest, hip bones strung with the sinews of an assassin. I arranged open jars around Lisa's body, and sang as I plucked the strings. Some of my mother's teachings I had tried to forget. For the first time in my life, I was glad I hadn't.

Bottled-up magic flew into the corpse, glowing under her skin like starlight. I sang, and played, and did not catch my breath until her chest rose, fell, rose, fell.

She opened her eyes.

'Sophie,' she said.

I took her hand. Her body shone with a life that wasn't hers, but the words, the longing were her own. The brief hope in her eyes faded into sadness, as she remembered, as she understood.

'I want to see her,' she said.

I nodded. Julie had taken her in, I told her, and fed her along with her own son. She sighed in gratitude. I didn't ask what else she remembered. She hugged me one last time before going through the door, floating like a cloud of moonlight.

They said one can only do the devil's work for so long before going mad.

I did not sleep that night. I let myself entertain a brief hope that Lisa would come back, then snuffed it like a candle. Not even my mother's darkest magic could bring the dead back for good, and she had important people to visit on her last night. One for love, one for... I shook my head and forced myself not to think about what she would say or do when she found the hangman. Instead, as the last of the magic evaporated from the jars, whispering anguished, dreamlike nonsense, I listened for wisps of my mother's voice, reaching to me one last time as her power fled the house for good. My mother. It was the hangman who had lit the fire. Merciful fire that had ended her life in unimaginable pain, but spared me the horror of being forced to buy back her corpse. I wondered if the hangman had thought of it. I wondered if he had truly believed that he had no choice at all in the way he lived his life.

I spent the rest of the night wondering how I would now choose to use mine. Then in the wee hours, I lit a candle and departed for the castle walls.

I was the one who lowered him from the gallows, laid him down on the ground. I didn't bother to close his eyes. A lock of hair was wrapped around his hand, like a lover's parting gift. Whether he'd ripped it out in a desperate struggle, or she'd cut it herself after this last night together, I would not try to guess. This belonged to her, and her alone. As for him...

They found him on the midden, clothes torn apart, a long strip of flesh peeled off his stomach where (they reasoned) wolves had fed before being scared away. It was October, after all. Autumn made wolves more daring.

Magic tingled when I prepared a thin sheet of velvety leather, for the last time in my life, or so I hoped. I did not pluck it away. On that parchment I wrote a story, and then I tied it together with a thread from the hangman's rope. The power that quivered inside was stronger than anything I'd ever made.

I knocked on Julie's door in the morning.

'For little Sophie,' I said. 'For good luck.'

She kissed me on the cheek and wiped a tear. She dangled the bundle in front of the baby. It was a nice gift, though a silly one, from a harmless old woman who fashioned trinkets to pass the time.

I watched the newborn squirm and groan, eyes dancing as she tried to catch a glimpse of the charm. The magic would be potent enough to keep her safe; it was the best heirloom the man who had fathered her could ever have offered. As clouds parted outside, a ray of sunlight fell through the window, bathing her face in gold.

She looked exactly like her mother.

French singer Georges Brassens was famous for his straightforward guitar playing (which overshadowed a fabulous talent for melodies), his anti-conformism, and for lyrics that celebrated a nostalgic version of the French countryside, ringing with his tenderness for vagrants, thieves, marginals and sexually liberated women. One such woman from his songs is named Lisa.

Most of Brassens's songs are light-hearted, and don't reflect historical reality; his dislike of ideologies often translated into a rejection of any kind of politics. Once, living at the margins could be deadly: vagrants, thieves, and anyone unlucky enough to become the town's scapegoat were routinely jailed, tortured or executed, depending on the time and place. But it is less often recalled that those tasked with performing the executions could suffer almost as much: they were feared, hated, and forced to take on the tasks no one else would sully their hands with, be they cleaning gutters or hanging criminals. Only in some cases could executioners thrive, often only thanks to corruption.

I have to credit fellow author Sheila Massie for pointing out that the main character and her antagonist actually had far more in common than I'd seen myself. Atavistic prejudice had wormed its way into my story, and my choice of heroine and villain had obscured the fact that in a social order built on injustice and violence, the lines between victims and perpetrator are less clear-cut than they appear.

On second thoughts, Brassens probably knew that well. Could he be faulted for trying to dream a new world into existence?

Ice Cream from Pluto

When I stepped into the garden, my son was jamming sticks into a bottle with great intent.

'What are you making?' I said.

'A space station!'

I smiled. He had been fascinated with space from a very young age – contaminated in the womb, his dad had said – and I'd been more than happy to regale him with stories of rockets and faraway moons. Then I noticed the empty cat bed he was sitting in. I swallowed.

'It's a beautiful space station,' I said. 'Don't forget the sleeping bags!'

'No. There's even one for cats.'

I stroked his hair. He was silent for a moment.

'Where has Oreo gone?' he asked, for the twentieth time this week.

I hugged him, hard. After a moment, he shook free and resumed arranging his contraption.

'Is Oreo with Granny Lola?' he said.

I wiped a stray tear. My grandmother's life had been long and happy. I missed her nonetheless. I'd hoped Tim, who had barely known her, would forget quickly. He hadn't. One too many deaths at the margins of our happy little cocoon, and we hadn't even worked up the courage to tell him what death was yet. I stroked his back as he carefully introduced one more stick into the bottle. He didn't break focus, but rested his head against my arm while he worked. I wished sometimes I could enter that buzzing, growing mind of his, shake that feeling that he and I existed in realities so different I could not find out how to communicate with him.

'You're not going to be gone too, Mummy?' he said.

I moved closer, at a loss for words, and this time he hugged me back.

'I'll always be your mummy,' I said, because at least I knew this was true.

That night, as usual, I checked Tim's bedroom before going to bed.

His bed was empty. I rushed outside, called out frantically. I ran to the spot where he'd been playing earlier. He wasn't there. Neither were the bottle or the cat's bed.

I steadied myself against the tree, too bewildered to be properly scared. It was summer. Door and windows were open everywhere. I'd have heard him climb over the garden fence if he'd managed to, and he wouldn't have, would he? It was a tall fence, with a thick hedge. He was hiding in there somewhere. He'd probably dragged the cat bed into the bushes and was playing at sleeping in it curled up like a kitten.

'Tim?' I called.

Over the trees, the moon's face was peering down, bright and sleepy-looking.

'Tim?' I called again, louder.

The moon started. Two of its seas opened like eyes.

'Oh, that was your little boy?' she yawned. 'So precious. And what lovely manners! He left a while ago. I'm to tell you he left a spare rocket for you, under the thicket.'

I stared at it with my mouth open. She frowned.

'Well, what are you waiting for? You wanted to look for him, didn't you?'

I straightened up at the rebuke, nodded and ran to the thicket. Sure enough, there was a mud-stained plastic bottle, bathed in moonlight and glowing faintly in dead leaves. I knelt down.

'I can't fly to the moon in a plastic bottle,' I said, which was rather foolish.

As soon as I'd spoken, the glow vanished. The moon made an exasperated sound.

'Don't say silly things! Good thing he left his lunar module with me. I'll beam it down to you. Just wait –'

'What are you going on about?' I cried, and wiped my forehead. From high above me, a beam of moonlight was stretching down, almost touching the top of the trees. 'I'm dreaming. This can't be real. This is just –'

'For Jove's sake, woman, I'm trying to help!' the moon exclaimed, as the beam vanished and the moon's halo settled again in its familiar round, hazy shape. A nearby owl made a small desolate *Tyooh*.

'Last attempt,' the moon said. 'Listen carefully. I'm going to beam *you* up, and you, my dear lady, are going to keep that big mouth of yours shut!'

My jaw was still hanging open when a beam of moonlight stretched down again, and down, and down… until it came to rest on the ground and caressed the grass in front of me.

I looked at the moon. At the moonlit grass. I stepped forward.

A moment later, my feet hit grey rock, I tripped, fell very slowly and landed bottom-first on the surface on the moon.

'Wow,' I said. Then I noticed the plastic cup, stuffed with a bed of dry leaves.

'Lunar module,' the moon's voice rang, hanging eerily around me.

'This? But…'

A sharp shushing sound cut me off.

'Hop in and don't ruin it!'

I stepped forward. I opened the door of the plastic cup module and sat, warm and snug, in a seat that smelled of dry earth. I fiddled with the controls.

'I… thanks,' I remembered to say at last. 'Any idea where he's gone?'

'None at all. Now shoo!'

I pressed a button, and the module took off.

Space was huge. But I knew a little about Tim's interests after all this time. He had never been too interested in barren Mercury; Venus and its scalding-hot clouds scared him faintly, and though the giant planets fascinated him, he found my stories of never-ending storms and icy rings intimidating.

But Pluto he'd always liked, that small, distant, forsaken world (so cold everything that touched its surface would turn to ice), with Charon hugging next to it – a mother planet and its baby, orbiting together in the far reaches of space.

The journey was much shorter than I expected.

It was dark on Pluto, and very cold. In the distance, the sun shone like an icicle in the dark. Charon hovered above, a smooth, plump crescent, as cold and pristine as the surface I was about to land on. The ground was uneven, strewn with rocks and hollows – silent traces of the violence of space, though I instantly knew as well that if I flew high enough above it, they would be the features of a friendly face, crinkled eyes and minute lines around the mouth. Right now that face was expectant, quiet.

And there was Tim, sitting cross-legged in a crater in his winter coat, eating an ice-cream cone.

'Hey,' I said, sitting next to him.

He smiled.

'Do you want ice-cream? Everything that touches Pluto turns into ice-cream.'

'Um, this isn't how it…'

I stopped myself.

'That sounds delicious,' I said instead.

He beamed, laid a chocolate bar on the ground, then picked up a round, dark, luscious scoop of chocolate ice-cream. We ate in the quiet, watching the universe dance.

'I told Eline at school about Oreo and Granny Lola,' he said. 'She said they'd gone to heaven.'

I nodded, slowly, and took his shoulders.

'So you went to look for them,' I said.

'Yes. But heaven is so big.'

I kissed his hair. His head lolled against mine.

'Time to go back to bed,' I said, and glanced at the bottle on the ground. *We'll never fly in this*, I first thought, but I knew better than to say it, or even keep thinking it. We climbed inside. There was room for two in the pilot's seat. I took the commands and we jumped through space, with Tim cradled against my chest.

He began to doze as we reached Neptune, blue as a giant bilberry, with its storms that could whip you around like a crazy merry-go-round. When we crossed the orbit of Uranus, his eyes were blinking open and shut, struggling to stay awake, and I had to admit, the spacecraft would have been a lovely place for me to fall asleep in, too. Just as we flew past Saturn, however, he looked up, shrieked and pointed out of the window.

Another spacecraft was flying by. Another window, lit from the inside. And against the window, a black-and-white cat standing, pawing at the glass. And behind...

'Oreo!' Tim yelled, jumping up with excitement. 'And Granny Lola!'

Oreo's mouth opened, as if he was meowing in recognition. My grandmother beamed and waved. Her eyes were wide, youthful, happy. She blew us a kiss with both hands.

And then they were gone.

Tim turned back to me, a bright smile on his lips. Then the smile grew grave.

'You'll go to heaven too one day, right?' he said.

I drew him tight.

'Yes,' I said. 'But now I have the lunar module, I'll know how to fly back home.'

He yawned and curled up like a kitten, and I gathered him in my arms and flew us back, the taste of Plutonian ice-cream lingering on my tongue.

Some children play at being superheroes; some are plucky princesses, some travel around in colourful cars, and some join crews of space pirates on Europa where they defeat evil robots by playing epic guitar solos. I'm a science fiction fan, and a very lucky mum. I'll let you work out which one my son is.

Many children learn about death sooner than their parents would have wished, and then they're full of questions that are too large for their little hearts. Like most parents, sadly, I don't have answers.

But I have stories.

Soaring, the World on Their Shoulders

The Swallows' Cave

The war claws at the coast, but up here in the dry blue sky, the only turmoil is the wind.

Over the wasteland the mountain rises unchanged, white rock that simmers with the scents of rosemary, juniper and thyme. Long ago, monks had settled there, built an orchard and a cistern I am now grateful for. Their home and their chapel now whistle with the north wind, and the only chant you hear is the stridulation of cicadas.

The monastery at the top of the mountain was too risky a refuge, but, just below, the Swallows' Cave was perfect for my purpose: a lofty chimney with stumped pines concealing a much smaller opening, the remnants of a bomb crater I have walled up with slabs of limestone, so securely one could clamber across its mouth without finding it.

The fumes from the factories block the view to the sea, now that they operate on a forced rhythm. The war needs weapons. A large stretch of land over there is unrecognisable, scarred barren in the scramble for the aluminium it contained. When the wind scatters the haze into the sea, you can make out black steam engines sputtering on their caterpillar tracks, endlessly criss-crossing the mud, like monstrous scarabs scaling the corpse of the land.

But they have not found me. Under limestone and pinewood, I build.

Cécile Cristofari

Motherland

Your country is your love and your destiny, they said.

Until the very last, I could not believe that so many would follow them. Even when my friends started turning, one by one (too many people taking advantage of honest folks; if we don't defend our identity, no one will do it for us; you know, what they say actually makes sense; our country will be great again), I could not believe that the angry mumbles would turn to screams of hatred, that our worst fears would come true and that, eventually, the country would begin eating its own children.

The day after the election, I was having coffee at the university when the newspaper came in. I read, dumbfounded, then I stared outside the terrace at the end of the tramway line; men in cream suits and women in summer hats came down to admire the cliffs where the sea bit into the land at the edges of Marseilles, and I wondered how long it would be before the wood and brass wagons were replaced by tanks and grenade launchers. It was a long while before my ears registered the excited cheers. In disbelieving horror, I realised that in that place where only great minds were supposed to matter, not gender or nationality or religion, the news was received with acclaim.

I remained silent, even when an acquaintance leaned closer with slashing malice (*'You look so gloomy on such a happy day, Madame Santucci!'*), even when I noticed the ghastly faces of the ones who were not cheering, and started to wonder what peril they would find themselves in, during the coming months.

Over the mountain, there used to be a sea. Long before, the land was a warm, tropical country. Dinosaurs lived near its marshy rivers, laying their eggs in the mud. Invariably, the rivers overflowed and covered the eggs in silt, where they quietly died and fossilised. Somehow the dinosaurs never understood, and the land kept swallowing their children, over and over and over.

Now I know what to do with the last of the fossilised eggs.

First Flight

Soon after the election an entire pine grove disappeared, chewed up by mechanical saws to make way for the new military base. One by one, the laboratories at the university were requisitioned. By then it was too late to balk. The first opponents had started to disappear, as well.

They couldn't imagine why I wouldn't cooperate. Wasn't I one of them? Could I deny my country the power of one of its most brilliant scientific minds, when we were about to rise from our ashes and reclaim our stolen might from the rest of the continent? Not even if you torture me, I wanted to answer, I should have answered.

Yet it was a long, long time before I made the right decision. A train whistling from Marseilles in the dead of the night, a horse-drawn carriage waiting for me north, out of the city and into the mountains. Then clambering up convoluted limestone, fossilised trees and high rocky chimneys in pitch darkness to the cache, the wind pulling me from the cliff, the pit below blissfully invisible. As I put the rock slabs back on my hiding place, its hisses froze me. There started my new life – hiding, like so many before had tried to, some whose voices I could still hear at night, remote and cushioned in silence.

Siguiriya

He danced with the might of a lion.

You would not think much of him at first: a short wisp of a man who kept to himself. You couldn't understand until you saw him dance. He could stomp up hurricanes. He'd start spinning, and your eyes would widen, expecting him to soar into the sky. He'd stride towards you and you'd recoil, fearing the wrath of gods.

He could dance them all. Happy ones, *alegrías* and *guajiras*, he'd uncoil with a sarcastic, womanly smile on his face. He'd swirl and jump around *bulerías*, slither along *tangos*, pouring joy into everybody's heart. But the sad harsh ones he was best at. When the guitar slid into the five-fold, staggering beat of a *siguiriya*, he suddenly looked like he carried the weight of a thousand worlds on his shoulders, lifting it step by step, then letting it slip and crush

113

him. Not a sigh would be heard until he had finished. Only then would his exhaustion really show.

He danced in run-down bars in the workers' district, to the tune of guitars that could not afford strings. Red wine flowed and solemn *Olé!* punctuated his steps, saturating the pauses in his fiery display. After dancing, he would come to my table and shout for the best wine in the house, 'For Armande Santucci, the greatest genius God gave our generation!' and he sat amid the cheers, laughing at my embarrassment. I knew he would never admit how wrong that was. There was a genius at our table indeed. But that genius was my childhood friend, the little man the Spanish workers called El Flaquito with reverence and I called Kuki as I always had, who could dance up wonders my best calculations would never touch.

One day he took me aside before the final dance.

'If things get bad, you have to let me in on this invention of yours, *tía*,' he said. It didn't make him laugh any more.

'Things won't get bad,' I said, though I knew very well that they would.

When they did, he went into hiding, as well as one can hide when betrayed by one friend after another. The *gitano*? they said, much later. Well, he hid around here for a while, and then he got into the back of a car and was never seen again. That's all we know. We never talked to him much anyway.

I had to thank them, the kindly neighbours, and pretend that the news didn't matter to me. That's war for you.

The Swifts and the Stone Egg

Through the window in the rocks, I watch the swifts that earned the cave its name. They are unusually large, white-bellied, but as crazily nimble as birds can be. My camera records every motion of their tails, every change in the angle of their wings, the minute moves they use to navigate with the precision of bats.

Hunting, preening, playing, dancing. So many different kinds of flight.

The last of the stone egg is suspended in its beaker, radio beams nibbling at it, chemicals recording every remnant of genetic material. Aside wait more sorcerous offerings: feathers, bones, pieces of skin.

A torch shines at the bottom of the cliff. I withdraw the camera and close the opening. At dusk, I am more vulnerable than ever: it is just dark enough for a strong light to reveal the tiny window in the rock where I have made my nest. They are still looking.

Somewhere Else To Go

'Just go away for a while,' Kuki told me once, coming down from the stage. He was still sweating. His face was blurry in the dim light of the underground venue he now danced in, since the government had forbidden foreigners to meet in public places.

'What are you going to do?'

'Woman, whatever God wants me to do.' He laughed and rubbed my shoulders. 'Some good friends have my back. Don't worry about me. Just go away for a bit. Let the madness pass.'

'I'm no more at risk than you are.'

'*Tía*, so many people saw you prance around with that girl from the university I'm surprised your parents didn't just marry you off. If my beloved mother were alive, she'd skin me for talking to you.'

'Arianne and I are not – '

'I don't care about that. But you're a scientist, you dress like a man. These days nobody likes a *gender theorist*.'

He twisted his face, so that for a second it reflected all the weight of unspeakable perversion people loaded those two words with, then he roared with laughter. He was a puny thing, my friend Kuki. But his laughter was bigger than the world.

'Nobody likes a dissident, either,' I said.

'I'm not alone,' he repeated. 'You'll see. We'll stop that war in no time.'

'And how can I know you're all right if I go?'

'Why, you can't make one of your cranky inventions tell you where I am? Come on, girl. You try to go to the stars and you can't invent something to tell you how poor old Kuki is doing?'

115

Before I had time to put on a more optimistic face, he patted my arm, laughing.

'Be sure to take me for a ride on that thing of yours, will you?'

He said it jokingly back then.

Kindling

It's like a microscopic sculpture.

DNA weaves itself inside the beaker, offering its facets to my magnifying apparatus. It is magnificent.

Now it only needs a spark to unfold into life.

The Invitation I Could Not Refuse

A man with a neat grey moustache and a brown uniform studded with medals. Behind him, a life-sized poster of our beloved Leader, one eye ferociously trained ahead and the signature patch covering the other; grateful blond workers kneeling in awe at his feet. And me, sitting as tall as I could in the too-small chair, dwarfed by the viciousness of the giant on the wall.

'Your collaboration is crucial to us, Madame Santucci – '

'And for such a noble purpose. I know.'

He crossed his arms. There was so much contempt on his face it was painful to keep my eyes up.

'Which side are you on?' he said.

'I was wondering when you would ask that. You've run your background checks, I'm sure. I have nothing to be ashamed of.'

Nothing except believing a friend who told me he would be all right, because though I knew it, I could not bring myself to admit we would never be all right again – and then keeping my head down, buried in my research papers in terror of one day hearing that fateful knock on my door, even though the university valued me enough that I might have been safe. I might have helped him, if I had tried to, if I hadn't let fear keep me from standing up. But I didn't say that.

'I am right here, doing the work I am paid for,' I said instead. 'I'm not fleeing from my duties. What you are asking goes beyond that.'

'There are many different kinds of flight,' he answered, cryptically. 'By the way, I hear that you were very close to that history lecturer – what was her name again? One Arianne...'

'Machenaut. She's not a lecturer any more. She takes care of her children now. She should be happy to send you her family's papers. Her record is spotless.'

So had our last conversation been: crisp, dripping with perfectly polite finality. *You know, what they say actually makes sense.* I'd answered with a tight-lipped smile. Keeping my head down. That was one friendship I didn't really mourn.

The other one, the vanished friend, remained with me like a stab wound. I still could not believe I had done what he'd suggested me to. We had grown up together, in the decrepit streets by the Old Port, he trying to make me understand the complex beats of flamenco, me sitting him down with his school books to re-explain the arithmetic he never managed to grasp. Numbers, his and mine, had been the only area where we could not understand one another. In all else, we were two shoots of the same tree.

This had been the one time in my life when I shouldn't have believed him. Yet when he'd told me he would be fine, I'd trusted him, as I always would. Only too late had it occurred to me that he had only been attempting to keep me safe.

The words were out of my mouth before I could think.

'Find him.'

The officer raised an eyebrow.

'Here are my conditions,' I said. 'He was a flamenco dancer named Kuki Fernandez. Disappeared two months after the war was declared. Bring him back. Then we'll talk.'

A grim nod. A stamp on a piece of paper.

Just like that, I had become a collaborationist.

The Tiniest Nest

I have a cell. It's unmistakably alive. Then I have two cells, then eight. An egg.

The liquid undulates around it like a living belly. It's much safer here than in a bed of silt. It will grow safely until it can hatch.

117

I can't take it out just now. The light and July dryness would be its doom. Luckily the bombs have made the path upward to the Swallow's Cave much more perilous, and climbing down from the top of the mountain before the swift chicks have taken flight is tricky. They're more numerous and aggressive than they used to be, and the limestone has been polished to a sheen by trickling water; a single false step could be fatal. It would be so nice to think that this will really stop them, when they find my hiding place.

I wonder if it will recognise me.

Soleares

They would stop looking if I stopped working. I would stop working if they stopped looking. Thus we locked ourselves in a dance, me and the regime I loathed most of all.

Outside, the storm swelled, week after week. New roads cut through the land to bring coal for the brand-news dreadnoughts. Beaches turned dark and the water oily. Planes droned in the sky like monstrous hornets, back from razing one unsuspecting village or another. Inside the university, doubt was not allowed. All those who did not work on producing slimmer, faster bombshells and more powerful cannons had been sent home. Most of those who stayed were happy to, greeted each other and reported on their progress in booming, aggressive tones. Occasionally I met the quick, lowered eyes of the few who took no part in the collective enthusiasm. We never went as far as exchanging a word. We were useful, and therefore probably safe – but none of us wished to put our immunity to the test by exchanging careless words, and we all kept on in our separate universes, with the ironclad loneliness of guilt.

I knew there were whispers about my work, though I said as little as I could. Sometimes officials came to check on my progress. Would it be delivered before the end of the war? Was I positive that we could leave the Earth's atmosphere, all without the help of steam? How much load could it carry? And above all, how good would be its aim?

I answered, as curtly as I could, that success would be ensured beyond anybody's wildest hopes. I did not tell them that I had mercifully been stalled for weeks, trying to find the spark that would push my invention from fancy into reality. Whispers went on, calling me unhinged, and officials came and went, reminding me that their search still depended on the energy I put into fulfilling my end of the bargain. I worked harder, still unsuccessful, every step heavier than the last, every day longer, time crushing on itself as if the gravity of the planet was swallowing it.

Kuki had danced with gravity once, his feet sinking *soleares* into the ground, his body blossoming from it instead of crumpling up.

I fragmented my work into the most meaningless tasks I could devise, scattering it across research assistants who photographed, compiled, drew, mixed, without the slightest understanding of the whole. The most crucial parts I attended to myself, alone. If I'd been asked why, I would have answered that my research required the greatest secrecy. It would have satisfied.

In truth, I never paused to wonder why I did this. I carried on nonetheless, urged on by an intuition I could not admit to myself – or I would be crushed, for good.

Alive

A membrane has formed around the egg. What a mother's womb would be like to such a creature I can only guess. In a couple of days I'll lay it in a nest of leaves inside the incubator. In a couple of weeks, it will hatch safely.

The searches in the mountain have become more frequent. They know I'm here. It's only a matter of time.

Kuki Fernandez 'El flaquito'

One day they called me back to the office in the new military quarters. I crossed the immense esplanade, newly sterilised with concrete, amid crawling tanks and gasmask-wearing soldiers. I sat outside the door as I would have sat outside the gates of hell, listening to the dreadful sounds outside, wondering if my ability to bear them without breaking down meant that I was no longer fully human.

They made me wait for hours, not out of necessity, but to remind me of their power. The official held out a printed sheet of paper. Male, thirty to thirty-five, Mediterranean race, probably Spanish. Gold cross around neck. Height one metre fifty-eight. Weight at death thirty-four kilos. Cause of death –

I didn't read on. The sheer length of that paragraph spoke for itself. I glanced at the picture, closed my eyes, and nodded. The officer put it away.

'You said you'd bring him back,' I said.

'And we did, as fast as we could. What happened in the meantime was not our initiative. We kept our promise.'

'To the letter,' I said.

He ignored the sarcasm.

They knew what I would do after that, of course. But they didn't know I'd been preparing for weeks. That intuition I had not wanted to face was all that allowed me to be quick enough to slip beneath their grasp, and fly to my hiding place in the mountain, with a large, unassuming suitcase filled to burst with the most valuable research the country had ever funded.

Under Pines and Limestone

I settled in the mountain cave, away from daylight and guilt. At night I climbed down the wall to forage for food in the abandoned remnants of a garden the monks had once tilled, when the mountain was peaceful, fertile. For days I went through my calculations again, reviewing the pictures, trying to understand why I could not seem to achieve what was right at hand. I looked for the last piece of the equation everywhere I could, before realising it was flying right above my head. Swifts.

Even after I have shared their hiding place in the mountain for so long, their agility still confounds me. Neither earth nor wind holds any power over them; they are movement made flesh, dance made corporeal. Sometimes it seems to me that I am one of them, and that I drift faster than the wind, bathing my wings in the scents of rosemary and pines.

There are many different kinds of flight.

Too Far to Turn Back

I should have destroyed my papers, on the very day they asked for my help. Whatever the wonders my discovery could give humankind access to, its destructive applications were much more immediate.

But not after I'd dedicated my life to it. I wouldn't stop; I could only forestall the worse. I kept working on the genetic patterns until nothing was left to chance. I gave the creature exacerbated care-giving instincts, programmed it to react to the presence of any foreign organism as a mother would to her chicks. I made it as large as I could, so it wouldn't have to fear attacks. I wired its aggressive tendencies so that they would be triggered only in the utmost emergency, in protection of itself or others. I gave it the capacity to emit and receive pheromones that most earthly species would consider friendly.

They had searched in vain for a machine capable of transporting humans to the outer reaches of space, to survey the Earth from above and quench their thirst for destruction on any target they might want with no fear of retaliation. The solution was right at hand, however. It was not a machine they wanted.

What a machine can do with years of patient programming, a living being can know from birth. Where machines fight the world, tear themselves from it in long shrieks of steel and steam, a living being can make a pact with gravity and soar only because its nature is to live in the skies. Machines resist. Life embraces, like a dancer weaves his steps into gravity and pain and comes out lighter, quicker, indefatigable, like a dancer laughs away the power of dictators and his dance and his laughter keep hanging over the world long after his body is gone.

The result is two weeks away from hatching after a lifetime of work. A bird as large as a city, its back bearing a solar sail like the dinosaurs that used to roam the mountain, its tail and wings fashioned like a swift's, to navigate obstacles with frightening speed and precision. Its skin will protect it against the vacuum, high pressure, heat, cold, poisonous gases. In its flesh, a network of vacuoles is embedded, where human beings could live for months in the warm comfort of its body, fed and quenched by its secretions without needing to transport their own food, or even clothes. My bird could carry humans across the galaxy, as safely as inside a mother's womb.

But they only want it to load it with bombs.

Fledgling, Futures, Worlds

The egg hatches into my hands, on the minute it is supposed to.

First the beak pierces the leathery membrane, then the head emerges, covered in velvety, chestnut-brown fur. Its eyes gleam golden. They are faceted and alien, behind a translucent nictitating membrane. It pulls out a wing, then another. Gods that may be, I've never seen anything so beautiful.

Then it notices me, and it... sings. Its voice is so sweet, fluttering like a nightingale's. My hands shake and it clings to them with elongated fingers. We look at each other for minutes, the little creature blinking and whispering fluted sounds at me. It takes me that long to dare stroke its back with the tip of a finger. Though it is probably more resilient than I am already, my limbs are made of stone. When I run my finger along its beak, it rubs its head on my skin.

Light inundates the cave. A stone crashes down the cliff. Someone steps inside.

'You're under arrest, Madame Santucci,' they say.

I make myself not move. Very gently, I put the Swift down on a shelf. It whistles mournfully.

'Don't move, *pitchounet*, little one,' I said. 'You'll be fine.'

It is clever enough to understand my tone. Then I remember I have gifted it with enough memory to remember my words until it can comprehend them.

'I love you,' I say. 'Little one, you'll be safe. I love you more than the world.'

A second person hauls themselves into the nest.

'You have to come with us now,' they say, a little less firmly.

They've seen it. Perhaps they are even starting to feel its calming influence. One of them puts a hand on my arm.

'It's court-martial,' they say, apologetic. 'You stole military property. They should be lenient, if you cooperate. A few months in house arrest, and you could still negotiate…' The voice trails off, as if they could not bear their own false promises, when there is only torture and the depth of a cell waiting for me outside. The second one approaches the shelf.

'Is it… How old is it?' he said.

'Five minutes.' Already the sun feels too hot on my neck. I retreat towards the opening.

'How long will it take to be fully grown?'

I don't look behind me. I know what I will see: brightness, white limestone and dark green rosemary and oaks, and the aluminium wasteland, and the cave, above, the young swifts getting ready for their first flight.

'My little one,' I say. Then I look again at my creature, spreading its wing with lovely clumsiness, and my heart bursts into a myriad of shards, from love and regret and grief I didn't know I could feel so keenly, knowing that this is the last look it will be allowed to take at me.

'Thirty years.' I savour the words. I have lost my love, my beautiful creature, but not to the war, not this one, anyway. 'It won't fly before ten years. It needs to learn, first, and grow strong. In a year, it will crawl on the ground, but it will already be stronger than you. You can try to make it carry your bombs for you, if you want. It will die of despair or kill you first.' I laugh, helplessly, and in my laugh I hear another, a roar of laughter from a little man whose dancing feet could make galaxies spin – a man who made beauty I will never touch again, but my little one will, when it takes off from the world. 'Yes. Kill them if you want, *pitchounet*. And take good care of everyone else when they're gone.'

I reach out one last time to touch its furry head, and the cold I feel when I draw my hand back is as gentle as it is cruel.

There are many different kinds of flight, and for a moment I had them all, blooming here in the depth of my nesting place. I have lived with death, with guilt, with grief, and very briefly, with immeasurable love. I have touched eternity.

I yank myself from their grasp and fly through the opening, among a cloud of swifts, mothers and fathers and fledglings just learning to soar.

And from that flight I never land.

I have never found out for certain where the deposit of dinosaur eggs of the Sainte-Victoire Mountain was. The number of eager tourists is high enough that archaeologists prefer not to say. The swifts of the Swallows' Cave I have seen, however. They swoop and swirl, arched like crossbows ready to shoot into the sky, dark against the wind-swept light, untrammelled, magnificent.

Like many French children, I grew up with passed-on memories of the war. Family memories for some, a grandfather hiding an American soldier in his farm and serving in De Gaulle's army, a great-uncle smuggling Jewish children into Switzerland, Jewish relatives hiding among a White Russian community. Collective memories, painted over until they grew bright and uncomplicated as myth: these taught me that save for some unredeemable collaborators (who, I hear, didn't really count as French anyway), ours was a country of *résistants*, bravely rising up against the Nazi invaders. Vanished memories, at last; some swallowed, perhaps, by traumas I will never know of; some that didn't fit with the bright light of myth, like that other grandfather who simply decided to carry on with his studies in Algeria, and in the end did... nothing, as many of us do, living alongside injustice and making do as best we know how to.

I would like to tell myself that when the time comes round again to stand up to a fascist tyranny, I will not baulk at any sacrifice. I suspect that the truth will be a less glorious one. I will be scared, and lost, and my first thought will probably be to protect those I love.

Still... I would like to think I will try my best.

Schrödinger's Children

Archie stares at the cat as if he doesn't know whether to laugh or cry. Well, the *cats*. Or cat, singular. I don't even know.

"You said it would come out either alive or dead!" he says in a tiny voice.

"I know, okay?"

Archie peers down the opening of the quantum bag as if searching for a decisive answer. I want to point out that the last thing you'll find in a quantum bag is a decisive answer, but I shut my mouth. I don't want him to start crying for good over that stupid idea. Hey, let's put the neighbour's cat in the quantum bag, it'll be so much fun! And now everything has gone wrong. We've let the cat out of the bag and it's still neither alive nor dead. One cat is licking its paw and looking sceptically at the whole business, and an identical one rests in a little limp, pathetic heap in the same place – its eyes turning glassy.

"We can't return him like this," Archie says. "Mum will kill us." He stares some more at the living-and-dead cat. "Kill us for good, too," he adds.

I snort in spite of myself, then the mood is gone.

"I'll figure something out," I say. "Let me think."

Archie should be the one doing the thinking. He was the one Mum and Dad picked out at birth to be a scientist, after all – hence the ridiculous name. Me, I got Eliza, which sounds better but not particularly prophetic when it comes to future careers. Flower girl, perhaps? Anyhow, they got their predictions mixed up. Archie may love playing with silly experiments, but count on him to sit here bewildered and expect me to fix everything as soon as something goes wrong. To be fair, he's right to expect me to find a solution now. We both got the idea for the quantum bag at the same time, after all.

And right now, I've got nothing. What do you do with a living and a dead cat in a state of quantum entanglement? Disentangle them and end up with two cats instead? If our dog digs up the dead one, we're in big trouble. Besides, I have no idea how a living cat would feel, living on the same street as its dead buried self.

That's when I realise that if the quantum bag had worked as planned, we would have taken a fifty percent chance of killing this poor kitty that had never done anything to us. Science is a cruel game, but I still feel bad.

"Maybe we could just tell Mr Newton and hope he'll understand," Archie suggests.

That's a rash solution. Our neighbour, Mr Newton, is the unpredictable sort. He might yell at us and try to kill our dog in retaliation. Or he might laugh off the incident. No way to tell until you're right there, confessing whatever new mischief you have to apologise for.

"Fine," I say with my best over-dramatic sigh. "Wait here. I'll face the beast."

Next thing I know, I'm in Mr Newton's garden, which only happens when Archie and I have messed up or he wants to give us fruit for jelly. Apples are scattered under his huge tree, some still red, some already smelling of cider.

"Mr Newton?" I call. My voice is only slightly shaky.

Mr Newton's head appears in the window.

"Mr Newton, I need to – *Ow.*"

Something has hit my head and I start panicking, thinking he's overheard us and is already pelting me with kitchen implements. But it's just a falling apple that's hit me right on the skull. I stare at the fruit on the ground. When it's jelly season, we divide the pile in two, take the good ones home with us and leave the old ones to finish rotting there...

Suddenly I feel a big grin stretch on my face. Mr Newton has come out running.

"Are you all right, Eliza?" he calls.

"Yes, Mr Newton," I say. "Just wanted to borrow a little sugar, if that's okay?"

As soon as I've dumped the sugar in the kitchen, I run to Archie.

"We won't end up with two cats in the same place if we disentangle them," I say. "We'll end up with two parallel universes, and one cat in each. Much easier to explain."

Archie's eyes open wide. Then we get to work. It takes us the better part of an hour. One thing that string theory doesn't teach you is that the strings in question are devilishly hard to pick apart with nail-bitten fingers. So if you need to make a discreet hole between parallel universes, you'd better have tweezers and a sewing needle at the ready. And then we have to tease the two cats apart whilst preventing the live one from playing with the fraying edges of reality around him. If we hadn't already been put off silly experiments by now, this would have done the trick.

The hole grows as our task nears completion, pulling at the dead cat. I step through it, waving to Archie. We agreed that I would go with the riskier task of explaining away the cat's death, then I would join Archie in the other universe and we would both stay there, in the one where the cat is still living and we won't have to live with the consequence of our mischief. Because, after all, we're only children. I take up the poor beast in my arms and ring Mr Newton's doorbell, sniffing.

"I'm so sorry, Mr Newton," I say. "Your cat wandered into our house, right at the moment when Archimedes was running himself a bath. He fell in and the push wasn't enough to help him get out. He just drowned there."

Mr Newton gives me a sad nod and a sigh.

"I always knew curiosity would kill that cat one day," he says, and lets me go. This is much easier than I'd anticipated. In fact, it is only when he raises a suspicious eyebrow at me that I remember: when he's in the mood for gravity, it makes him even more inquisitive than ever. I'd better scamper before he realises that something is wrong.

I should return to my universe straight away. But instead I make a stop at our house. Inside, I find a red-eyed alternate-universe Archie.

"Poor kitty," he says.

I give him a hug.

"No more stupid science games for us," I say. "We can wait until university. Or if you don't want to become a scientist at all, it's okay. Nobody will love you less."

"Maybe I could change my first name," he says.

"Good idea. Hey, it's over. Don't cry."

I head back towards the garden. No time to wait for my alternate-universe me and brief her on what happened; I trust her to figure it out. For a future flower girl, I'm not so bad at this science thing.

Grinning, I walk through the hole in space-time in the garden and head back home. Time to return a healthy cat to his owner, and then we can put this business behind us.

"Hello, Mr Newton," I call from the fence. "You cat just happened to wander into...'

I stop when I see him crouching in his garden, grumbling and poking at something with a sewing needle and a pair of tweezers.

"Um. Mr Newton?"

He looks up with an ominous frown and jerks his chin at something dark and blurry on the ground.

"Mending holes," he says. "Looks like the mice have been playing while the cat was gone."

He glowers at me and snatches the cat from my arms. I try to hold on to my grin.

"Sorry to hear about it, Sir," I say. "Well. I shouldn't..."

His glare is so intent I don't even finish. But before I can disappear, he calls after me.

"Don't forget to let me know about your baking experiments," he says, tersely.

"Baking...?"

"Or preserve-making. Whatever you really needed that sugar for."

I nod very hard, turn and dart back inside.

Archie waits for me in the living-room, the quantum bag folded beside him.

"Do you think he knows there's a parallel universe where we killed his cat?" he asks.

I shrug and sigh, which is easier to do now that our daunting neighbour isn't around.

"Killed, not killed," I say. "Whatever old Newton thinks, it's all relative anyway." Then I take my brother by the hand. "Let's put that bag back in the garage. How about we try some baking now?"

One of the joys of learning to write in another language is the treasure trove of words and phrases that don't quite match those from your native tongue. That joy is so strong that on occasion, it's been known to rise to the head of novice language learners; it's easy, then, to wax pedantic about how some ideas can only be properly expressed in one very specific language, or languages radically transform the way you think, and by the way, did you know that Kilamburgish has seventy-five different words for chick peas?

I still find tremendous pleasure in the minute shifts in perspective I experience when switching languages — or, in some cases, when catching my breath between two more serious pieces, in the silly games one can play when trying to figure out how many cat and science idioms can fit into a story before it bursts open.

Don't look at me like that. You already knew there was more than one way to kill a cat.

A Diary from the End of the World

Worlds depart; their light endures.

Over five years before, I had arrived on the planet we call DA3(1), the Third Daughter of star Alkahran and only life-bearing body in the system. As most planets, this one had no specific name in the language of its natives: they called their sun the Sun, their world the World, and its inhabitants People. This world was not dying, but signs of extinction of its dominant species were already there: squeezed between a voracious and utterly unviable relationship to their habitat and a generalised sense of doom, the people of DA3(1) might yet recover, or they might not. The main savants of the galaxy already mentioned them with the tinge of regret reserved for disappearing beauty. Recording the glow from their fading embers was the perfect job for an exoethnologist, and so I was given an assignment there, to gather as much as I could of their culture in case it was lost forever.

I had spent the past few months in a place called Montevideo, sipping *mate* tea from a gourd and adding sketches of parakeet vendors to a string of unsorted field notes, when the mental call from Brood Mother came.

'The Grand Central Reactors have failed for good,' she said, her voice shaking with more than interferences from stellar winds.

The implications did not reach my brain at once. It takes longer to form an adequate reaction when you have transformed your body into one from another species, and for a moment, all I could think of was the warm *mate* cup in my hand and how annoying it was to be unable to receive space transmissions properly.

'We have to evacuate,' Brood Mother said. 'Me, your sisters, we all have to leave. They say it's hopeless. There will never been enough fuel to start them again.'

I put the cup down. In the dying throes of our sun, the Grand Central Reactors were all that kept the cold at bay. If we had only known they would run out of energy so fast...

'How long is there left?' I said.

'A month or so. We can't be sure. Please, daughter... please come back.'

I blinked. My eyes, native eyes in a native body I had composed five years before, suddenly seemed to remember the soft red light of my native sun, and the glare of DA3(1) blinded me. Getting near my ship would be simple enough: air transportation operated all over this planet. It was the last few dozen kilometres that worried me. I had left my transporter hidden on a remote island to make sure it would come to no harm, but that meant it would be days, at best, before I could reach it.

'I'll be there, Brood Mother,' I quickly said before she could sense my uncertainty.

And I snapped out of transmission.

There are thousands of records of worlds ending, but I had never seen anything quite like the place they called World's End in Tierra del Fuego: a colourful city sprawled between mountains still capped with snow, with the sea glistening greyish blue some distance away. Boats swayed in the port under a weak breeze: mostly travellers, people of means and wanderlust, with little need for extra crew. It might take days before I found someone to take me to the other end of the channel lying between a maze of islands, where the transporter waited for me.

It was a strange city, Ushuaia, a place where no one seemed to linger, and yet where everyone appeared to come seeking a truth of some sort. 'End of the World' it said everywhere, as if this was a great thing. I sat in a café full of tourists in expensive hiking gear, like a very expensive interstellar tourist myself.

I tried listening to the conversations around me, out of habit. But there was little I managed to record. After five years on another planet, in another body, taking notes on everything until it became second nature, all I could now think about was a reddish sky illuminated by a huge sun, with purple trees bending in the wind.

It had taken me days to find a ship that would have me on board. I had finally embarked upon a sturdy steel-hulled schooner, sailing towards the end of the Beagle Channel and manned by three Frenchmen – a sailor, a violinist, and a biologist who taught me about birds between bouts of peering at seawater through a microscope. Less than two days into our voyage, there was already no trace of human occupation left around us. Glaciers dropped into the sea from black, naked mountaintops. Flocks of penguins, albatrosses and petrels fled before us, inaudible with the whistle of the wind in the halyards. Aside from these, and the occasional sea lion surfacing like a black blot in the distance, there was no animal presence, although many roamed the depths of the sea, my companions had assured me. I had never seen the near-mythical beast they called a whale, but around here, those animals were undisputed queens.

On my home world, there were very few places that were so entirely devoid of people.

'Hasn't anyone ever lived here?' I asked.

'They used to, yes. They were slaughtered.'

I remembered encountering countless black-and-white pictures in Ushuaia, of a long-gone people, wrapped in furs and staring at the camera with nostalgia. Their names, Selknam, Yaghan, Haush, Kawésqar, were mentioned with reverence. Nowhere did anyone allude to the fact that they had been slaughtered, exterminated in less than a century to make room for cattle and fishing boats.

We'd had our genocides at home too. We did not like discussing them in the open, either, and I could only suppose that now the end had come, most people would prefer to feel sorry for themselves and forget past guilt. That was how it seemed to be happening on DA3(1), at any rate.

'Would you like a sip?' my biologist companion offered, handing me the *mate* cup, once the waves calmed down a little.

It was a welcome respite from thinking. We sat together in the cockpit, enjoying a few minutes of warmth from the tiny, bright yellow sun.

'You're very silent,' one of them observed. 'Is everything well?'

It was. It had to be. The panicked call this morning from Brood Mother was nothing; you would expect her to feel nervous in a time like this, and I was going to the transporter as fast as I could. I had acquired a decent command of most of this species' expressions by then, so my broad smile reassured them.

'Penguins,' I said, pointing out to the now-quiet waters of the channel. 'Look.'

As the ship approached, the tiny black-and-white shapes dropped one by one into the waters. I gazed at a massive ice field cascading into the sea, surrounded by smooth rock where the ice had retreated. When I was a hatchling, my brood used to worry about the ice creeping up to our village, not away from it. I grew up to dread the sight of ice. Yet for some strange reason, despite two hundred metres of cold dark water under the hull and steep banks covered in impassably convoluted trees on either side of the channel, here the situation felt peaceful, comforting.

The loss of an intelligent species is not the end of the world, I reminded myself. It was hard to keep that truth in mind sometimes. If humans disappeared from DA3(1), this place would hardly change at all.

Three days in, we approached the other side of the channel.

'We could see whales around here,' my biologist friend said. 'We're close enough to the ocean, and the waters are deep. I hope we'll see them.' He grinned like a child, a hand on the rigging to steady himself as he half-hung above the water – two hundred metres of kelp and darkness and massive wandering beasts.

'Everybody seems fascinated with whales,' I remarked.

'They should be. Whales are as intelligent as we are. Just imagine, we could learn their language one day! How cool is that?'

I thought he was joking, but his grin was one of excitement, not of irony.

'I thought you –' I checked myself. 'I thought *we* were the only intelligent species on this planet?'

'Lots of species are intelligent,' he retorted. 'They just don't write books about it.'

I had never thought of it this way, not even back home. I stared into the depth. But the water was so dark you couldn't see anything one metre below the surface. I realised that, after five years on DA3(1), I knew next to nothing about whales, or any other species, for that matter. Perhaps I had talked with too few biologists.

There were not many whales left, I heard, but this was one of a few places on Earth where they regularly came to hunt. Now I thought about it, on the day I had landed, I had seen a dark shape rise over the surface of the water and sink back down in a couple of seconds. I had not known about whales back then, although I had taken time to study local cultures through the haphazard messages they sent to outer space.

'I hope we'll see whales too,' I said, to keep my thoughts from straying towards those years when I studied exoethnology from the comfort of my doomed home.

Ahead of us the sea spread like a sheet of metal, so smooth the reflections looked as vivid as the mountains themselves. I gazed into the distance for the tapping of albatross feet in the waves, waters poked open by the back of a Chilean dolphin, or perhaps even a tall plume of spray that would announce the coming of a whale. The rumble of the motor blurred all other sounds, isolating hearing more than silence itself. But the broadcast echoing in my head bypassed exterior noise.

'It's over,' Brood Mother said.

I did not answer for a moment. I was taking the news surprisingly well. I was not sure how the body I had adopted was supposed to react, but so far it hardly seemed to react at all.

'You said there would be a month left,' I said.

'They ordered evacuation today. It's over. We won't ever come back.'

She said more things afterwards; that we had always known after all; that my sisters were not adjusting badly, all things considered;

that the barracks on GDKZ5-3 were clean and pleasant. She did not say how our planet looked as the ship soared away. I imagined it would have shrunk to the size of a ball, then a tiny, cold silver pebble, alone and dying in the emptiness.

Something warm started to flow from my eyes, as if, of its own accord, my borrowed body knew about the beauty of the lakes on my home world at moonrise, the bellows of the storms in the trees, the cries of river birds in the morning. Water ran down my cheeks, so familiar after five years of use, yet so foreign in that moment. I tried to push myself out, to throw my mind towards the transporter however I could and fly away I didn't know where. But grief tore my focus apart. I'd have to reach the transporter before I could get away from the form I had adopted, and so I just stayed there, clutching the rigging, trying to remain motionless even as my mind cracked down piece by piece.

There was a hesitant touch on my arm.

'Are you all right?' one of the crew asked. I forced my face into stillness.

'I...' My voice croaked. I blurted out the first justification that would not sound too strange to them. 'It's... the anniversary. Today. My mother's death.'

I did not turn to face him, but I received his words nonetheless. They were kind and awkward and brief. People here did not know how to deal with endings. He walked away soon and they left me alone, respecting a grief they understood so much less than they thought.

Island after island, channel after channel, the labyrinth unfolded towards the edge of the Pacific Ocean.

I did not discuss my supposed mourning any more with the crew. Instead I asked them about whales. I asked about whale song and what calves might learn from their mothers; whales helping out other beasts although nobody knew why and giving each other names; whales staying behind when hunted so that their pod members would not die alone; whales approaching ships without fear and being slaughtered for their flesh even though nobody ate it any more. We talked about albatrosses and penguin families and the tiny passerines that flocked to watch what curious sorts of beasts we were, when we neared the shore and shut down the motor. We talked and talked, warming our hands on *mate* cups and sipping the bitter warmth of the tea with delight, but we hardly looked at one another. Our eyes remained riveted on the blue and white humps of the mountains around us, the silver stillness of the sea.

Once, as we passed a waterfall gushing from under a glacier, I said, 'There was a river near our house, when I was a child. And a waterfall, just like this one.'

My biologist friend nodded gravely and let me go on. So I told him about cold mornings bathed in red dawns, and taking walks near the water to pick tart little berries in woods rustling with beasts he knew no name for. I told him how I heard the voices of my grandmother and aunts in the wind and he smiled, no doubt thinking I meant it as a metaphor. I did not tell him about the daily reports on the central reactors that kept the core of our planet warm even after the warmth of the sun had failed – about peacefully waiting for an ending everybody thought they would accept without question, as if we would always be able to hear the voice of our world and of our dead sun in the galactic wind.

I heard my own voice splinter before I felt it in my throat. I stopped talking.

My friend looked away and pointed at the shape of a sea lion, to give me a moment of privacy.

'We lived in a house by the sea when I was little,' he suddenly said.

I remembered what I had learned about warming climate and rising sea levels on DA3(1).

'Is it still there?' I asked.

He nodded.

'It's not going anywhere,' he replied. 'It's just that there are more storms now. It gets flooded more and more often, and it won't get better. I haven't been there in a while.'

He did not sound as buoyant as he usually was, and I did not insist. But his smile came back after a brief silence, as he told me about a childhood on the beach, glimpsing octopuses and hermit crabs in beds of seagrass, eating bitter red berries from trees that grew short and dense in the salt seaside heat. The more I listened, the more I seemed to hear another voice under that of the seasoned sailor: the voice of an excited little boy reading about fish and dolphins, running on a beach and lecturing his family about the cuttlefish bones and seashells he found there, building up a steadfast love of the sea when everybody thought he was just playing. I remembered lying down in the grass and gazing at the stars, revelling in the certainty that there were other worlds to explore even as the first reports of alien probes reaching our orbit were broadcast. Without the strange shape of his limbs and face, this alien could have been a sister of mine.

'It will stay there,' I said. 'None of it is going away.'

But I was not sure what I was talking about.

I recognised the shape of the island even though it looked exactly like all the other islands around. It was the first thing I had seen of this world after landing, the place where I had left the transporter five years before.

But the familiar pulsing noise at the back of my head was absent. Aside from the song of the halyards against the masts, there was nothing to be heard. I reached with my thoughts. The body I had adopted was less sensitive than my native one. But there was no sound even as we neared the island. When I tried to empty my mind, I could not find the familiar echo. It was as if my own heart had stopped beating.

I stood still on the side of the ship as the realisation dawned on me. The transporter was in constant contact with installations on my home world. There would have been no reason to keep them running as evacuation neared completion. Without its transgalactic anchor, my ship could not function. It lay there inactive, dead as the world that had made it.

I would never be able to go back.

Hours passed and I still stood, gazing at the island, probing with my mind even when I knew there would be no answer. Far ahead, the islands grew farther apart, the wind and waves more insistent. To a sailing ship, the passage to the open ocean was trickier than the crossing of half the universe had been to me. But when would my people start exploring the galaxy again if they had a whole world to rebuild?

I was alone, and stranded, and even if I ever found a way to go back, there was no 'back' any more. I would only land in yet another new world, one where I would speak my native tongue and where people looked familiar again, but where the rustle of the trees and the smells and tastes and bird songs would never be the same.

As I desperately reached into the silence, a hollow sound burst through the sea, immediately followed by shouts. I jerked back to the ship as the sailors rushed to the prow.

A huge shape broke the water, shiny and black, its blowhole visible for a second, then the length of its back, then the tail unfolding out of the water and sinking again, as large as my entire body, not twenty metres from the ship. The sound of its blow had split the air like a horn, but it sank soundlessly, while the crew whooped and ran across the ship in hope to see it surface again. But in the wasteland of my mind reaching out for a signal that would never come, another sound rushed like a wave, the echo of a mind bigger and deeper than any I had ever encountered –

Little one little calf on the water hurt are you hurt I am here little one I will help...

I stepped on the bowsprit, as far as I could, a strange feeling of weightlessness washing over me, as if I had reached the transporter and was changing into my native form again. I spread my mind open. Concern, gentle worry for a strange creature flooded my thoughts, and I probed for a way to respond, *no hurt I'm fine I'm fine stay please stay here...*

The sound of the blow echoed again amid cries of wonder, and perhaps I saw the whale surface again, although sight and thought were too mingled to tell apart. Amid hissing waves and grey summits, I let myself drift for the last time, letting go of my borrowed body and perhaps of my native one as well, too far away from the safety of the transporter to know how it would end, and too far gone to care. The shouts of wonder turned to cries of warning, but overlaying my senses came the vast drifting thoughts again –

Little creature little stranger I will help you hurt no hurt you're safe you're safe...

My feet lost the bowsprit, but there was no cold to meet me. I greeted the water like a long-lost home, I felt my mind change into one I had never imagined, and just before I lost words to enter a never-ending song, I realised that I was swimming home, in the only place in the universe where the world was not ending.

**

To Sonate and her crew: Robin Cristofari, Florian Maury and Jean-Christophe Gairard

The Beagle Channel in Tierra del Fuego was not always empty of human presence. The Selknam, Yaghan, Haush and Kawésqar people once lived on its shores or nearby, before being killed or driven away by white settlers; their descendants now live all over Argentina and Chile, where they carry on the heritage of their people. The Selknam were finally recognised as one of the original people of Chile in September 2023.

Today the wilderness is back in most of the Beagle channel, however; the mountains on either side echo with birdsong, and nothing suggests that people ever lived there. The old names are gone, and even the stars overhead bear the names of colonisers from Europe.

I have never felt so tiny and out-of-place as when sailing the Beagle channel with my brother and his friends. As a tourist, first, forging my own bond with the place but being nonetheless aware that I could not understand its depth and complexity; as a human being, as well, crossing waters that happily existed outside of human presence and showed as plainly as possible that the universe didn't revolve around us. The sense of how little humanity mattered there was almost mystical in its intensity. Unexpectedly, it was also comforting.

One of the newspapers in Ushuaia is titled *Diario del fin del mundo*. Thoughts of the end of the world come with fear and distress, much of the time.

But maybe they don't always have to.

The Third Time I Saw a Fox

'You know what I think, the world is going bonkers,' the circus man says.

I nod, draw a gulp of burning coffee from my thermos flask. A decent night watch needs to start with a little bitterness on the tongue, the first drink just a little too hot before the next cups fade to lukewarm. It's the only excitement I'm afforded, after all. No one ever breaks into natural history museums.

'Who needs the world when we have this?' I say, encompassing the anatomy exhibits with a wave of the hand. 'And the two of us, of course.'

The circus man nods, sagely. Even though I'm not looking at him, I can hear it from the creaking of his vertebrae, grinding against the copper wire that holds them together.

My shift always starts after the cleaning crews have left, and I always take my first walk alone around the quiet halls, as the ghost of another crowded day fades into the night. Some say I'm too old to be working night shifts, but I say I'm too old to stand by as hordes of school children squeal over dinosaur bones. Fake dinosaur bones at that, though children don't realise they're standing in front of casts.

It's easier to tell real skeletons apart when night falls.

'Hello there,' the minke whale yawns. It stretches its big head left and right and sighs, a whisper of wind through polished jaws that snap uselessly, as if attempting to trap shoals of ghost fish in imaginary baleen. It must feel lonely here, hanging above the ground, floating in a make-believe sea. I pat its bony knuckle and walk on.

In the zoology gallery, discreet sounds emerge upon my entrance. Sawdust rustles from inside stuffed bodies, glass eyes whirr in their sockets. Their old bones move even more awkwardly than mine, but they acknowledge me nonetheless. They don't make new stuffed specimens for natural history museums any more. Resin models may look glossy and sprightly forever, but the night shows just how dead they are, in their perfection of plastic. All my friends here, posing on their mahogany stands, tired but still proud under their bald patches and protruding wires, are from another time. Just like me. The thought makes me grin. Sometimes.

In their glass cabinets, ancient enough that the glass bends in places, the birds stretch the tips of their wings. Some of them groan the way I do when I wake up with stiff limbs on a cold morning. An albatross sways on the thread that holds it up, gliding in the same spot, day after day. I wave, nod, ask about their health. They tell me the same things every night, but I can tell they're still pleased that I asked. They need distractions, just like all of us, and they have no one else to talk to.

Farther on, the leopard stretches its paw, lazily hanging from a fake branch, and rests it on my shoulder as I walk by.

'Nice evening, isn't it?' I say, petting its front leg.

'A little damp for me,' it replies. 'I feel bloated.'

Of course. All that sawdust stuffing won't do well in damp weather. I turn down the humidifiers at once. The leopard nods its thanks.

I don't know how long this nightly ritual has been going on. It seems that they've always been waiting for me, dormant by day but awake and already stirring the moment I come in, though part of my mind also holds the memory of a time, long ago, when I considered those night watches to be lonely and dreary. I'm not certain why I should pay attention to passing time anyway.

As I leave the gallery on my way to my favourite seat – next to the circus man, in the anatomy exhibits – I greet a fox sitting on a tuft of fake grass. It doesn't greet me back. I raise my eyebrows and say it a little louder, but the fox doesn't budge. A little miffed, I leave the hall.

*

'It's just a grouchy old fox,' the circus man says. 'It must make it grumpy to see those rabbits cavorting just outside its reach.'

He's making sense, as usual. But I can do nothing about where the rabbits are set, alas. You'd expect the fox would know that. It's rude of him to pretend it's my fault.

'Strange creature,' I mumble.

It's uncommon to meet foxes these days. They're unpredictable, too; some of them will sit by your car, expectant, as if used to being given food, while others will scamper away as if they had been prey all their lives, not predators. I grin as a memory hits me.

'First time I saw a fox, I was not yet ten,' I say. 'I'd been walking in the rain for hours, trying to find mushrooms. It wasn't a good day and I wasn't in a good mood. And then I see this fox, right here on the path in front of me, with eyes as big as saucers.' I smile at my own words. It doesn't sound like such an exceptional experience when put like that. But the circus man keeps nodding, waiting for what comes next. 'So we just stood there and stared at each other for a whole minute. He was thin as a rake. At some point I wondered if he was hungry enough to try and attack me. Then he just left.'

'Nice story,' the circus man says.

'Have you ever seen a fox?'

'You see a lot of things on the road,' he replies.

He doesn't like to talk about his life, the circus man. It can't have been happy. He was very tall, too tall for most ordinary jobs. He ended up on the road as a circus freak. Eventually he died of tuberculosis, or so the label under his glass case says. Once I told my friend that it pained me to know so little about his old life, and that all of it came from a shiny brass plate in a museum, but he kept silent. I think it pained him more, for some reason I'll never know. I didn't press the matter any further.

I don't press him about foxes, either.

'There was this other time I remember, I say. Two other times, in fact.' I grin again. Three encounters with foxes in the wild. It sounds like something out of a fairy tale. 'I was in the woods, looking for mushrooms. And all of a sudden I saw this fox right before me, looking as if it had never seen a human in his life.'

The circus man cocks his head.

'Isn't that the story you've just told me?' he says.

I stop. Pictures overlap in my head, the difference between them fading, like the logic of those half-dreams that come to you when you're just starting to fall asleep. I frown.

'Same story, yes,' I say. 'Sorry, mate. Got distracted.'

'Happens to everyone,' he replies. There's something sceptical in his tone, though. But he changes the subject too quickly for me to ask about it.

'I'm telling you, this world is going bonkers,' he says, and I nod.

Just before I leave the gallery the following night, I turn back to look at the fox. It's just sitting there, empty-eyed. Yet there's something in its gaze that almost feels like malice.

'Still sulking?' I say.

No answer comes. I shake my head and sigh. Really, those rabbits aren't even right under its nose anyway. And they've always been there. Why would he start fussing about them now?

Why do you expect a dead animal to greet you?

I pause at the incongruous thought. There's nothing dead here; only old, rusty creatures that nonetheless haven't lost their will to live.

None of us have.

When I sit down next to the circus man, something comes back.

'So, that story I was going to tell you yesterday about the second time I saw a fox,' I say.

I can sense he's happy that I've remembered. I am, too.

'We were going out for a picnic, my girlfriend and I. Driving in the woods to this spot I knew.' I'd felt like a regular woodsman that day, taking city-bred Louise along the forest road, although in truth I would have been just as lost as her if it had come to surviving there for more than a day. 'The weather was beautiful and I was head-over-heels in love. When we saw the fox by the side of the road... you should have heard her squeal.'

'I can picture it,' the circus man replies.

This is, I realise, one of the happiest memories of my life. I'd forgotten about looking cool and detached and started squealing along with Louise – who, as it turned out, much preferred this side of me anyway. The fox had been oblivious to us, only glancing our way while licking its skinny leg. We left after it trotted away, and ate sandwiches and blueberries in a clear patch between birch trees, all the while kissing and laughing and talking.

Innocence can't last, precious and lovely as it is. We parted ways one day as quickly as we had fallen in love, over a misunderstanding I couldn't even remember. I lost track of her after she got married, and went on to build a family of my own, then another. All my life, however, the memory of our pristine infatuation flickered over the faces of the women I met, until there were no women left, just children who didn't call often enough and the memory of young love, lost.

Regret is what I should feel right now, I suppose. Or I could be wise and observe that my past is just another of those things that make up who I am; I might as well regret having hands or ears. I feel neither wistfulness nor bittersweet peace. What really bothers me is that I can't picture Louise any more in my mind. All I get is the fox, and the blur of our combined laughter.

'It's terrible that happy memories can become the saddest ones to remember,' my friend says, with unexpected gentleness.

I gulp down some coffee. Terrible, yes. That's probably why the memory wouldn't even come back yesterday. I'm too old to be pained by recollections of a happy youth.

On every one of the following nights, as I tour the museum before turning off the lights in the exhibits, I stop by the fox. It never blinks. Once I even try moving two of the stuffed rabbits around, to their gentle protests, but get no reaction. There is no expression in its glass eyes. The emptiness I see there has its own depth, though, like murky waters where too much silt prevents you from feeling the bottom.

When I walk out of the gallery, I'm loath to turn my back on it. *Dead thing*, something in me whispers, as if it made sense. Just a couple of weeks ago, the fox greeted me at night just like all the others. It's uncanny that when I try to remember its voice, its words, however, they keep eluding me. I suppose it never was a talkative creature.

'Didn't you say you had three memories of foxes in the wild?' the circus man once says.

Did I say that? I don't answer for a while. Three, like fairy tales. Yes, that's right. There was a whiff of the otherworldly every time, I remember that well. Except that when I attempt to recount them, they sound trite to my own ears.

'That's right,' I say. I force my face into a grin. The circus man never has to make any efforts to smile. My skin feels like the remnants of his, stretched and dry over yellow teeth. I close my lips, shake my head. Good memories.

'There was that time when I was picking mushrooms in the rain,' I say. 'I've told you about this one, right?'

A creaking nod answers.

'Then that other one with Louise. She was so beautiful that day.' And every day after that, though we spent too few of them together.

Another nod. He knows about that one, too.

'Then the third time…'

I pause. It was right here. A moment ago, it was obvious, fully-formed in my mind.

I close my eyes and join my hands in front of my face. Is this one of those nightmares when you think you've woken up, only to find yourself in another, stranger construct of your brain? The cup of coffee warms my skin, just a touch too hot to be comfortable, as real as one could feel. The memory, on the other hand, has evaporated like a dream.

'I don't know what's going on with me, old boy,' I whisper. It sounds like I'm starting to cry.

There's a shift in the glass cabinet next to me. I glance to see the circus man move his arm. Slowly, awkwardly, he raises his hand towards me. His bony fingers scratch the glass and he makes a frustrated, helpless little groan. I lean on the cabinet and feel the vibrations of his bones that creak against the pane where he moves his hand up and down, trying to pat my shoulder through it.

It takes me unexpectedly long to compose myself. The coffee is cooling in my hand. I drink the tepid brew that's no longer comforting.

'Do you reckon,' I say, as steadily as I can, 'maybe I could ask them not to bury me at all when I'm gone?'

'And just leave you there? What for?'

'Maybe they could embalm me instead. And put me in here.' I tap the cabinet. 'We can chat all we want then. Just the two of us. Wouldn't that be fine?'

The answer doesn't come straightaway.

'You know,' my friend says at last, 'embalming doesn't work that well. They left one of those Egyptian mummies here once, remem–' He stops. I could almost hear him bite his parched lips. 'Well, that was a while ago. Before your time, I reckon.'

I don't remember it, no. But I'm glad he would tell me about something that happened before I met him. He so rarely does, and now this is just what I need. 'Anyway. Poor chap couldn't even move his neck. With all the fuss they make about Egyptian embalmers, there's one simple thing they never figured out. You don't get younger, ever.' He makes a cackling sound. 'Especially when you're dead.'

'You're not dead,' I protest. And then the sight of the dried-out remnants of his skin, stretched like a membrane over the huge expanse of his body, hits me like a slap. I take my head in my hands.

A horrible, irrational fear of walking back through the museum courses through me like fever. Behind closed eyelids, I feel the glass eyes of the fox bore into my soul. There's nothing behind those eyes, only a growing pit. *Dead. Old dead things.* I start to whimper.

'Bernard?'

The word comes from very far away. I'm certain it means something. I have it right here.

'Bernard? Hey, it's all right. Don't be so upset. Come on, old friend.'

And then it comes back to me. Bernard. I turn my head towards the cabinet. The circus man leans forward, its hand on the glass.

'Yes, that's me,' I say, and smile. 'It's all right. I felt dizzy, that's all.'

Bernard. No, it's not like I was beginning to forget my own name. Bernard Gagnon. I was only scared, that's all. I am Bernard Gagnon. I've always been.

The thought is so satisfying I feel an urge to get a piece of paper and write it in capital letters. I am Bernard Gagnon. I've never doubted that for a second.

'What are you doing?' the circus man asks.

I put down the pen and read the words again. I am Bernard Gagnon. What a simple, beautiful truth. I put the piece of paper in my breast pocket.

'You should go home,' he gently says. 'You need some rest. You'll feel better tomorrow.'

Home. Yes, that's what one does when one starts crying in the middle of their work shift. November is never kind on anyone.

'You're right,' I say, and get up, grinning. 'I should go home. Can't keep Louise waiting for me all night.'

Three times I saw foxes in the wild, encounters that smelled of magic, such a fragile sort of magic that even talking about it could destroy it.

Or maybe chasing memories is like looking at the stars. Stare at them and they'll disappear. Catch them from the corner of your eye and they'll strike you in all their brightness. Except that, for untrained eyes, this is the best way never to see the stars; as soon as you've caught something, you can't help staring at it, and then, unavoidably, it escapes your grasp.

The following night, the minke whale, the albatross, the snake swimming inside its jar, all of them greet me with a worried air. I hurry past the fox without looking at it. The circus man is the only one who doesn't look distressed.

'You were right to take a few days off,' he says. 'Feeling better?'

I grin.

'Ten years younger, you mean,' I say.

And then I stop. The circus man stares ahead, tense and silent, and I pick up his hint and turn around.

There is someone in there. For a moment I am too shocked for words. I haven't had human company in the museum in… in…

It's a middle-aged woman I know; mousey hair, grey jacket, sensible shoes. We work together. Or at least we both work here. She's never shared my watches, that's for certain.

'Bernard? What are you doing here?'

Friendly, concerned even. Still, I frown.

'Hello to you too,' I say.

Beside me, the circus man remains still, in appalled silence. She has the grace to look embarrassed.

'Good evening, Bernard. Sorry. I wasn't expecting to find you here.'

Still that gentleness in her voice, as if she was attempting not to frighten me. A picture flashes in my head, a fox staring under drizzling rain, taut, ready to dart away. We eye each other cautiously.

'Why didn't you expect me here?' I say, trying to sound genial, though in truth, her intrusion is as irritating as it is unsettling. 'This is my schedule. I've never missed a day in all my time here. You know that.'

She sighs. Now she straightens her back. I don't remember what she does here, but she must be some sort of manager. She expects me to listen. I do, but only out of courtesy.

'You were in the hospital, Bernard,' she says. 'For the last five days. Someone called an ambulance for you while you were...'

She trails off. Now I'm angry.

'While I was what? What hospital, anyway?'

But just as I speak, a new, foggy picture forms in my mind: unknown parts of the city under yellow lights, cars flickering by, high brown walls, all looking similar. Cries for help echoing around, like a small boy begging for his parents, only it was not a child's voice but a man's, a shaky male voice I knew but could not place.

I finger my breast pocket. There's a piece of paper there, all crumpled. I remember a voice reading, word after word, 'I am Bernard Gagnon.' That must be the person who stuck that in my pocket. What for, I cannot imagine. Of course I know who I am. Did they mean to make fun of me? People like to make fun of solitary old men. Yet they seemed so kind, their voices so reassuring, when they helped me on that gurney and into the car, under revolving lights.

149

'After you got lost on your way home,' she says.

I don't know if she's trying to play a joke on me. Then I realise that she's not laughing, not even suppressing a mischievous flicker around the eyes. Hospital. A long straight corridor, painted green, flickers on and off in my brain. A steel bed. I've never liked steel beds at home, reminds me too much of a...

'I'm certain you'll be better very soon,' she says, softly. 'But now you're supposed to be resting. At home. I was coming to show your substitute around.'

But this *is* home, I think. 'This *is* my home,' a voice echoes, a thin whimper of a voice that sounds like my own.

Unexpected pain seizes my throat. There is pain in the woman's eyes, too. I turn to the circus man. Explain to her, I want to say. Tell her I've never been away, never lost my way home, this is all a misunderstanding, we were right here all along, the two of us, drinking coffee and chatting the night away. If I'd been lying helpless in a steel bed, behind the walls of the hospital, surely my friend would have noticed? But the circus man can only stare in dismay as the woman lays a gentle hand on my arm and leads me away from him.

Once I saw a fox while picking mushrooms in the forest. I was a child then. I had a happy childhood, a very unremarkable one.

The second time, I saw a fox while driving through the woods with my girlfriend Louise. I had an unremarkable adulthood, of the sort that flies past leaving behind more disappointments than memories.

The third time...

My name is Bernard Gagnon. My best friend is a dead circus freak who waits in a glass cabinet between other museum specimens. I hope I'll never be buried. I hope they'll put my body in the glass cabinet beside him. People will gape at us, the giant and the short, thin old man. They'll notice me for the first time and I'll grin an endless grin in response. Maybe one day my children will walk by and say 'Hi, Dad.' Maybe Louise will walk by and recognise my smile even if she doesn't recognise my bones.

None of this will ever happen. They say I'm too old and worn to work. They've sent me home. There's no sweetheart waiting and no children visiting and the nurse is kind to me but she doesn't know me nearly as well as my old friends did and one day she'll stop even pretending that what I tell her makes sense and I'll have nothing left but... memories...

And then they'll find my lonely old body one morning and they'll put me in a grave and I'll be all alone, falling and falling and falling forever, with the empty glass eyes of a dead, stuffed fox staring at my back.

Out of kindness perhaps, or because everyone can forget things that don't matter much, they didn't take my badge from me.

I take one last stroll through the museum in the wee hours of the morning. My friends are weary, but they say their enthusiastic goodbyes all the same. The minke whale settles back in its iron braces. It has another long day ahead of it, weathering squealing children and amateur naturalists by the hundreds.

'Take it easy, my friend,' I say.

'Always do,' is the answer.

My last stop is in the anatomy exhibit. The circus man sees me come in. His grin stretches on his lips, tinged with a sadness I don't have the heart to dispel.

He knows I'm not coming back.

'Tell them about me,' I say. 'We've had some pretty good times, haven't we? Some good memories we have together. Next time you make friends, you tell them all about us.'

'I'll do that,' he says. As I turn around, he adds, 'And if we ever meet again, you'll tell me about that third time you saw a fox. I'm dying to hear about it.' I chuckle. He cackles.

'I promise,' I say, though I have no idea what he's talking about.

It's not dawn yet when I leave the museum. The slush and dirt of November have dyed the pavement brown. I walk through a city that's just waking up, under maples whose leaves have turned from their vivid reds and yellows of September to a dull russet colour.

It has been a long time since I last drove a car. I remember how, though. It's a long drive away from the city, longer yet to get away from the sparse houses dotting the last suburbs. When the sun rises, I open my window. It turns chilly at once, and the first light of the day makes patches of snow glitter by the side of the asphalt.

When I was a child I liked to wander away from the path. I never went far; I knew the depths of the woods could swallow me whole. There is no path by the side of this road. I step through the undergrowth, brushing young snow against my trousers.

Light filters through the trees and only birds break the silence. It's been so long since I've seen anything like this, wildlife that hasn't been trussed, dried up, filed and neatly arranged in cabinets and galleries, with tidy labels underneath. The crisp scent of the snow, cold air on my cheeks, rustling branches, all spells peace and quiet, yet the slightest sensations are overwhelming in their presence. A bird, bursting with energy, takes flight and sends snow cascading through the needles of the tree it was perched in, and the whole tree shakes like a chime. A whiff of breeze stings my cheeks, wakes up warm blood through my skin as if a sudden spring had melted it from its sleep. The rays of the sun branch and snake through bare boughs and dark needles until they caress my face, like a golden vine, like a delicious wine warming my throat all the way down. Everything is boundless, alive. Everything is trilling, crackling, humming, whispering. I hadn't known what I'd been missing, how much I'd been missing it. If I stood in front of a glass case, I could tell five species of albatross apart, but I cannot recognise the trees from my own childhood when their boughs are close enough to graze my hands and my neck. And it's all right. The trees welcome me all the same, and let me breathe in their life, overtaking any need for words, any lingering fear.

I walk into the woods, slowly, taking in every scent, every birdsong. With every step I try to send my mind back in time for precise memories of the forest, and with every step I fail. Yet I remember, completely, organically, as if I had never been inside the woods, but the woods had always been inside me.

In a clearing, I pause to drink the last of my coffee flask, the only drink I took on that trip. And then I see it.

The fox sits on its haunches and watches me with narrow, yellow eyes. I stop moving. It makes a small jerking motion, as if to run away, then stops. In its gaze, I read curiosity, wariness, perhaps annoyance at being surprised on its own grounds.

My grin spreads on my face like an invigorating brew in my blood. The third time I saw a fox in the wild, I was lost in the woods, too far away from home to ever hope to return. We stared at each other for nearly a minute. The whole forest was alive with invisible rustles, with the cold glitter on the ground, pins and needles in the breeze that made my blood rush with the exhilaration of life, life everywhere, never extinguished, only dormant through the winter until it bloomed again. I could feel snow under my feet and I was happy, happier than I had been in years.

Then the fox cocks its head at something I cannot hear and darts into the trees.

Still dizzy with happiness, I follow it, my footsteps disappearing in moss and crumbling snow, off the road, off any trail known to me or anyone else, and we sink into the wilderness.

This story was born of music – more specifically, three songs by Québécois band Beau Dommage and its frontman Michel Rivard, songs that I listened to as a child but only understood as an adult.

'Le géant Beaupré' tells of the fate of Edouard Beaupré, one of the tallest men in the world, who spent much of his life in a travelling circus, and whose body was exhibited as an anatomical curiosity for decades after his death. 'L'oubli' is a tribute to Québec filmmaker Claude Jutra, whose last years were marred by Alzheimer's disease. 'Le Picbois' is a song of the joy found in birdsong and the presence of the woods, after too long in the city.

One last piece haunts this story, though I only realised it after I'd written it. Bach's Prelude No. 8 in E flat minor tells a wordless tale of winter and frost and darkness – and of buds rising through the snow, carrying a glimpse of spring.

Kings of Snow

A snowflake lands on the lump of soapstone in Mel's hand. It stays there for a second before the wind blows it away. Today the snow is thick as tar, which is fine. Sunny days are so unbearably cold we can't walk any more. And we still have a long way to cover.

As we rest for a few minutes under a ruined shed, we shake snowballs out of our scarves. Bart mutters a 'Global warming my foot,' purely out of habit. Mel glares at him. She pockets the soapstone again.

'Does your cousin know anyone who can work it, anyway?' I say. That's a lot of extra weight to carry. With days of walking ahead of us, every ounce counts, and it's not like we're spring lambs either.

'Doesn't matter. She'll like it.'

Mel gets up to face the snow. The road is visible in places, where people travelling before us have trampled a path. In a couple of weeks, it won't be. Everyone will stay put for the rest of the winter, digging through their caches of cabbage and salt pork, and all that tarmac will just lie here useless.

Bart readjusts his fur coat. It's a fine one, thick beaver fur that belonged to someone's grandfather. He got it in Wendake for a cask of salt fish. As he tried to haggle in broken French, Mel made fun of him, but I see her look of envy when the weather gets bad. I don't make fun of them any more. We're three old fools crossing half of Québec on foot in late December to visit a woman who hasn't heard from us in months. None of us is in a position to laugh at anyone.

Backs bowed, heads sunken in our shoulders, we start walking again. The next town we cross is deserted. Bart tosses Mel a nasty look. We bickered for weeks over the way we should take: walking along the north bank of the Saint Lawrence river, where some people still lived according to Mel, or crossing the river in Québec

City to walk along the warmer, more populated south bank, as Bart thought we should do – longer, but far safer than travelling through the wilderness on our own. Mel won the discussion and we stayed north, only to find out that most towns on the way had turned empty. As Bart put it, as soon as the oil had ran out every sane person in the country had fled west, to Montreal where a few solidarity camps had managed to thrive, or to Vancouver, where at least the weather was close to decent. There were only three not-so-wise folks to keep walking east, and that was us.

'And we're right, too,' Mel said. 'My cousin is a brave woman. We can't leave her alone in a time like this.'

Not that bringing her soapstone is going to help, but Mel insisted we should bring presents, and that's the only thing we possess that's not immediately vital. Even the two thousand dollars in my jacket have proven useful. Paper is nice and insulating once you get used to the permanent crinkling sounds. Still, I can spare some to insulate a tiny mattress once we get there. Mel likes that. Bart is the only one with no present yet. He says there will always be a rabbit he can skin if Mel's cousin is offended.

Soon the path ends and we have to put our snowshoes back on. Everything is white, everywhere – white and smooth, except for the river which looks like a chaotic wasteland where the ice has cracked and reformed. There should be another town soon, Port-au-Persil. I faintly remember stopping there as a child, on the way to a popular whale-watching resort. It had a lovely white church surrounded by wild roses, and not much else. As we walked away from the pier, my brother started jumping up and down. A pod of beluga were swimming near the horizon. It was the prettiest thing I'd ever seen.

That was before the last of the beluga dropped dead from all the poisons we dumped into the sea. Back when rich blockheads could still tell all of us poor blockheads to keep pumping oil into our cars like there was no tomorrow, and get away with it. The thought that we messed up every nice thing on the planet because our cars and fancy houses were so important to us drives me nuts. When I point it out, Mel huffs and says her ancestors told our ancestors so centuries ago and we wouldn't listen – but I know that before it all went south, she drove a Skidoo through the snow like everybody else. Plus, it's not even true. My ancestors wanted nothing to do with this continent. They were brought here anyway, and now we're all trudging together, White and Black and Wendat side by side, bickering about our forebears because it passes time.

We pause at the top of a pass. Although we can't see our destination yet, the clouds have parted overhead and unveiled the glint of the defunct space station in the sky, like a bright signpost hanging right above where we're headed. If we're lucky, there will still be a church in Port-au-Persil where we can take shelter for the night. And in a couple of days, we'll glimpse the opening of the Saguenay. There should be people there. I've heard whales still come to that place to feed, and now there's a sort of cult that believes whales will save what's left of mankind by pooping into the sea and making it fertile again. That's where Mel's cousin Marie lives. That's where she's supposed to give birth, a little before New Year, if Mel's estimates prove better than they have so far.

'Don't look so down, Gas,' she says, patting my arm. 'Marie's a great woman. Bringing a child into the world in times like these? That's just admirable of her. We should worship that baby, I tell you. This is no little thing.'

'If she's still in Tadoussac,' Bart grumbles. 'If she hasn't jumped on the sane people bandwagon and gone to Montreal.'

'Not a chance. She wants to keep count of the whales. It's really important to her.'

We start walking down again, our feet the only things crushing the snow.

I hope we'll make it to Tadoussac before the baby is born.

The Christmas tradition of nativity scenes is so strong in Provence it permeates even some thoroughly irreligious families. Rather than focusing on the birth of Jesus, they usually represent an entire village, with joyfully anachronistic characters going about their business while somebody gives birth in a stable somewhere. Angels meet 19th-century poets, schoolteachers, wild boars and flamingos, and of course, Melchior, Gaspard and Balthazar, the three kings come to greet baby Jesus. According to one tradition, their figures should be placed at the very edge of the scene, then moved towards the stable a little every day, until they reach their destination on 6th January.

My father came up with the idea of rewriting the Three Kings' story in a frozen, post-apocalyptic Québec, one December when we were setting up the nativity scene. I added the soapstone and the defunct space station, and my own memories of the Québec winter, perhaps the most alien aspect of that transatlantic experience.

The Owl Woman

Nobody noticed when the owl-faced stranger ate my mother's heart and took her place by the family's hearth. I had been sleeping between two thick deerskins, with my feet as near the embers as I could without catching fire. I opened my eyes when a hand – so much like my mother's I thought it had been her, at first – buried some eggs and a clay vessel full of gruel into the cinders, sending sparks flying. She was humming the tune that had lulled me to sleep for longer than I could remember.

Her face, though, was flat and white as an owl's, her hair tawny like a wing crushing through the night and disappearing into the forest. I stared at her, too horrified to scream, until she noticed that I was awake and appraised me with dark, dark eyes.

My father came back just then, with the hind leg of a deer and a basket of chestnuts. He grunted to the owl-faced woman, and sat by the fire to munch on a strip of dried meat.

'Miika's awake. Come, girl. Have something to eat.'

She held out the bowl to me, oblivious to the way I glared at her. Her voice was like my mother's, only with a new, feather-soft quality, like a predator readying itself to swoop.

Heart pounding, without taking my eyes off her, I inched my hand towards the eggs in the fire. She slapped it away and shoved the gruel towards me.

'That's for the men. This is for you. Eat.'

I took a long breath, and burst out in a scream. Terror, grief, hunger all overwhelmed my throat where words should have been, and I kicked and wailed and clawed, until a slap sent me sprawling back on my deerskin.

I ate nothing. I watched them, the owl woman and my father, eat the eggs and the gruel, and when I closed my eyes and pretended to sleep, my father grunted and huffed on top of her on the deerskins next to mine, as if there was nothing wrong with the creature wearing my mother's shift.

Fear kept sleep at bay for a very long time. I remained as silent as I could, like a mouse frozen when beasts of prey roam the undergrowth. But I could not hold the tears through the night. I held my breath while they flowed, and stayed silent.

Not silent enough. She sat up, and when her talons touched my back, my blood turned to ice. She pressed her hand into my skin, and sang.

'*Shhh*
Soft you
Little dove
That coos
In the woods
The woods…'

My mother had sung that song every night. It had sounded like love then, like the warmth of the embers, of her milk running down my throat.

Now it sounded like a bird hooting in the night wind. I whimpered. But sleep won in the end, as it always would.

I mourned my mother in sullen quiet, and in fits of temper my father would silence with sharp backhanded blows. That first morning after her arrival, the owl woman took me with her into the forest. She gathered wild asparagus, sloes, rowan berries and handfuls of herbs I couldn't recognise. All through the morning she sang, in that mournful, rounded voice that sent chills of fear through my spine.

We were back at noon, and she set me to work pounding chestnuts under a stone, while she sorted through the herbs and laid them out to dry on flat wicker plates. She looked up intermittently, to point at the shape of a leaf, or crush a stem between two fingers and force me to smell it. I could not remember her explanations. More than once, I hammered on my own fingers, and bit my lips so she couldn't see my pain.

Neighbours came by in the afternoon. I held my breath, expecting stones to fly, revenge at least, if not reparation. But the neighbours did not show any more reaction to the owl-faced stranger than my father had. They came to work as usual, singing and dragging their children by the elbow to sit them down on the ground and hand down menial tasks to them. I sat near the wall pounding chestnuts handed to me by the older girl who removed their husks. Her mother had come with her and was resting in the shade of the clay walls of our hut, fanning herself with her hand and groaning. She would have a baby very soon.

They sang songs together, and once in a while peered down at the valley below, the place where the woods dwindled into tough bushes and the hills fanned out into an expanse of smooth red clay, where you could run up and down without having to climb and where my mother used to forage for the best herbs and dig the ground for pungent, tasty mushrooms to warm up our gruel in winter.

'Barma was raided just before the full moon,' a woman said, suddenly.

The others perked up. The pregnant one propped herself against the wall, alarmed.

'Barma? Are you certain?'

The woman who had spoken nodded.

'They took three girls, killed a couple of men. Took the last of their winter supplies.'

The pregnant mother took her scarred face in her hands. From the conversation that followed, I gathered that her mother was from Barma. She had still been alive last time she'd heard from her.

The mood turned sombre. Many of the women here had come from somewhere else, taken as girls to become brides in neighbouring hamlets. Some had not heard from their families in years. Very few ever travelled back, but at this moment it seemed that all they could think of was whether there was still a childhood home somewhere, or their parents lay in the dust with their throat cuts, hoof prints mangling their bodies.

The older girl learned towards me.

'Have you ever seen a raider?' she whispered.

161

I shook my head. Of course we heard of raiders every so often. No one built villages down there in the open ground, where they could be laid waste by an attack in the time it took for the sun to rise. Horses couldn't climb hills, and raiders had no interest in going where their horses couldn't go, it was said. And so younger women huffed and sweated under the weight of the pails of water they had to carry all the way up the hill from the streams at the bottom of the valley.

The girl nudged my arm with a mysterious smile.

'I have. Two of them, once. They rode black horses. They were very tall, and they had flowing hair, brown like yours. One of them wore the skin of a wolf.' She leaned even closer, her eyes wider, and for a moment their darkness reminded me of the owl-woman's eyes. 'He was carrying a girl away. You wouldn't believe how she was *screaming*.'

She said it as if it was not a bad thing at all.

'I don't believe you,' I said, reflexively. 'Why didn't they take you if you were right here?'

'Because I was hiding. And anyway, I'm not old enough.' She grinned and glanced at the women, who weren't paying attention to us. 'They want us old enough to stick their *thing* inside us and make us have babies.'

'You're disgusting,' I said, and flung a handful of husks at her.

She laughed and flung them back at me, until someone snapped at us to get on with our work.

The women left at sundown. I caught the girl gazing down at the valley, as if listening for distant hoof-beats, then the owl-woman took my hand to lead me back inside.

That night I dreamed of wolves howling around our house, a great owl prowling the skies above, and a little mouse in the grass, running, running with nowhere to hide.

Every morning upon waking up, I put a hand to my chest and didn't rise before I'd ascertained that my heart was still beating there, still mine. I could no longer remember my mother's face. All I knew were the alien, heart-shaped features and low hooting voice of the woman who had taken her place.

In time I grew old enough to hold a stone blade, and it was my turn to peel chestnuts and acorns, skin rabbits and dry their pelts in the sun before chewing on the leather until it became soft enough to wear. When the village women weren't around, the owl woman took me with her into the valley, following the edges of the woods, so we could run away between oak trees if the raiders came.

One day I woke up with blood staining the deerskins I lay on. I stared for a while, and didn't notice at once that the owl woman was looking over my shoulder.

'I'll call the women,' she simply said.

I sat there, frozen, until she opened the door and said something to my father, who sat on the threshold carving a new blade from a hard stone. I made out the word *blood*. And *today*.

He only grunted.

I sprang up and ran to him.

'No,' I panted. 'Please. I don't want to. Don't let her.'

My voice broke. He frowned at me.

'What are you talking about?' he said.

'Don't let her. Please. I won't go into the valley any more, I…'

I clung to his arm. He looked at me with his mouth open and a scowl on his brow, then he backhanded me across the face and sent me sprawling in the dust.

He resumed working as if nothing had happened. I was still crying and pleading when the owl woman, and other women from the hamlet, came for me.

They dragged me until the edge of the woods. A couple of children perked up at my screams. A baby began to cry. They laid me down, pinned my arms and legs to the ground, while the owl woman held my head straight. An older woman wiped the tears of fear and rage from my cheeks.

'Now, now,' she said. 'If you wail like this now, what will it be like when you give birth?'

I yelled incoherent things in return. I didn't want to give birth. I'd stuff my own womb with stones if it came to that. But she only frowned and grunted and then, after checking under my shift for the blood that proved me a woman, she took out a blade and began to sing.

The women chanted, only stopping to snap at me or pinch my arms every so often, when my screaming grew too loud. The pain was nothing to the throes of impotent rage that overwhelmed me as the old woman carved my face, one quick, precise cut after another, until I couldn't see for the blood running into my eyes.

I had thought to bolt when they let me go, fling myself at the old witch and gouge her eyes out of her scarred face. But I could only lie there, trembling and hiccupping, vision blurred and limbs paralysed with exhaustion. It took me a very long while to notice the silence. The women were gone, and the owl woman was helping me up, and holding a bowl of pungent-smelling liquid to me.

'There now. It's all over,' she said, her voice soft, though her beak of a mouth could not form anything I'd term a human smile.

I stared at her. The feathers on her face rustled in the breeze. I brought my hand to my own face, the myriad of cuts now marring my forehead and cheeks like feathers of my own. I stared at her wordlessly, as if my look could drill a hole into her soul and pour all my rage in there, the hatred I'd built up over the years and which words could not, would not convey.

I knocked over the bowl. The medicine spilled on the ground. She sighed.

'Would you rather be taken?' she said. 'Like the girls in Barma? In Vorabran? They don't cut their faces over there. They parade their girls, pretty as orchids, and then when they get taken you can hear them scream in three valleys at once. Is that what you want?'

I didn't recall her saying so many words at a time, save for the songs she sang. I grunted in answer, got up, and wobbled away.

On the way home I stopped at the top of the ravine, where the hills opened up into the wide world below.

There were men roaming the valleys on horseback, tall and wiry where my father was squat, sharp as blades where he was blunt as an uncut stone. Men who took smooth-faced girls away, rode with them to the end of the land, and then rode them in the night while they cried out, strange cries that almost sounded like pain – almost.

Something rustled in the grass by my feet. I shot my hand and snatched it up. A little brown mouse, squealing and squirming between my fingers.

I twisted until it snapped in two and was still. Then I dangled its corpse in front of my face. The scent of blood made me hungry.

The scars on my face still pained me sometimes, when I laughed or cried too hard. So I stopped doing either.

I was carrying pails of water up the slope when one of the other girls screamed and pointed at the end of the valley. Immediately after, pails dropped to the ground and we ran for the cover of the woods.

From behind a thicket of lentisks, we peeked at the open ground again.

'There,' a girl whispered, voice thick with fear and excitement. 'Don't move!'

Down there in the valley, a dark shape was moving up, his horse stepping carefully between clumps of tough scented grass.

'It's a scout,' the girl said. 'There will be others.'

Her hand went to her face. For a moment, the light dappling her scars and her receding chin through the leaves turned her into a trout, glimmering at the bottom of a brook.

The scout rode up, relaxed and unafraid, though he was alone. We cowered in silence when he drew close enough for us to see his face. His hair and beard were a rich honey-brown, his eyebrows thick, his nose jutting like a rock on a cliff face. The dead snout of a wolf rested on his shoulder.

Eventually he rode away, unaware of the four pairs of eyes that following him, rapt, unblinking, and of the turmoil unfolding in his wake, thoughts and dreams and fears we had no words for.

The hill folks knew what to do. For a few days it would only be the men going into the valley for water, with stone axes and clubs, and the women would forage under the deepest cover of the forest, where horses could not go. The young ones were locked up inside their huts. I hadn't seen the sun for three days.

I was fighting the boredom by listening for mice in the thatch and trying to grab them before they slipped between my fingers, when I heard the shouts.

The door open, a blissfully warm ray of sunlight fell on my face, then the owl woman got in and shoved me to the back, right before burying the hearth under ash.

'They're coming. Hide!'

I stared at her back, at the door.

I thought of the scout's lean, broad shoulders, his hair framing a strong-boned face, his arms resting in front of him like the paws of a wolf. I had never seen a man who looked like that. When his horse had come close to our hiding place, I had drunk in the sight as earnestly as I had hidden myself, terrified he would find us, terrified that the he would ride away in disgust of our marred faces.

I bolted for the door, threw it open, and ran down the slope up which, in the distance, five armed men were riding to us.

Behind me, there was a screech, and soon the owl woman's footsteps followed mine.

'Miika!' she screamed.

I didn't turn back.

'Miika!'

She swooped down on me. I cried out and raised my arms in front of my face. Instead of tearing me apart, her talons closed on my arm and she pulled me to her.

'Come back inside. Miika, please!'

I lowered my arms, bewildered. For the first time in years I had tried to escape her. She was about to lose the prey she had been nurturing since she'd killed my mother, and instead of seizing her chance and attacking me, she asked me to *come back inside*.

I shoved her away, laughing with disbelief.

'You think I haven't seen through you, in all these years?' I said. 'Just because nobody can see who you are, you think I'm blind as well? She was *my mother!*'

She grabbed my wrists, anger simmering now.

'I don't know what this is about, but you're going to –'

'You murdered her! You ate her heart and you took her place, and now you think you're going to eat me too?'

Her black eyes opened wide, and she made a sound that very much resembled pleading.

I looked down. The raiders were close enough that I could see their faces. With a jolt, I recognised their leader.

I wrenched my arm from the owl woman's grip, and ran towards then, and then I waited, while behind me, pleas turned to words I couldn't understand, a curse, a prayer, I didn't know. I raised an arm in greeting and watched the scout's horse gallop closer, and closer, and closer.

He didn't stop. When he grabbed me around the waist, air whooshed out of my lungs, followed by a dull pain when he threw me across the horse's back. An arrow flew in the owl woman's direction. I couldn't help glancing back. She was still chanting, pointing her finger at us. The arrow flew wide. But the raiders were already leaving, and whatever curse she had thought to cast scattered itself in the wind.

The last I saw of her was her figure crumpling to the ground, and the last I heard was a despairing wail.

I had never left the valley. The horses crossed another one, and a river I'd never seen, before stopping at a large settlement surrounded by a wall of raised stakes.

I was battered from the ride, hungry and breathless. But he was hungry too, in a different way. He did not dismount before reaching a large stone house, and there he pulled me off the horse and dragged me inside.

I took the pain with clenched jaws, and when he slumped on top of me, I took stock at last of my own astonishment at having dared to leave my house, the pride of having withstood yet another challenge of womanhood, and underneath the ache, a sensation I had no name for, one that had woken me up on nights when I dreamed of the scout's handsome face, one I'd been thirsting for with a mute desperation.

I smiled at him through tears when he sat up.

'I'm Miika,' I said. 'I'm your bride now, aren't I?' He frowned, so I touched my chest and repeated my name.

'Miika,' he said. He touched his chest in turn. 'Kerwaen.'

He touched the tips of his fingers to my cheek, and brushed my scars, gently, tenderly, the hint of a smile playing on his lips.

No one had touched me like that since my mother had died. For a long while, I forgot to breathe.

A moan from across a door interrupted us. Kerwaen stood. The door opened directly on another house, or perhaps another part of the same house. I followed him, wincing, and waited while he knelt by a mat of furs where an old woman was huddling and moaning, her forehead slick with sweat.

He spoke to her for some time, his face growing grave. I wondered what distressed him so. The fever wasn't nearly as bad as some I'd seen back in the hills. The herbs the owl woman gathered would have cured it in no time. I waited, but the only drink he gave her was something white and opaque that smelled like an animal's litter.

'I can help her,' I said.

He frowned. I sighed.

'Wait for me,' I said, walking out of the house and of the settlement, and towards the forest.

The moon waxed and waned nine more time over Kerwaen's hearth. One night, his mother – healthy as a horse since I had cured her of her fever – and three of the neighbours held me up and chanted encouragements while I screamed and cried and begged for the agony to end.

I hadn't known such torment since the owl woman had let them carve my face open. There would be no release. I was not strong enough, could not push the child out. My world would end in unbearable pain, death sneaking up my womb and curling up in the place my child was now leaving.

Kerwaen's mother said something in her flowing language and shook my hand, squeezing it. She crushed a handful of herbs in her fist, the ones I'd taught her to use in moments like this, and waved them under my nose. I clung, forced breath out.

Without knowing what I was doing, I began to sing.

'*Shhh*
Soft you
Little dove
That coos

168

In the woods
The woods
The w…'
The song ended in a long screech of agony.

Then there was another cry, and exclamations of victory, and then the pain was over and to my amazement, Kerwaen's son and I were still alive.

The milk in the cauldron was setting, ready to be cut and piled in wicker baskets. The men were fond of milk, drunk still warm from the pail, left to ferment in the shade, or the heavy, pasty concoction I was now busy preparing, which would last all winter and taste more pungent every day. Milk turned my stomach. I'd watch as someone else slaughtered the lambs in front of their dams, then I'd have to cure their stomachs so I could seep them in their own mothers' milk to curdle it properly, and I'd try not to retch. Most of the women, who had been abducted here and there, felt the same way. I'd come to suppose that this was simply another difference between the strangers on horseback and us, like their pale skin, tall frames, and their frightening, fascinating viciousness.

A child tugged on the bottom of my shift, whimpering.

'Sevinda,' I called. 'Your son's hungry.'

The words tasted strange on my tongue. After learning the raider's language, I'd seldom used the one we spoke in the hills, to the point that it no longer showed up in my thoughts or dreams. The only words left from my childhood years were the names of plants, which I'd taught the women of the village over the years. The hill folks had never talked much anyway. I only held the ghostliest memory of my father's voice, and did not miss his grunts nor his rebukes. I remembered nothing of my mother's.

Or rather, I smashed the recollections down as soon as they formed in my mind – and all I could see was a white, feathered face, and I could hear no words at all, but only a long scream of despair, fading as Kerwaen's horse bore me away.

I had very soon stopped being foolish enough to believe I had freed myself by allowing the raiders to take me. I rarely wondered if I had made the right choice, however. In the hills I had been a

169

fearful little mouse, ordered about, slapped around, held down without a single word of apology when the time for disfigurement had come. Here, I had to hold my tongue around the men; but the women nodded to me whenever I walked by, and left gifts and words of thanks whenever I healed their husbands or helped bring their children safely into the world. That was good enough.

Sevinda's scars made her face look like the pebbly bank of a river. Kerwaen's brother had brought her back from a raid last spring. She'd spent the first nights wailing and pleading, and the days sobbing through split lips and blackened eyes. I'd gone to her then, talked her through the beginnings of her new life. She still wept at times, and acted sullen on her best days, but she'd picked herself up at least, and kept going. Life wasn't that different from what we'd known. Make food, sew clothes, sing our babies to sleep.

Sevinda now eyed hers with distaste.

'He's always hungry,' she said.

'All the better for you. The longer you feed him, the longer it will take you to make another one. Trust me.'

She sighed and pulled her neckline down.

'What's the name of that plant you said we shouldn't let ewes eat?' she said. 'The one that makes them lose their lambs?'

'Rue. And it can kill you.'

I got up, stretched my back. It didn't show yet, but a baby was coming, again. I didn't mind. I'd grown rather fond of the three I already had. I'd prepare broths of pungent herbs before each birth, then sing through the process while the other women held me up. In the last few years, I'd been called to assist with most births and illnesses in the settlement. I reckoned I had little to fear myself, at this point.

'Take the little one,' I said. 'We're going to the woods.'

She sighed, again – she did that a lot – but followed. I had been disappointed to discover that the woods did not soothe her as they did me. I walked slowly, towards the spots where wild asparagus grew.

I'd chewed on the rich, bitter shoots while following the owl woman into the woods, years before. Her unnaturally keen eye had spotted anything edible even through the thickest branches. With

Sevinda trailing behind me, I trudged up the rocky slopes, just damp from the presence of underground water.

The air should have smelled of loam here, and green leaves, unlike the strong herbal scent of the bare ground near the settlement. Instead I smelled smoke. Sevinda cried out.

'It's the wood! Over there!'

There was a gust of wind, and flames licked the sky. We scrambled back, running as fast as her son and my quickened womb allowed. When we left the cover of the trees, we slowed down. The area around the village walls had been grazed again and again, and fires would die down on that thin layer of grass. A couple of shepherds were watching the flames, farther away, as if nothing was wrong.

But I'd grown up to fear fire. I shouted until some women walked up to us.

'What's wrong with you, Miika?' one of them said, with undertones of glee I didn't like at all.

'The forest is burning. Someone must have been careless with their camp fire.'

'That? Oh, no. The men need more ground to take the horses to pasture, that's all. They're burning the green oaks, the useless ones.'

She gave me a smile of fake solicitude.

'Did it scare you?' she added.

'Scare me?' I repeated.

The forest was burning. The woods were shelter, providers, allies. The hill people revered them. This village did not know how much it owed to the woods, how many children would have been lost to fevers without the herbs I brought back from my walks, how many elders would have succumbed if the woods had not stood right by them with their healing gifts. And now they were *burning* them.

'Owl woman is afraid of fire,' someone snickered in a low voice.

My head snapped up.

'What did you say?' I growled, stepping forward.

The smile on the woman's face melted into a look of alarm.

'Nothing! Don't take it like that, it's just…'

I screamed and raked my fingernails across her face. The others fell back, crying out, not one of them daring to get in my way, or say a single word when I ran towards home, and Kerwaen.

His brother and he were respected raiders. Surely he would be listened to. I grabbed his arm, spoke too fast, the words of the hill folk and his colliding on my tongue and turning my speech into an incoherent plea.

'The beasts need more ground or we'll starve this winter,' he said, frowning.

'Then make a clearing. Fell some trees. You don't know how far fire can spread. You could be destroying ten villages and never know it!'

Kerwaen stared at me. He was a good man, one who had never eaten without making sure I would have enough left over to eat my fill, one who rarely hit me or his children. He would understand. He would help.

He pried my hands from his arm and pushed me away.

'The hill folks have never meant us any good,' he said. 'Besides, why would you care? Aren't you one of us now?'

'This is not...'

'Miika.' I recoiled. *Rarely* did not mean it could not happen. 'You are our wise woman. The village respects you, and everything you've done for us. Don't you bring shame on my house now.'

He strode away, and moments later, the breeze brought in a smell of smoke and death, while the village carried on as if nothing was happening.

Fires could go on for days. At nightfall, I ventured out, eyes still stinging with the smoke.

It had been years since I had last wondered if my father was still alive. If the hamlet still stood, if the women still softened deerskins with their teeth and pounded acorns into mush while singing their droning songs. If girls still begged and screamed under the knife that parted their faces, in a futile attempt to make them invisible to the men on horseback.

I wondered if the owl woman was still waiting, still hoping I would come back, since that day when she had collapsed into the dirt, a spell she had never had time to teach me melting into a wail of pain, tears streaming along the scars on her face.

Panicked birds were leaving the woods. Earlier in the day, men had cheered after catching a doe with her fawns as they fled the fire. Prey – deer had never been anything more. The women of the hills had never been anything more.

I wondered if Kerwaen would ride again to get me back. Our next meeting would be a different one. You could pick a mouse from the ground and twist its neck, toss a stone spear at a deer, even snatch a screaming girl and carry her away – these things were allowed because they were, by and large, harmless. The world did not stop for one more bit of pain.

But you did not get to destroy the world.

I breathed in the night air, raised my arms, puffed up my chest. Spread my feathers.

With a last defiant hoot, I flew away towards my home.

Back to Provence, after a trip across the ocean; to the past, and a time that archaeological records do not currently cover in that part of the world, leaving imagination as free as does the future.

I have a fascination with biological, evolutionary and anthropological explanations of gender roles in early humans. I am hardly qualified to have a valuable opinion on their merits, but what they say about our own assumptions and frameworks is a topic of reflection in and of itself. When acknowledging that women often left their native settlements to join their husbands', for instance, it is so easy to imagine a strong, brutish man dragging a hapless woman by the hair that popular discourses rarely deviate from that narrative.

Scientists, however, may be more nuanced. Reading about the rapid spread of Proto-Indo-European culture and genes across Europe, I came across a simple hypothesis: Proto-Indo-European people may have been better organised and more brutal, perhaps, but, also, very simply, more attractive to local women. A slight shift in perspective; it merely invites us to remember that the women of the time had minds and desires of their own — and to wonder what else might have slipped between the cracks of too-simple explanatory stories.

The Goddess's Spear

The wise woman wiped the blood and birth-grease from Lukalla's sons, cooed approvingly when they gave their first cry in unison, laid them together on Lukalla's chest and pulled up a corner of bearskin to shield the three of them against the cold. Then she told Lukalla that when her babies had drunk their first milk, the snow goddess would need to eat her liver.

Lukalla was staring into her babies' eyes and the words didn't register at once. She had just survived pain, exhaustion and distress like she had never experienced before, in warfare or hunting. She had babies to feed. There would be an end to meet, one day, but it would be a fair one. One that made sense. Not an unjust, absurd...

She stopped thinking and brought her corded arms around the little boys, holding the bearskin tighter. No man or god would take them away. She was their home, their shield. She stared at the wise woman and set her chin.

'Then tell the goddess to come and tear it out, if she can,' she said.

The goddess could. She did.

The nights had grown as long as they would, and so much snow blanketed the mountains that no living woman or man recalled there being so much of it. Wolves had taken three children already, and a lean long-toothed cat had been spotted, prowling close and raising new dread.

The snow goddess wanted her due: a warrior, from a line of warriors, one who had come into the world with a guardian spirit made flesh, one who had been marked from birth – one who had refused to acknowledge it, until the holy men of the tribe ripped her from her babies and her bearskin pallet and dragged her, screaming and biting, to the snow goddess's cave.

They took her furs, her seashells, her stone axe. She managed to stun one of them with a blow of her head to the chin before they kicked her legs from under her and forced her against the burning-cold rock. They poured something into her mouth, and kept pouring when she gagged, when she spat, when she broke down in sobs.

Chanting prayers to the snow goddess, they shoved her into the cave and rolled the boulder back across the entrance.

Lukalla willed her eyes open. She willed her legs to move, and when they wouldn't, she willed a scream out of her throat and hammered on the boulder with her fists.

Then light flickered over the face of the rock and when her own shadow looked back at her from the boulder, Lukalla turned around and saw fire.

Numb, shivering, her body moved of its own accord. The fire drew closer. She could not see behind it, and didn't care, only crawled towards the warmth, until she realised that she was close enough to the fire that there ought to *be* warmth, and there was nothing, only red lights painting the walls and the horrid cold of the snow goddess's cave, and as she understood that even fire would bring no warmth in this sacred, awful place, the flame drew even closer and she saw a face behind it.

The goddess had come to demand her due.

Lukalla snarled and tried to pull herself up. She managed a crouch, hands clasped to the floor like the claws of a wounded animal. The goddess paused. She did so like a wolf, pausing to assess whether its prey was weak enough to be worth the chase. Lukalla could not look weak. She could not *be* weak.

She had exhausted the last of her strength and the goddess saw it. She took a few more steps forward, holding her cold white flame above her. She held something supple and bright in her hand. She threw it over Lukalla's shoulders.

Lukalla tried to scream and only managed a whimper. There was no weight upon her back, though now something shimmered there, a surface as smooth and glossy as the inside of a seashell, but gossamer-light.

The goddess said: 'I'd wait here, but you're going to die of cold if you don't come now. I have furs, over there. Will you?'

They both waited, in wary silence. When Lukalla tried to move her feet she felt, to her surprise, the excruciating pain of blood flowing back into her toes. She pulled the gossamer fur about her body and began moving, half-crawling, after the receding shape of the goddess.

She had never entered the cave before. The place was sacred, forbidden to all but the holy men who could not touch blood. Red stone walls gleamed under a sheen of ice, and frozen mud covered a low, narrow passage they had to cross on all four. She rose when the white flame did, and for a moment she stopped moving.

The light stretched up and lost itself into the night. Instead of the smooth walls of the entrance, the rock around her rose and fell, like snow melted and frozen again, transformed into still cascades of yellows and reds and whites, hanging from the ceiling, overflowing into rounded shapes rising from the floor. A sheet of ice took up most of the bottom. It looked thin, but there was nothing to see but darkness underneath.

'Over here,' the goddess said.

She pointed to the end of the cave. Lukalla squinted. There was something new there, like a bubble of ice, stretched and rounded and incredibly clear. It rested on a pebble-smooth surface, with grey-white sticks sprouting underneath and resting against the blossoming rocks. The goddess walked ahead, and at her touch the ice moved. A portion of it floated up, then stopped. The goddess propped herself up and sat on the edge of the new cave of ice, then when Lukalla tried and failed to crawl up, she took her arm and pulled until they were both in, and the ice closed on itself again.

Lukalla breathed in. It was *warm*. A warmth she had not felt since summer, a warmth nothing had equalled save for the skin of her twin boys against her chest. She closed her arms against herself. Her sons, her flesh given life. She let out a choked breath. She was not going to fail them.

She stared the goddess down.

177

'I'm not afraid of you,' she snarled. 'Listen, whatever you are. You're not having any piece of me. I'll fight you to the last, and then I'll bring your head back home and it will be summer forever, and they will make songs about me and my sons will sing them when I die. I've killed wolves. I've killed a cave bear. If you think I owe you anything, come and try to take it!'

The goddess looked at her for a very long time.

She had looked like a woman, from a distance, enough to lull Lukalla's fear away. From here, it was plain that she wasn't. Her face had the smooth paleness of seashells, and her hair, though grey, flew around her face in fine strands like a new-born's, as if she had never touched dirt in her life. The furs cloaking her body were the colour of the winter sky, clear above, dark below, and wrapped around her limbs as if they had grown there. Everything in her cave was the same, rounded, impossibly smooth, as if all of it came from the embrace of the sea. There were furs on the floor too, coloured like flowers. Lukalla's heart pounded faster. She stilled herself. It took predators less than that to decide to pounce.

'Will you tell me why they brought you here?' the goddess said.

'You know why,' Lukalla growled.

The goddess seemed to hold her breath for a moment, then released it, slow as wind.

'May I hear it from you?' she said.

You could challenge the gods. Being petty to them, however, was shameful. Lukalla kept staring.

'My mother was born with her guardian spirit,' she said. 'A child that looked just like her. Her guardian withered away, and my mother grew strong, a great warrior of the tribe. When she bore me into the world, my guardian spirit grew inside her womb as well. After that they said my mother was marked for you. The holy men took her and you ate her liver in exchange for the spring. They said I would become a great one, like her. Honoured, feared.' Reflexively, she groped around her throat for her seashells, the proof that she was speaking the truth. But of course they had taken them, to hang by the cave and receive offerings of thanks, once her sacrifice put an end to the winter deaths. 'They said that if a guardian spirit was born with my child, it would be the ultimate proof that I was holy and

178

would serve the tribe when it needed it most. Well. You see, my sons were born just in time.'

She forced a harsh laugh out of her throat, cut short before it choked her. Her arms groped for the small bodies she had held for so little time. One of them had been a son of her flesh, they said, though they couldn't yet tell which it was; the other, born to lend him strength, was meant to waste away as its twin grew plump and strong, as was right. Only, remembering the way both their heads had rested on her chest, both their mouths had sought her breasts, it felt ridiculously wrong. She had borne two sons. And now she didn't even know what woman would nurse them.

'And your son, I suppose...' the goddess said.

'Will become the greatest of them all, and when they need him, they'll bring him to you so you can eat his liver.' She gritted her teeth. 'Only they won't, because you'll be dead. There will never be another winter. I'll eat the flesh from your skull and hang it in front of your cave, and they'll all know I defeated the snow.'

Blood had come back to her hands and feet. She had moved into a crouch while she spoke, slowly, taking stock of the way the furs shifted between her feet and the warm ice of the cave walls. This time an expression crossed the goddess's face, though Lukalla didn't try to understand what it was.

'What if I said I have no wish to... eat your liver?' she said.

'No?' Lukalla bared her teeth. 'You want to see us all die, then? Is that what it is?'

The goddess shook her head from one side to the other. Lukalla tensed.

'I want nothing of the sort,' the goddess said. 'I...' She made that head motion again. 'Come on. I have furs for you. Food, if you want it. You can decide what to do after.'

Lukalla was not hungry. Had she been, she doubted she could come back to the world of the living after partaking in the meal of a goddess. She took the furs, after some hesitation; there were layers of them, and they were shaped like human bodies, so that she had to writhe to fit herself in. Despite their thinness, they soon brought her warmth enough that she stopped wriggling her toes to keep numbness at bay.

The goddess remained seated nearby, munching on something flat and glossy. She never made a move. That was what frightened Lukalla most. Even a bear would have adopted a fighting stance, not just sat by as if there was no way Lukalla could be strong enough to harm it. The ice walls of her cave were barely cool to the touch. There were shapes in a corner that she could not make sense of, sharp and straight glossy surfaces, like crystals.

She could have gone to sleep on her own here, enjoyed the pleasure of spreading her limbs like she did on the warmest summer nights, without having to huddle someone else's body for warmth. At that thought, her hands closed of their own accord, clutching the air. Her sons. Babies died in weather like this, went to sleep in the cold and never woke up. She pressed herself against the wall of the cave, but all she could see was the rock beyond, falling from the top of the cave like ice tears, or teeth.

Her distress must have shown. The goddess stared at her again, and this time there was an expression on her face, one that could have been compassion more easily than aggression.

'I'm afraid you won't be able to leave,' she said. 'I'm really sorry. I would help, if there was any way to.'

'Then make the snow stop,' Lukalla said.

She was surprised at hearing that the fight had gone from her voice. Her sons were out of her reach, perhaps already dying. Glory could wait. She was a sacrifice. She had one part to fulfil, one thing she could do with honour, even if she had to beg for it.

The goddess let a breath out in a long, steady breeze. She was silent for a while.

'Fine. I will,' she said, eventually.

What the goddess took from her, Lukalla didn't know. She went to sleep and woke up, after some time, sprawled on the furs of the ice cave. The goddess was sitting in front of her planes of crystal, gazing at them, sometimes tapping their surface with light, fast fingers. Divining something, perhaps, like holy men did when they threw pebbles in pools of melted snow. Lukalla didn't intervene. She refused food when the goddess offered again. She did not feel hungry.

After a while she felt restless, and asked for permission to leave the small spot that was beginning to feel more like a nest than a cave. The goddess nodded. The ice wall opened up and cold air came rushing in. The sense of imminent danger was gone, however; the draught only pricked her skin. The goddess must have made good on her word to bring about the end of the winter.

She took a few steps forward, leaning on jutting rocks when the terrain became too slippery. Membranes of stone dangled overhead, so thin that for a moment she expected them to billow like leaves. The rocks around stretched up and down from the floor and the roof of the cave, in shapes she had never seen in the world outside. With sudden dread, she realised that this was what had happened to her. She had stepped into a new world. It was not the boulder at the entrance of the cave that prevented her from going back. She had gone... somewhere, to a place where the gods could be seen, where colours were too bright and the ice too clear, where the mountain itself was turned inside out, where the rocks melted like ice and sometimes rose where they should have fallen.

She wondered if the holy men had known. They passed through the world of the gods, when they retired high up in the mountain and spent icy nights in the sacred dells. They were permitted to see magic, and live. Sacrifices... sacrifices were only permitted to see magic.

She heard footsteps behind her. The goddess had come down from her cave, much steadier in those strange tight furs than Lukalla was.

'Careful,' the goddess said. 'There are sinkholes in there. They look like puddles, right until you step in and there's no bottom.'

Lukalla met her eyes. After a long while, she decided to bow her head. The spark of defiance was still there, whispering at her to attack the seemingly frail creature at her side; nonetheless the goddess had granted her a swift end to the winter, and she owed her courtesy, if not submission.

'Is that what the magic of the gods does?' she said.

The goddess frowned, then shook her head.

181

'No. Not this. That's just the way the cave is.' She peered at Lukalla. 'No one of your tribe has ever been in there? Not even the holy men?'

This time Lukalla drew herself up in offence.

'We keep our word to the gods!'

The goddess nodded and held up a hand. Then she took the last few steps to where Lukalla stood and pointed at the mud.

There was a skull there, human-looking, yet its shape felt wrong in a way Lukalla couldn't have explained. She recoiled.

'A god?' she whispered.

'Not exactly. Someone who lived around here a very long time ago. There are bones at the bottom of one of the sinkholes. I believe they may have stepped in and broken a leg, or remained trapped somehow. They died here.'

'They trespassed,' Lukalla said, subdued now.

There was a longer silence. Abruptly, the goddess walked towards a smooth spot in the wall, took a stone from the ground and scratched a long chalky line in front of them. She jabbed her finger into one extremity of the line.

'Say you're standing here, and throw a spear this way,' she said, pointing at the other end. 'This is the path your spear takes.'

Lukalla frowned. Spears did not take *paths*; they flew true, or not, but that was a matter of strength and skill, not of walking. She thought she could understand the goddess's meaning, nonetheless. She grunted.

'But before the spear can reach its destination...' the goddess pointed at the middle of the line, 'it must first come halfway. All this way,' she explained at Lukalla's perplexed frown. 'And then before it reaches its target, it needs to fly...' another finger pointed at the remaining section, 'halfway across what remains. And then halfway again. And this is how the spear never reaches its target.'

Lukalla stepped away. Dread was welling up again inside her. The goddess was describing something impossible, but with such certainty that she made it exist somehow; she had just created a spear that kept flying and flying with its end in sight, and never reached it. This was what happened in the world of the gods. She had touched a magic she was not meant to see, or understand.

'May I go back inside?' she whispered.

The goddess took her arm to steady her. When the wall of the ice cave closed again, Lukalla slumped on the furs, gathered herself into a ball, and closed her eyes. Her breasts ached with gathering milk. Her whole being ached with a new urge to get out.

They did not try to kill one another after that. Lukalla knew better than to lay her hands on a being whose magic she had seen. The goddess left her alone much of the time, and when she seemed to notice her again, she only wanted to talk.

Holy men listened for animals speaking to them in human voices and deciphered the messages whispered by the ripples in ponds and streams, but no one Lukalla knew of had ever spoken with a god. The goddess's conversations were unnerving. You could not feel the magic that laced them, at first. And then after a while it would become plain that the goddess had twisted Lukalla's questions so that Lukalla would be the one answering instead, driving the converstion towards things hidden, arcane, which would take root in Lukalla's mind and slowly change her from the inside out.

The goddess had names for what did not exist. Words from the gods' language would sometimes slip into her speech, and then she would be talking of *nothing*, of *numbers*, of *infinite* and *probability*. Not only did she talk about these things as if they were natural, they were, she maintained, an essential part of the divination she performed each day. She figured out the world that was through the world that wasn't. As little as it had made sense at first, Lukalla slowly began to understand. Things had shadows, or reflections in water which sometimes tricked animals and young children; the goddess's language held both the words and their shadows, words that wrapped themselves around absence, or brought to life things that could have been, or might still be.

Her own name was absence, Lukalla once understood, a pit opening deep inside her. She would still be talked about among the tribe, the way they still talked about her mother. Her seashells adorned the poles at the entrance of the cave, and her sons would learn that their mother had been a fearsome warrior, gone to the goddess's cave to bring them warmth. But they wouldn't know of

Lukalla herself. The memory of her arms around them and her milk on their lips would fade, and the name they would grow up with would mean… *nothing*.

That was what the goddess's words meant. The dark void, the absence that shaped the world.

The holy men had words of their own, a language they taught among themselves and that no one else could learn, on pain of death. Lukalla was changing, as they all did during their retreats. Changing, perhaps, more deeply than any of them had dreamt.

She had been silent for a while, with only the sound of her footsteps to echo through the cave. She was getting better at crawling and clambering between upraised poles of rock and through passageways she would have thought barely large enough for a child. What she had taken for a white flame in the hand of the goddess was in fact a stone, which gave off a steady smokeless light, far more powerful than a torch would have been. When they walked together, it cast stark deformed shadows on the walls of the cave.

She thought of asking about what the holy men learned in their dells. But every time she attempted to bring the subject back, she was the one who ended up talking about the holy men and the tribe and the hunting season, and she never knew how it had happened. So she pointed instead at an undulating wing of stone that descended from the top of the cave and tapered into a thin point halfway down.

'Did you see this grow?' she asked.

The goddess looked up with one of her rare smiles.

'It would have been very boring if I had,' she replied.

'Then how do you know they have *grown*?'

The goddess stopped, directing her light up.

'I see,' she said.

Then she touched the reddish point. There was a drop of water there, which travelled down to her finger and dropped to the ground.

'You are right,' she said. 'In a way, I do not know. They are just here. A part of what the world is. Whether they grew or not is not material.'

How strange it was, Lukalla thought, that she could now understand the goddess's answers at once, with all their shadow-words, their *whethers* and *is* and *nots* that carried worlds of absence inside – just as the goddess had understood at once what Lukalla meant, and answered that when they would have talked and talked around the point days before getting none the wiser.

She had talked to a goddess, and understood her. There was power in that, a strength greater than weapons had ever lent her.

On their way back, she walked a little way past the goddess's dwelling. The entrance of the cave was not far. She had not dared to go, not wanted to know if the boulder would still be there, or if the cave would go on into the gods' worlds *as if* its entrance had *never* existed – the shadow-words rolled inside her mind and settled there, defining her fear in a way she could not have before.

But if the cave still came to an end and the boulder was still in place – she could not have rolled it back by herself before, but she was stronger now, powerful with the goddess's own magic. She could imagine it gone, and perhaps…

She reached the end of the cave. There was still an end. The boulder still fit snugly in the entrance. From the outside, it would look like any other part of the mountain, if not for the poles and seashells poking out of the snow.

She turned around when she heard footsteps. The goddess was right behind her. She did not look angry; if anything, she looked very sad.

'I just wanted to know…' Lukalla said. She trailed off.

The goddess didn't say anything. Lukalla strode off to the warm embrace of the ice cave. She could not challenge the goddess, not after giving her word that she would stay in exchange for the end of the winter. But there had to be something else she could try. She had passed through the gods' world, survived, learned.

She had to find her sons again.

For much of her waking hours the goddess sat in front of her crystals, sometimes brushing her fingers over them, sometimes just holding her head in her hands and staring in silence. She had looked up, at first, when Lukalla found out which spot of the cave to press in order for the ice wall to open. She no longer did. Lukalla came and went, even borrowing the blazing white stone, whenever the need took her to look through the cave. She had gone back to the entrance several times. She had tried to listen. Once she thought she could catch a chirruping sound outside, though it faded so fast it might as well have been a trick of the silence.

She had tried strength. She had tried subtlety, picking up sharp rocks and digging where the wall around the boulder seemed prone to loosening. Nothing had worked. She had the disquieting sense that this was the last trial, one last thing for her to learn, and that it was just out of her reach.

She did not hear the goddess come. She was scratching at a crack which seemed to have opened when the water in it had frozen, and when she glanced back, the goddess was there, looking at her with sad, sad eyes.

Lukalla dropped the stone. The goddess had not given her leave to go. One did not cheat the gods of their sacrifices, not without expecting some terrible retribution. There was no forgiveness for even attempting it. She had always known.

And yet she had never accepted it. She had struggled from the first, kicked and bit and screamed and bloodied at least one of the holy men before they got the better of her. She had been ready to kill, men and gods alike, and she had never meant to give up. One last trial, and she would be free. She probed the crack with her finger. It was damp with melting ice, though no wider than before.

One last trial, and she was failing.

All of her anger came back, the defiance that had led her to believe that she could kill a being of magic, the anguish as her empty arms closed on *nothing* every time she needed to rest. She had failed. But the one who had decided that she would fail was standing right here, watching as the cave bested a woman who had never sought to be anywhere but with her sons. Lukalla threw a handful of dirt and let out a long scream, and then she stared at the goddess, who had not even moved.

'What did I do wrong?' she yelled.

There was no answer. Lukalla strode to the goddess and grabbed the furs that covered her shoulders.

'What did I miss? What did I not do? I did everything you asked! I stayed, I told you what you wanted to know, I obeyed every word...' She shook her, screamed at that wall of silent sadness. 'Didn't I learn? Didn't I pass through? Why won't it open now? What have I done?' Her voice broke, but she kept screaming. 'When will you give me back my children?'

Do it, she thought. *Punish me. Attack me. Show me how you fight so I can learn how to best you.* The goddess raised a hand.

The goddess bit her lips, shook her head, and, wrapping both arms around Lukalla, pulled her against her and stroked her back.

'I'm so sorry,' she said. 'If you could only know. I'm sorry. I wish I could... Oh, dear.'

She let go, stepping away from Lukalla, who didn't move, still reeling from the shock.

'If there was any way to send you back, I would,' the goddess said. 'If it was just a matter of opening the cave. I...' She took her head in her hands. That gesture, so familiar, had never meant anything until now. When she spoke again, her voice was very gentle. 'You can't go back, Lukalla. You're dying.'

They still stood by the entrance of the cave. Whether any time had passed at all, Lukalla didn't know. The goddess's hands now rested on her arms, as if it could change something.

'They eviscerated you,' she said, slowly, almost hushed. 'They drugged you, then cut your liver out when you began to lose consciousness. They left you in the cave. There's no way I could cure you, even... there's just no way.'

Lukalla felt around her midriff. It was fine. She felt fine.

She had also not been hungry or thirsty once since arriving in the goddess's cave, and even sleep had come out of distress or boredom, not tiredness.

'What's happened?' she said. 'Why am I still here?'

There was a long silence. They were sitting on the damp ground now; Lukalla wasn't certain how that had happened.

'Picture yourself throwing a spear,' the goddess began. 'A spear that will shatter on impact.'

'A spear,' Lukalla repeated, remembering.

187

The goddess wiped the corner of her eye.

'When it flies out,' she said, 'it will first need to fly half of the way. And then half of what remains. And then half again. And then...'

'It will never land,' Lukalla whispered. 'It will never break.'

'That's it,' the goddess said. 'Oh dear. That's exactly it. It *will* break in time, of course. Except... at this point, there won't be a spear any more. If you watch it fly, you will see it... you will see it shatter, when it lands. But picture yourself *as* the spear, and... and then the spear will never land. It will never break. Because as long as that spear exists, it will be flying. Half of the way, and then half of what's left, and again half of the rest, smaller and smaller, but... still there. As long as it *is* a spear, it will keep flying towards its goal. Its last moments will stretch forever.'

Lukalla grasped at the shadow-words. She was still alive. And yet not. Her being understood in a way her mind couldn't. She clutched her own face. This was the most impossible kind of magic she'd faced yet. And the cruellest.

She had pleaded. Challenged. Shouted in anger. All this time, the goddess had known she was speaking to a dead woman who couldn't possibly hurt her. She had kept her, taught her. Given her hope that she could, in time, pass through, when there was no hope to be had, when this had been all the afterlife she had waiting for her: a cold dark cave, beauties that weren't meant for her growing up from the ground, the blazing memory of the only moments she'd had with her sons, and a death that would stretch on and on until she went mad.

'Is this what sacrifices do, then?' she said. 'You never wanted my liver. You wanted all of me. All that would be left when I died.'

That particular spear seemed to hit. For a moment, the goddess's impassivity was shattered, and it was her turn to clutch her face, albeit briefly. She wasn't looking at Lukalla when she spoke again. She didn't really answer, either.

'Life binds us to time,' she said. 'Our minds perceive it only as a steady flow, just as we cannot hear the cries of bats or see certain colours. It is a trick of our perception, one we require in order to keep living. In death... we become untethered. We leave the flow.

188

Moments can stretch for an eternity, and we relive years in a blink. As long as we exist...'

'Like the spear,' Lukalla whispered.

The goddess moved her head up and down. Her chin trembled.

'But in a very long time,' she said, 'years and years and years from now, the living... they will find a way. They will never travel through time, not with their bodies, at least. But they will find the means to untether the living mind, and once untethered, to communicate with other minds that have left the flow of time as well. Dying ones. Mind to mind, with no need for even a common language.' She wiped her eye again, through her voice was steady, gentle. 'And once they know how to do that, they will send... people. Observers, people of knowledge. To talk, to learn from those who could not leave messages to us. It will be... a haphazard process. It will sound right. It always feels right when there's something to learn, and when you don't kill anything in the process. But this... I didn't know it would come to this. I only wanted to bring knowledge back. I've never meant to make you believe... I've never wanted...'

She fell silent.

Lukalla tried to sort through her words. But there was no point to it any longer. She stared at the rivulets trickling about the boulder, life carrying on at the centre of the earth.

'You made the winter end,' she said. 'Didn't you?'

The goddess let out a long breath, and there was a long silence before she spoke again.

'Yes,' she said. 'I promised I would. Lukalla... close your eyes. Please?'

Lukalla obeyed. The goddess took her hands.

'The snow is melting already,' she said. 'Do you see it? No, don't open your eyes. See it in here. See the rivers grow. Very soon it will feel warm when you stand right under the sun. But this winter, there were other babies born. Two of them won't make it. There will be two mothers, with enough milk and warmth left for both your sons. They will grow. They will see another winter.'

'One of them will waste away,' Lukalla muttered. The goddess squeezed her hands.

'Listen to me,' she said. 'Both of them will grow up. And in time, when it becomes plain that they are both going to live, the clan will see what they are. They will see that they are warriors, from a line of sacrifices, and that they are holy, both of them. They will turn to them for guidance when food gets scarce, and when long-toothed cats roam. They will both become great hunters, and fathers, in turn. They will wear the furs of wolves, and gorgeous seashells. And every winter, they will come back to the cave. They will touch the shells you left there, and thank you for making the gods spare them, and pray to you so that you do it again. They will ask the elders for stories about you. They will never forget. Do you hear me, Lukalla? They will never forget.'

Lukalla reeled. But she remembered the goddess's orders, and she didn't open her eyes.

And so the goddess kept speaking, and her tale was words of life and light, not shadow, yet the magic rose inside it nonetheless. It was a tale of brave men, and a great clan, and the great dead women and men that had helped make it so. It was a tale of how a warrior had bought her sons a mild winter with her love, and how for all their lives they knew of that particular magic, even if they never knew of her. It was a tale with no winter in it, where the snow only appeared in order to melt, and leave fruitful rivers, forever thriving. A tale she could hope for. A tale she could live in.

A tale that kept going, even when the goddess's hands opened, and her voice fell silent, and Lukalla kept her eyes closed, and the world went to sleep around her.

In the Toirano caves in Northern Italy, there is a place where you can still see the traces of hands and feet and knees, where people crawled through the mud ten thousand years ago; what they were doing there can only be guessed at.

How we interpret what we know of our origins is a matter of fascination in itself. How we think of *knowledge* itself is another. Are abstract concepts a true part of reality, or an elaborate system of representation humans (and many animals) use to navigate the world? Do numbers and scientific concepts enable more elaborate reasonings than our perception of tangible things? Have our minds progressed since the formation of our species, or merely changed?

Many have pointed out that there is much in common between oral storytelling and university lectures; or between shamanic initiations and academic training. It is striking how often these good intents barely hide a layer of condescension: the word *primitive* has been erased from polite discourse, but not from our culture. We can go far enough in the past that humanity gets diluted; a few centuries to dig up graves, a few millennia to exhibit corpses in museums, ten thousand years before we think nothing of placing a solitary skull behind a glass and gaping at its animalistic features.

I would never question that we need knowledge, if only because it can be weaponised far less readily than ignorance. That does not make ethics any less necessary. Mad scientists playing God are, or should be, a trope of the past; but it does no harm to remember that research can harm, that animals feel pain, and that the skull grinning in its glass case may once have been buried and mourned.

Nine Lives, One to Spare

Be reckless if you must, but make sure you always keep one of your lives in store for an emergency, the witch used to tell her cats. She had not expected them to follow her advice; however, when she woke up one morning in the great silence at the end of the world, and found them on the roof of her greenhouse, cleaning their ears and bickering lazily in the sunlight, she was pleased to find out that they had.

One nagging question was now answered: cats did indeed possess better control over their impulses than humans ever had.

She might tell *him* that, one day. Not that the matter had ever arisen between them (not that they'd ever had anything approaching a polite exchange, come to think of it), but seeing as there was no other human alive now, no one else could take the role of the listener in her daydreams.

She thought of him more often than she would have expected. The thoughts weren't unpleasant – why would they be? He had never been a real threat. A mortal foe, certainly; but that had been his fear of her, his unwillingness to understand (she had no doubt he would have been capable of it, if he'd tried; as daft as he could be, someone who could build spacecraft and lasers all by himself couldn't be *entirely* hopeless). She had only wanted to be left alone, and pushed back a little when he hadn't.

Yes, some matters between them could have gone... very differently, if he'd listened before trying to blast his way through every problem he saw.

The world had been very quiet, but she had been paying growing attention to new sounds, of late. What she heard that morning had nothing to do with leaves rustling. She rose, unhurried, grinning in spite of herself, her heart picking up with an emotion she'd forgotten how to read, the excitement of an upcoming battle or the anticipation of pleasure to come, she couldn't say.

The witch walked out of the greenhouse just as the spacecraft made a precarious landing on a crumbling terraced field. She shielded her eyes against the dust cloud. If that big lout had damaged one of her lemon trees, he would hear about it. But when the dust settled, the trees were still standing, bright with fruit hanging like stars in the void. Good. She would have fought over her trees, but violence was not what appealed to her most right now. She watched, instead, as the door of the spacecraft opened, and she cocked an eyebrow.

'Look what the cat dragged in,' she said.

'Good day to you too,' the knight replied.

They stood, face to face, for a long while. Lightning crackled in the witch's fingers, begging to be let out. As for the sword hanging at the knight's belt, she could feel it vibrate from here, begging to be wielded for justice. Well. She was ready to defend herself, if she absolutely must.

No doubt he had the same thought. Her hand relaxed at the same moment his let go of the sword's hilt.

'Cup of tea?' she said.

He nodded, and she beckoned him in.

She would have made that tea, too, if upon entering the greenhouse, the knight's eyes hadn't drifted towards a bottle of Campari she'd salvaged from a wrecked bar by the coast. It would have been petty not to offer. They drank it warm, from mismatched mugs, with a squeeze of fresh tangerine juice. She didn't miss his sigh as he unwound, took in the inside of her home – just as dilapidated as the rest of the world, but she'd never minded decay – and relaxed on the bench.

'So this is where all the evil came from,' he said after she refilled his mug.

He sounded appreciative. She allowed herself to smile. The greenhouse did not look like much these days, it was true. The polycarbonate panes of the roof were missing chunks; the tool shack in the corner was the only part that was still water-tight. Bright

194

sunlight came in, and one of the cats was peering inside, probably wondering how on earth she could be talking to someone who didn't meow in answer. The knight followed the direction of her gaze.

'And they said that cockroaches would be the last animals to survive. Shows how much we knew, eh?'

'The cats didn't survive,' the witch replied. 'Most of them had at least one spare life left.' He frowned. 'Yes, the nine lives thing is true,' she said. 'They began to resurrect a couple of months ago. I didn't mind the company.'

'Pretty ironic, coming from you,' he said.

She smiled again and refilled her own mug. There would be no sense in drinking on her own after he left. It was a long time since she'd drunk with someone. Loneliness suited her fine, but having someone to talk to was a pleasant kind of spice, especially when the person in question had put their sword away in a corner, as she'd kept hoping he eventually would.

'I like company, as it happens,' she said, and poured him some more.

He drank again, shaking his head. It was still warm inside the broken-down greenhouse, sheltered without feeling like a prison. She didn't like feeling restrained. One could surmise that this was part of what had started everything in the first place, her love of freedom, never being told where to go, what to do, what she was or wasn't allowed to experiment with.

The knight put his mug down and inhaled with his eyes closed. Even he must realise how peaceful and lovely it was here, though she didn't figure that he was a great lover of green, growing things. In fact, it was the first time she had seen him without some kind of metallic contraption enclosing his body. He had worn armour when she'd battled him on the ground, and had been strapped up in his craft when they'd battled in space. Not a great idea, that one, but then it had been his choice. She had never worried that he could defeat her. She'd got a good long look at the shape of his shoulders through his porthole while they fought. Say what you will about knights, but they knew how to stay fit.

'I'd like you to tell me something,' he said, with his eyes still closed. 'If you didn't hate humanity, why did you do it?'

'Do what?'

'You know what. The curse.'

'Oh. The virus, you mean.' He waved his hand. 'Why, dear, I don't know. Why wouldn't I?'

He chuckled.

'You don't even know,' he said. 'Is the evil truly that strong in your soul, that you'd destroy humankind and not even know why?'

'Very little would have been destroyed if you hadn't tried to blow up that asteroid in my face,' she replied. 'Honestly, what were you thinking?'

The knight's back sagged and he rested his head in his hands. She might have been a little heavy-handed with the Campari. She patted him on the back.

'Not that I'm blaming you,' she said. 'You had a split second to make that call. Anyone could have got it wrong.'

She didn't think she would have, but she didn't say that. In the knight's place, anyone not blinded by pride and anger would have understood that they were outmatched. She could understand the pride, though she was less sure where the anger had come from. She was not the first witch tinkering with new life-forms, surely. She could recall his face at that moment, the grim set of determination and despair, and also, she thought, something knights seldom exhibited when going after witches – respect, and regret. Oh, how she had understood. She had begun to form a spell, a warning, but it had ricocheted against the hull of his spacecraft – and then it had been too late to craft anything but a shield to keep herself safe, as the gravity generator of his ship caught the asteroid, swung it, and propelled it in her direction.

And towards the Earth's atmosphere, where it exploded in a shower of meteors and falling debris raining down from the sky. Towards seas, cities, fields. Towards the vault where her virus was stored, safely, she had thought – had kept hoping, right up to the moment when a shooting star had blown it up into a million shards, scattering the virus into the atmosphere.

'A virus,' he said. 'And to think you eco-warrior types couldn't stomach the thought of GMOs!'

'I don't know what *eco-warrior types* are. I'm a witch. This is what I do.'

She pointed at the countryside around them. For a long while, it had been silent. But she had caught some noises at night, lately, sounds of things chirping, lurking, scurrying. The world was recovering, as it always did. She sensed it in the greenhouse itself, overgrown as it was with specimens she had tried to classify once, before growing bored and moving on.

'They're all still here, you know,' she said. 'Humans. Animals, even if you don't seem to miss them much. They merged with plant life when they caught the virus. They didn't disappear at all. They're still changing. The world is a very interesting place, these days.'

'Interesting. My.'

'Interesting, yes.' She rose and pointed at a shrub growing in a corner. 'I have no idea what this one is, but it started growing robin's eggs, a few days ago. I doubt they'll hatch, but still...' She gestured towards a clump of flowers. 'I thought these ones were mimetic, reproducing the shape of bees. Turns out, one of them flew away yesterday. At least it won't run out of flowers to pollinate.' She grinned. 'It could become the first bee in the history of the world to have pollinated a seagull, for all we know. Imagine what could grow out of that!'

The knight didn't say anything. She doubted he fully understood; she didn't think she could fully explain, either. He was a man who thought one should have a *motive* for wanting to try something new. The workings of his mind were a greater mystery to her than dog embryos sprouting from pear trees.

She was growing bored with words, so she poured them both another drink.

The knight rose, after some time.

'Well,' he said. 'This has been... surprisingly nice.'

She grinned.

'I don't suppose your engine is about to run out of fuel and you'd care to stay the night?'

His eyebrows shot up.

'It's a fusion engine. But thanks for the offer.'

He walked towards his spacecraft, a little unsteadily. She had to run after him to hand him back his sword. He took it absent-mindedly, stared at the vehicle, and sighed.

'What are you planning to do in that thing?' she said.

'Roam space. Seek penance. Look for a sign of... something. Whatever knights are supposed to do when there's nothing left to fight for.'

She was about to protest, but closed her mouth. He was right. There was no need to *fight* any longer. Just sit back, watch things grow, prune a little here and there. Scavenge some tinned meat for the cats before they decided to prey on her.

'I'm not planning to move around much,' she said. 'If you're ever in need of a drink and a chat...'

He answered with a nod and a smile, weary but grateful, it seemed. Then he climbed back inside.

She watched the rocket soar in the silence and blinding light of its fusion motor, until it looked like a little sun, then a shooting star, then nothing.

Then she walked back into the greenhouse to tend the robin's eggs.

I ended up writing a mad scientist story after all. Or maybe I didn't; nature doesn't play God. It exists, it will not stay still, and it doesn't see any reason not to experiment, even if you explain carefully. Even if you get forceful: root out fig saplings growing between the pavement and the wall and they'll be back in a year. Throw glyphosate at weeds and they will only bide their time until you get tired and they can grow back. Pour concrete one metre thick over the ground, and it's only a matter of time before roots push it up. Tear down forests, and watch the human world grind down to a halt as it wrestles with the viruses it's unleashed on itself. If this is a war, there is no way we can win it.

If this isn't a war, then what are we sacrificing ourselves for?

Wind, River, Angel Song

The first scourge is the wind. It descends from the north, or rather it crashes down, cold and pitiless, scouring the land for days on end. Great barriers of cypresses break some of its strength, scatter it away from the fields, but in the shells of villages and cities crumbling houses whistle and tiles clatter on the roofs.

The sky, however – the sky gleams like a jewel when that wind blows, and there is no more delicate pain than the light that overwhelms your eyes whenever you look up.

I gave birth on a fair September morning, in the windowless bosom of a country hospital. I sweated and swore and dug my fingernails in my man's hand, collapsed into an exhausted sleep when the pain ebbed and jerked awake again when it came back. Painkillers were delivered to the large hospitals in the cities first, and only reached backwaters like mine when there was enough fuel and someone to drive and the universe was feeling benign.

The universe was not feeling benign today. Instead of the horn of a providential lorry, it was the scream of the siren that drowned my sobbing cries.

The nurse gasped and the midwife looked up with pained eyes. There was a commotion outside the room and Julien tensed, but even if I could have moved, it would have been a terrible idea to leave. The midwife surveyed the monitor. She squeezed my hand with a smile.

'The safety doors are all shut,' she said. 'We're on autonomous ventilation now. It's all right.'

The sounds outside subsided. There only remained the fierce gusts of the wind that had risen while my body tried to cleave itself in two. Now my body reminded me what we had come here for, and so I screamed and swore and sank into fits of panic; but in the end my daughter was born, and for the first time in nine months I did not tell myself it had been a terrible idea to bring her into the world I lived in.

The midwife laid her on my chest and I folded my arms over her, my eyes into her uncomprehending blue ones, and smiled until it hurt.

Then there was a sound of a door slamming, and a sudden cold in the room.

The nurse blanched. Julien clamped a hand on my mouth and one on our daughter's, as if that could do anything. The cold draught subsided. The midwife shook her head with a weary groan, and collected herself much more quickly than the rest of us. Understanding dawned on me.

She was already infected, living on borrowed time until the angel's song sank her life into the ground. She had nothing left to fear of the wind that had seeped into the hospital.

'You said the safety doors had worked,' Julien breathed.

'They have.' The midwife rose, all reassurance now. 'Someone must have slammed a door nearby. Don't worry.'

But I had missed neither the draught, nor her despondent groan.

My daughter squirmed in my arms and I knew that no wind on Earth would change what I felt, that she was here and never in my life had I felt more right. I looked at Julien. I was still smiling, and not because I forced myself.

'Babies don't catch it,' I said. 'And there's never been more than one infected every time the wind comes. One of us will be there to take care of her, whatever happens. And it doesn't even have to be one of us.'

I was rambling, and it was only when the nurse darkened that I realised I had said something callous. I searched for words to explain, but soon gave up. I didn't wish infection on anybody else. I was only holding my baby for the first time, and no one and nothing would make that moment unhappy for me.

It was an exhausting three days after that, locked up in the hospital with the wind still raging outside, and the occasional bursts of the siren when filters picked up the presence of the spores, or whatever they were. One night, drifting between sleep and wakefulness as my daughter fell asleep against my breast, I thought I heard a voice humming outside, though it was two o'clock in the morning and everyone had been warned to stay home.

After three days, Julien showed up at the doors of the hospital with a pedicab. Sweating and laughing between grunts, he ferried us along the potholed road. It was a gorgeous late summer day, too hot still, but the only warmth I felt was of my daughter's head resting against my chest, lulled by the bumps and lurches of our carriage.

Home was in view at last, the garden hidden behind an overgrown fence. Birds chattered in the ivy, and when I raised my eyes I saw a flock of swallows, gliding south before the winter.

I called out. My mother would be waiting for us; with the hospital closed against the wind, she had been unable to visit. She had called once, from a phone booth. As always, I'd felt a brief stir of panic, before remembering that she had been infected, years ago. She had nothing to fear from the wind – as long as she didn't hear the song.

I pushed the gate. She was waiting, indeed, already standing in the garden, arms raised in greeting.

Not in greeting. I faltered. I ran. I cried.

'Mum, it's me!'

She held her arms outstretched, as if she wanted to touch the sky. Her eyes were half-closed, her lips stretched out in bliss. The baby stirred and groaned. I held her against my chest, and grabbed my mother's shoulder, shook her, shouted in her ear.

It was too late for her to hear, to feel. But it was much too soon for me to accept that. I pleaded and shouted and shook until Julien took my arm, and only then did I realise that my baby was wailing, and the tears on my face were mine. But no sound came out of my mother's mouth, nothing save for a contented sigh, and her hands shivered like leaves as she settled back into stillness.

Her fingers seemed longer already.

The second scourge is the river. In summer it runs in a trickle, streams criss-crossing in a vast bed of rolled stones, young poplars and wild mint thriving with sunlight and silt. It only takes a rain shower for the watery threads to swell to ropes, then cables, then hurtling, ravenous snakes swallowing earth and stone and saplings. It changes course with every storm, eats up roads and gardens in its fits of hunger.

It leaves death in its wake, sometimes. And silt, a fragrant putrescence that makes weeds and trees soar towards the sky.

I stared out of the window as Lou finished her breakfast. Outside, just below the roof, a third family of swallows had built a nest. Butterflies swarmed the garden. Something would have to be done about caterpillars, though there had been less damage to my vegetables since I'd let huge clumps of borage thrive around the place. Beanstalks writhed up their poles, tendrils tickling the sky and thick pods already hanging; tomatoes would flower soon.

A gentle shadow stretched over the garden, a beech tree with two thick branches stretching up, and, in between, my mother's features, still visible enough to make out the last, ecstatic expression on her face, when roots had first sprouted from her feet.

I smiled as my daughter spread honey on her bread with an air of utmost concentration.

'Let's make sure we're on time at the doctor's, love,' I said.

She wolfed down the rest of her bread, wiped crumbs off her hands, sending them flying all over the floor.

'Will Daddy be there?' she said.

I tried not to let the strain show through my smile.

It was a beautiful ride to the hospital. The fields by the road were still thick with grey mud left over from the last time the river had left its bed, but all around, flowers had burst out in dew-covered pinks and yellows. A breeze shook the tall stalks of woad and bedstraw. Out of habit, I checked the sky. But it was only the Southeast wind with its trail of gentle cloud, not the deadly gusts from the north. I pedalled faster, to Lou's breathless singing and exclamations of joy.

Julien was already waiting for us at the doors. I slowed down, gave us time to trade uncertain smiles. It had been some time already, but my first impulse in the morning was still to pat the empty side of the bed, my body forgetting again that I would not find him there, even though my mind knew that some rifts would not be mended. The world was ending, and he could not stay with someone who couldn't accept it, he'd said. Or with someone who accepted it without question; I was no longer sure.

All I knew was that one day we'd been shouting and tearing each other apart because in the garden there was a tree that used to be my mother, and before either of us could remember how the row had started or why we'd said things we once swore we would never hurl at one another there had been Lou's silent tear-streaked face lifted towards us behind the plush kangaroo she pressed against her chest... We'd known that we wouldn't be able to go on.

I composed myself, drew a deep breath.

'Sorry to keep you waiting,' I said, as gently as I could – there were so many ways harmless small talk could sound like a barb these days.

Lou jumped off the bike as soon as I unhooked her from her seat, hugged her father and sauntered into the hospital. Julien and I passed the door at the same time, bumping shoulders and hastily parting.

'Memories,' Julien said.

Memories. Too many of them, emotions too diverse and violent to handle right now. I forced a non-committal chuckle out and hurried after my – our – daughter.

We had known a different world, once, one where having to spit in a Petri dish every other month would have filled children with anxiety. Lou didn't think it any more of a hassle than going to school in the morning. Doctors always welcomed her with cakes and good humour. There were few people left, and far too few children to waste an opportunity to see one beam at you. Lou was already seated in the doctor's office, nibbling on a small almond tart and grinning, when we came in. Waiting for test results didn't bother her as long as she had someone new to talk to.

'I rode my mummy's bike all the way,' she announced. 'And afterwards, we're going to the river!'

'The river, is it?' the doctor said. She glanced at me, and I made a small shrug of apology. Few adults enjoyed walking by the river any more. Whether the rich soil and water had drawn so many of the infected there, or they had sought to use it as a cure, no one could remember. All we knew was that a thick wood of alder trees now lined its banks, some old enough that their bark had lost the shapes of the faces or the limbs of the people they once were.

Lou had been delighted to discover that some trees had faces. Happy trees, she called them, same as the ones we sometimes found in the pictures of old children's books. She loved the river, and as much as I disliked it, I found no reason to saddle her with my own discomfort. The doctor didn't insist, and instead handed Julien a piece of paper.

'All good,' she said. Lou was beginning to fidget. The doctor gave her another smile. 'Why don't you go play outside with Daddy?' she said. 'Mummy will join you straight away.'

She didn't look at me when she said this. My legs began to tremble.

Julien looked at me. I forced myself to breathe.

'Paperwork,' I said. 'Go wait outside.'

They left together. The door slammed behind them. I remembered another door slamming, five years before.

The doctor was not smiling any more when I looked at her. I felt as if my blood had stopped flowing.

'How long do I have?' I said. She opened her mouth, but I stopped her. 'Stupid question. I'm sorry.'

She had no more idea than I did. For my mother, it had taken over a decade. But I'd heard rumours, people taking root a few weeks after breathing the deadly wind, sometimes without even having had time for a proper diagnosis. I took my head in my hands. The future was taking a very different shape now.

'I would be grateful if you kept coming here,' the doctor said. 'We need as much data as we can get. You will receive priority for experimental treatment, if you want.'

'Treatment?'

She mumbled something apologetic. Infection could be fought, for certain. But everybody knew it was not what mattered. You could live with the infection for years without noticing. It was the song – a hum, some had said, unintelligible words, according to others, an ethereal melody that came from nowhere, or from a silhouette drifting like mist through the night – that sealed your fate.

The Singing Angel, journalists had dubbed it. Whatever it really was, I wondered why they didn't call it a devil.

'There's something else,' the doctor said. She bit her lips. 'Your daughter tested positive as well.'

She stopped, waited for me to take in the information, probably not realising that I was waiting for her to explain what she meant by that, if she meant positive for something else, something entirely innocuous. I waited. She looked away.

'No,' I said.

I held my hand up when she started to speak. I could feel no air coming into my lungs or leaving them. This could not be.

Lou. Not her. Never.

'She cannot be infected,' I said. 'You mixed up your samples. She can't. It's only one person at a time, remember? And never babies. It's unheard of. They hadn't even cut her cord, for crying out loud! And I tested positive, I was the one, she can't be...' That draught, the door slamming, right when I held her for the first time. The cord was still intact, wasn't it? She wasn't even properly born, not a separate person from me, not –

Not separate from me. And I was infected.

'The chances that you were infected on the day of her birth are almost non-existent,' the doctor said, gently. 'Latent infections do exist, but not for so long. I know you did your best. Nothing can protect you completely, ever. Listen to me. You did not fail her. However it happened...'

She talked, talked, talked.

Afterwards I was back outside with them, and Lou was bouncing around and asking if we could go to the river now, and I didn't know what words I used or what face I pulled that made Julien blanch as he understood. I strapped Lou in her seat on my bike, and I thought that she'd really been looking forward to this trip, and that at least she wouldn't have to ever put on a gas mask again.

By the time we reached the river, Lou was squealing with excitement, asking if I thought we would find crayfish and not listening to the answer, distracted by a butterfly.

I took a few paces with my feet in the icy stream. Alders dipped their boughs in the clear waters. I shuddered. There were clouds overhead, snow-white and slowly drifting. There would have been planes, once. I had enjoyed watching them as a child; they were a rare occurrence now. I wondered if Lou would ever see one. She was playing on the bank and hadn't spoken for a few minutes. I glanced at her.

She was standing with her arms outstretched towards the sky, her face turned up, beaming, blissful.

'I'm a tree!' she breathed out in a long, drawled-out sigh of contentment.

I screamed.

I ran, stumbling and wailing, but before I had taken two paces, her arms had fallen down, and she was staring at me with fright. I fell on my knees in the mud, pressed my hand against my mouth to hold in a sob.

'Mummy? Are you hurt?'

She ran to me and hugged me, and I held her, smelled her hair, listened to her worried voice, and made myself laugh before she started to cry.

As for the third scourge, every century had its own.

Once it was a parliament of wealthy, corrupt men, with the blood of innocent unbelievers on their hands. There hasn't been a parliament since the first revolution took us back to being the quiet backwater we should always have been. In time there were cars and glass windows to protect everyone against the wind, and the river was dammed, at least for a time, its floods and its spirit tamed. Until everything broke down. Until there were storms and floods all over the world, and oil ran out and finally the wind came back with a new curse.

These days the third scourge is a single person, maybe not even a person.

The angel, and its song.

The train shuddered, and the city came in full view, cut against the canvas of the sea. By the tracks, the empty motorway stretched, asphalt broken up by ailanthus roots.

Lou could have gone on her own. She had not been annoyed at me for wanting to come with her, however. She watched the scenery unfurl with the lurches and shudders of the train, stamped over with drying stalks of fennel and colourful blotches where locals had once spray-painted their names. It hit me, watching the back of her head, the brown curls that had once been blond wisps, how little I'd noticed her change all these years. I wondered if I had been paying too much attention to stray sounds in the night, dreading the moment when I'd hear the song that would mark her end, or mine, or both, and had failed to seize the full joy of seeing her grow up.

And now she was going away.

I must have made a sound, though I'd sworn to myself I wouldn't. She turned to me and smiled.

'I'll be home for the holidays,' she said. Then she grew more serious. 'I meant it, you know. In three years, I'll go to the university, and I'll find a cure. I don't care what it takes. I'll find a way to cure you.'

Over time, I'd got used to the way she talked about the infection as if it didn't concern her. I no longer tried to argue. I certainly wasn't about to now, when she was going to settle down with her father in Marseilles – the only place that still had high schools running – and I wouldn't see her for weeks.

Or never again. I didn't want such thoughts, had come to convince myself they were not even rational; it had been a decade since I'd discovered we both were infected, and nothing had happened to us. There was no reason to think something would at this juncture.

No reason to think it wouldn't, either.

Slowly, as if exhausting the last of the vitality in its old bones, the train came to a stop under the awning of the station. Lou pointed and waved. It took me a couple of seconds to recognise her father.

We stepped down, and she hugged him with an exclamation of joy. Julien smiled at me, tentatively. He would be taking in the white in my hair, too. Ten years should have been more than enough time to bury the hatchet. But for that we would have needed a hatchet to bury, rather than a stifling blanket of misunderstandings and petty differences. His last letters from the city had hinted that I should come live there, too, but had always remained just allusive enough that I couldn't decide whether he feared offending me, or hoped that I wouldn't accept.

'I'll be back in October,' Lou said. Suddenly she swallowed, smile gone. 'Take care of Grandma for me?'

I nodded, embraced her, and then they were gone, and nothing remained but the cracked grey of the station, and the South breeze caressing the stones.

Two trains were about to depart. One left for the north and home. One went south along the coast, and I tried to remember how long it had been since I had last seen the sea.

The wagon was empty. As the train sank into the more derelict parts of the city, I remembered that I had forgotten to check whether I would have time to get back. I didn't have to care any more if the wind rose while I was outside, but it could still turn fiercely cold, and few people opened their door to one of the infected. But the train moved on; I neglected to rise at the next station, and decided to let the lull of the rails make the decision for me.

There had been over a million people living here once. Now pines and ailanthus trees crowded the rails, some with faces still visible in their bark, fading smiles and half-closed eyes. The buildings behind the canopy were falling apart, though clothes still hung from some windows, and here and there, small groups of people lounged about, sometimes with gas masks hanging from their shoulders. The train often stopped for no reason. Everything was quiet, until I began to make out the low, rhythmic sound of the sea.

I got off in a town that had once enjoyed a reputation for scenic beauty, at a time when people bothered to wander away from home. The station was just as deserted as the train itself. I wondered how many bits of the old world were still in motion but slowly winding down, like a swing still swaying for a while after a child has hopped off, before it quietly stops, forgotten. I tried to make out the face of the person who had been driving the locomotive. But it was too far away, and the train was already creaking, lurching, sinking away along the coast – and there was nothing left to do for me but walk, noticing, as if for the first time, how deserted the world had become.

So I did. I walked along overgrown vineyards, through a small town, pink and white, its streets cracked by the roots of so many slender pines, almost black against the gleaming sky. I walked until the sea sparkled ahead, and then out of the town and up the cliffs, towards the sky, towards a place that was blue and empty and unbearably beautiful.

At last I stopped, and sighed. There were hundreds of metres of orange cliff between me and the sea and, in the middle, a couple of scrawny pines, incongruously planted between sea and sky, as if they had been alpinists once. I was out of breath, bizarrely proud of having made it so far, though deflation was catching up with me. There was nothing to do now but go back home, maybe ask Julien if I could spend the night if I was too late for the last train. And I didn't want to go home.

That was when I heard the song.

The rustles of the bushes carried a frail droning to me at first, then notes, then words I still couldn't make out. I froze in place. The sea hurt my eyes.

Then the sounds got closer and I recognised the tune. 'My Funny Valentine'. I turned around, startled, and a short, slim, very old lady grinned and waved at me.

I took a few steps towards her. She was walking slowly, though she didn't look winded. She must have been in her late eighties, at the very least. She heaved a sigh when she reached the top of the cliff.

'How beautiful it is here,' she said. 'Have you seen my tree?'

I frowned, but then she pointed downwards, at the pine clinging to the cliff.

'It was so small when I first noticed it. And look how gorgeous it is now! I check on it every day.' She stared at me with a smile and wide open eyes. 'Aren't you a lovely sight, too. What a pleasure to meet you.'

I smiled back. It must feel lonely here, if she had to walk all this way on her own. We looked at the sea in silence. The glare finally forced my eyes down, to the mid-afternoon shadows darkening the ground about my feet, under clumps of gorse and pine saplings.

There were shadows everywhere, sharp and cool against the ground. Everywhere, except around the feet of the lady next to me. Light permeated her body as if there had been nothing there.

I looked up, my smile withering from my face. She had begun humming again. I felt my legs grow weak, the emptiness pulling. It was over. I'd left my daughter for the last time, and how would she ever know that the place I had grown my roots in was the very top of a cliff where I had not set foot in so many years? She would go home, perhaps, and it would be silent, only her grandmother would be waiting, alone, without a trace of her old features to show that she had been human once. I would never see my daughter again.

I looked out at the sea, weariness smothering what was left of my heart. I had always known it would end like this. It was never going to be the right moment, the right goodbyes, because we couldn't live as if we were forever on the verge of dying. We had to keep living, so we'd forgotten —as we'd forgotten the broken roads and overgrown houses, the power lines flickering on and off, the world narrowing down as daily news stopped coming from across the planet, then across the continent, then across the country, as we'd forgotten that the world would not end in flames and storms after all, but in silence, a silence that had already begun to take hold of us.

The woman was still singing, swaying left and right with her eyes half-closed. I would die to the sound of a broken-down voice singing 'My Funny Valentine'. I stared at the sea again, smooth, empty, silent but for a soft rumble that had nothing to do with life, the sound of the universe carrying on without us.

In the distance, the waves broke. A plume of mist broke the air with a whooshing sound, a black shape emerged, lingered up for another second, and dove back down.

I had so rarely seen the sea. I had never seen a whale before. I never would again.

I turned to the woman who beamed at me.

'How lovely you look,' she said, as if she'd forgotten she'd said it moments before.

And I broke.

I pressed my hands against my mouth, but it wasn't enough to hold in the tears. I said something, I think, a plea, a protest. Then I felt a hand on my shoulder and before I'd understood what was happening, I was crying in the angel's arms, she stroked my back and sang more gently, breaking the song at times to whisper reassurances.

Nothing changed. I could still feel the emptiness, the quiet, except that it was no longer suffocating, only peaceful, blissful, almost. And through the quiet, sounds came back. The sea, and its subtle rumour I'd mistaken for an absence, fish and seagrass and the whales that were free to roam again. The rustle of the wind, birdsong, everywhere, movement disturbing the grass, earth crumbling in burrows. And trees, more alive than I'd ever understood.

I lifted my head at last.

'I need to see her again,' I said. 'Please.'

She patted my head.

'Why, of course,' she said. 'Run along, dear.'

I ran. Down the slope, through ancient vineyards, towards a train that might not come until the morning, or ever, for all I knew, I ran.

Towards you, my darling, my little one. My Lou.

I'm running. I wish I could say it will be all right. You will not find a cure in time, my dear. It is too soon for me, for us, but then it was always going to be.

But it's not too late, no matter what I ever thought. The world was ending long before you came along, long before the wind came, even, drowning in hurricanes and heat waves. Every generation grew up in a world that was doomed to be lost before the next generation was born. And that doesn't matter. It would have taken more than a mere apocalypse to keep me from wanting to have you. I bore you, loved you, watched you enter a world that was already closed to me, a world so much more wonderful than the one I lived in, where trees are happy forever and where the wind can only prickle your skin. I thought I brought you into the world and didn't see the world really was my gift to you, and no matter how much of a downward spiral it is, you would see where I was wrong, you would tilt your head just so – and then the spiral would be flowing upwards for you.

Maybe I will never see you climb. Maybe I was the only one who was ending, all this time. I don't care – I'm smiling now, even as the air deserts my lung, even as I run to you, to embrace you one more time and let the end be damned. Because that part of me will never end.

Hold on, my darling. Live for me, for all of us.

And remember that there will never be too little of me left to keep running to you.

Picture Provence in your mind and you will likely think of an idyllic place, where the sun is always bright but never searing, where the sea breeze is never far and where somehow, your glass is always full of excellent wine.

Live in Provence for some time, and you will realise how miserably inhospitable it was, not so long ago. 'The Mistral, the Durance River and the Parliament are the three scourges of Provence', the old saying went. A hundred years ago, the land I live in did not exist. Ghosts from its past still roam, however, between motorways, well-insulated houses and the artificial lakes and canals scattered here and there to fight the dreadful barrenness of the land. It is in the mountains you hear them best, in the Sainte-Victoire and the Luberon, where shrub-sized oaks and the ruins of monasteries cling to the rock against the wind.

We are bound to wonder how long such a fragile balance will hold, when climate heating pushes the desert up. Change has defined Provence for millennia, and it still bursts with seeds. To be destroyed or to blossom in new and unlikely ways – that is now up to us.

Elephants in Bloom

'Join me in prayer for atonement and hope,' Ilana said, 'and for the Holy Cross in Our Lord's heart.'

Not his heart, his guts, my mother would have grumbled. *Assuming there are guts in there, or anything human.*

'For He who loved humankind so much that he gave His only Son, and now His own being…'

Mum would be back at the cathedral with the rest of her team by now. If I got there early enough, we could have a glass of fresh milk in the cloister, and maybe pears and grapes.

'… in sign of hope, for the day when He will rise again and lift us all to Heaven… Victor, are you with us?'

I blinked. From her makeshift pulpit on a grassy height, Ilana stared at me, her back straightened in an attempt to look intimidating. Behind her, the mountain loomed, half again as tall as it used to be before God's gigantic body crashed down from the heavens and came to rest, broken and sprawled, over its rocky spurs.

I grinned. Ilana tried to purse her lips, but her eyes smiled nonetheless.

'Sorry,' I said. 'Amen.'

I made the sign, to please her. She smiled, fully, this time. Ilana was nineteen, our appointed school teacher, and the prettiest girl who had ever smiled at me. That I was five years younger did not discourage me yet.

'Good. Botany, now.'

Just as I found my notebook, the sound of a bike rattling on the rocky path made all the class raise their heads. It was Farès, the postman, with his jacket slung over his shoulder and his cap propped sideways.

'Victor. Good to see you. Here's a letter for your mum.'

I sprang to my feet. A letter could only come from one person in the world. Farès held out the large, heavy envelope, with our names written in bold capitals. I clutched it as if the wind could rip it from my hands and turned towards Ilana.

'Can I bring it to her now? Please?'

Ilana sighed, but smiled.

'Fine. See you tomorrow?'

I nodded and ran. Ilana was always afraid of not seeing me come back to her classes. I actually liked school, even if she made us pray much more often than I had the stomach for. As far as I could tell, Mum didn't mind my going, either. Of course I avoided bringing up Ilana with Mum, just as I did not discuss Mum's work with Ilana.

September was warm, though not as much as older people remembered them. A breeze disturbed the large leaves of fig trees, more imposing and lush than ever since the Pope had declared them sacred and scientists had pronounced figs unsafe to eat. Behind stone walls, hens clucked in the remnants of once-impressive houses. I made my way towards the cathedral through empty, quiet streets. By the time I reached its dark gate, the envelope in my hand was stained with sweat.

Inside, the usual machinery was buzzing, with research assistants grunting and straining on the bicycles that powered the main computer. Two scientists in lab coats were taking notes on the pictures that flickered in and out of sight on the screen. They waved at me, absently, when I made my way to the cloister.

Mum was there already, sitting under a fine stone arch with her feet hanging behind a raspberry bush, sipping *mate* from a hollow gourd – a habit Dad had brought from his native Chile, along with a cellar-full of the stuff their conjoined efforts still hadn't managed to drink through. As always, I felt a moment of relief. Another day at work that hadn't seen her crushed under tonnes of rock, or the mysterious materials that made up God's body.

'Letter from Dad!' I shouted.

Cheers erupted across the cloister, where Kahina and Emma, Mum's oldest team-mates, relaxed on an old creaky bench. Mum leaped over the bushes, snagged her trousers in the process, splattered dark green *mate* leaves and swore very loudly. Emma and Kahina had got up, too, strolling to greet me.

'A regular little mouse, your mother,' Kahina said. 'You'd never believe that such a tiny thing can make such a racket.'

Mum gave her a whack and craned her neck, grinning, as I opened the letter.

There were a couple of handwritten sheets, which she snatched straight away, and some blurry photographs.

'*Haven't found another yet...*' she read. 'Well, what did they expect? It's not like it started raining gods on Earth all of a sudden! *Decent weather, for the Arctic... Polar bears are making a beautiful recovery...*' She read on, silently, for a minute, before I looked over her shoulder.

'Our godly corpse is still the only one, then,' Emma said.

'I've always told him so,' Mum replied. 'He just wanted an excuse to go sailing again.' She said this without animosity, though my throat constricted a little at her words. Dad had been gone for nearly six months, on a mission to find whether there were other gigantic alien bodies littering the Earth, or if our god was only one indeed, broken and silent on our mountain. I'd keep pretending not to mind, to anyone who asked. The truth was that I missed him beyond words.

'Victor, look at the pictures,' she suddenly said.

I did. Kahina propped herself on tiptoe to take a look, and sucked in a breath.

'That's horrifying. Oh crap. That's beautiful.'

The first picture only showed a large, dark shape under the ocean's surface. The next ones, however, had been taken underwater. Dad's team had found no god, but come across something that, to my eyes, was infinitely more fascinating: the body of a right whale, sinking towards the abyss, dissolving week after week as clouds of fish and algae clung to its dwindling flesh, life blooming in one last, crazy boom after the animal had died.

We gazed at the pictures in silence. Dad and his crew had spent weeks diving, photographing the decaying giant from every angle. Much of the letter was an enthusiastic description of what they had observed there.

215

'Would be fun if we could just take pictures of God from a submarine instead of wriggling up his backside every morning, wouldn't it?' Emma said.

'Get lost,' Kahina replied. 'You'd try to crawl through the wall after two days.'

Mum kept going through the pictures, a quiet smile on her face. After a while she looked up at me, ignoring her friends.

'Let's sit over there, shall we?'

I followed her to an ancient wooden bench, grateful for the respite. I liked Mum's team-mates, but their boisterous ways made me feel awkward at times, not least because I knew that I would never have the nerve or willpower for the harrowing job they did, digging through God's body for clues of what had happened to him, or of where the plagues that had taken the Earth by storm around the time of his fall had come from.

It was cool in the shadow of the cloister, and the air smelled of stone and damp earth.

'You miss him a lot, don't you?' Mum said.

I shrugged. If I told her, I sensed that I'd feel even more uncomfortable afterwards. She gave my elbow a squeeze and didn't insist. In the arches of the cloister, the weathered statue of a woman gazed at us with the last worn-out hint of a cryptic smile.

'The Queen of Sheba, apparently,' Mum said, changing the subject when she noticed me staring.

'Really?' I said, glad to steer the conversation towards innocuous topics, though this one wasn't of great interest.

'Who knows. It's a church. It's not like they have too many queens to choose from.' She smiled. 'Other people said she's much older than that, a spirit of the land or something. The snake loves her, regardless.'

'The snake...?'

That was when I saw it – a thin mottled shape coiled around the crown of the statue, its head resting on her locks. When I tried to move closer, it reared, but then remained still.

'Had to let go of the sniffer dogs,' Mum said. 'Too expensive to feed. Snakes keep us free of mice, and they're just as good.

216

Whenever this one acts like he's frightened by a sample, we get the DNA testing computer started.'

Our elderly neighbour had told me of a time long ago when electricity was so plentiful you could simply plug half a dozen computers into the wall and have them run all day for no reason. Until a couple of years ago, I'd thought she was pulling my leg.

'Did you get anything useful?' I asked.

'A couple of leads. Some unrecognised genes. Something that might be an equivalent of DNA if you squint hard enough. It takes time for the doctors to figure it out, you know. And we still haven't managed to get very far below the surface. That big brute is hard to dig into, and they can't work from too few samples.'

The doctors weren't the ones who burrowed through God's body, squeezing themselves into corridors barely large enough for a cat, retrieving foreign materials with their bare hands before knowing whether they were harmful. I didn't bring it up. Mum needed a way to keep us fed; it was either this or going away like my Dad, and she wasn't about to entrust the house to me, or leave me in the care of the Children of Charity.

I still hadn't become good enough at hiding my feelings. She rubbed my back, shaking her head, but stopped when I pulled away, resentful.

'Let's go home,' she said, after sipping a last splash of hot water from her gourd.

Ilana offered to walk me home the next day. The Children of Charity had given her the evening off, she said, and she wanted to enjoy the weather before the equinox. I was surprised and delighted, and had no ready words for the occasion, so I just cocked an eyebrow and said, 'Why not?'

Thankfully, she wasn't put off. Down from her pulpit, she was, unexpectedly, much shorter than me. Most people already were, but I hadn't expected to look down at her as she walked by my side on the narrow, broken-down road that led to my home.

'You're getting very good at botany,' she said.

I started. Without thinking, I'd been inwardly cataloguing the plants that clung to the side of the road: wilted celandine, clumps of purslane, lush pellitory and wild lettuce, amaranth, chicory, white bedstraw.

'We still organise Sunday walks, you know,' she said. 'To gather wild herbs, draw flowers. And just talk and enjoy being together. It's quite nice.'

I looked at my feet, searching for an answer. I liked Ilana, but couldn't shake the creeping sense of disquiet I felt around the other Children of Charity. Their professed love for God and each other rang like a well-rehearsed song, unlike the messy, loud camaraderie of Mum and her team. I didn't want them to talk to me about God, either. In their presence, I couldn't help feeling guilty for what Mum did for a living, though I would never have admitted it out loud.

Ilana's smile faded into sadness.

'You're welcome anytime,' she said. 'I know your mother won't approve.'

We'd come under the shade of a lush, wide fig tree. I stopped, grateful for an excuse to change the subject, and pointed up. Its billowing branches were covered in bursting ripe fruit. Tiny wasps flew from one to the next, worrying at the flowers tucked away in the folds of red, seedy flesh.

'I climbed up here once, when I was little,' I said.

Ilana's eyes widened.

'Did you? What was it like?'

I walked close to the tree before answering. Its bark was a soft grey, smooth to the touch. The first time I'd been aware of it, the fig tree had reminded me of a family of elephants in a picture book I owned. A slow, benign mother pachyderm, whose wide legs had taken root in the rocky ground by the road, but would still lift me gently with her trunk and hold me close if I fell from her branches.

'It was...' Harder to describe with every passing year. The moment I stepped on the branches, the world had shifted. I'd looked up to see leaves parting, impossibly far, and the colour of the sky had flickered, as if the Earth had been sent bouncing through space, propelled forward by a cathedral of leaves. 'It felt bigger than it should have been,' I said, pushing away the sense of dread and displacement, which had never quite replaced the fascination I felt.

Ilana looked up in awe.

'You felt it,' she said. 'That was Him.'

I nodded, unconvinced. Fig trees, along with a handful of less spectacular species, had been declared holy and untouchable some time before my birth. Scientists still shook their heads, but didn't protest. *Something* had touched the trees, whether that was alien DNA or an unknown toxin, and until they found out what, it would be much better if people refrained from eating their fruit.

Mum would hear no talk of alien toxins. This was no alien, she would say. This was God, the same as he'd always been: a ponderous, useless carcass, taking up so much space you couldn't help running into him even when you tried your best to live your life away from his influence.

'You know, there are many people who would love to hear about your climb in this tree,' Ilana said, tentative hope creeping back in her voice.

I looked away. I might have suspected that the point of inviting me was to talk to me some more about God. I still couldn't help feeling disappointed.

'Yeah,' I said. 'Maybe I'll come. I need to meet my mother at the cathedral now.'

She tensed, as if in sudden pain.

'They desecrated it,' she said.

I shrugged, unable to hide my embarrassment. I couldn't imagine how believers would take it, knowing that the place they once prayed in was now cluttered with the machinery that attempted to make sense of pieces broken off God's body. It was the only place both large and cool enough left in the city, but of course I couldn't tell her that. Being incapable of imagining her feelings beyond speculation made me uneasy. I said something meaningless and scampered off.

I heard the sounds from the cloister right when I set foot in the cathedral: laughter, loud jokes and brags, glass clinking. I took a peek. Mum, Emma, Kahina and a few younger members of their team sat in the garden with two of the doctors, cheering and congratulating one another.

'Here's the boy!' Kahina shouted right before I could disappear back into the cathedral. 'Come give your mum a hug. She's earned it.'

Bewildered, I did. That surprised her; she made a delighted sound and hugged me back. When I pulled away, she stared at me with a grin, eyes wet.

'Want to try some beer?' she said. 'I'd say we all deserve it.'

Emma pulled some bottles from under her bench. All took them, save for Kahina who shook her head, smiling. Emma rolled her eyes.

'Come on, woman. You really think the old man will get angry at you for drinking?' she said.

Kahina shrugged, unfazed.

'And what will I do,' she replied, 'if next time we crawl in there I meet my grandmother's ghost and I stink of sin? Give me some water. That's plenty.'

Everybody laughed and so did she. We raised our glasses – Mum had poured me a little swig, which was intimidating enough – and I tried to hide my frown when the bitterness hit. I still didn't know what we were drinking to.

'We found a new way in,' Mum said. 'A safer one, too. And much deeper. We may make this breakthrough yet.'

'So how did you do it?' a doctor said.

'That was Emma. She remembered about the Monks' Staircase. You know, that tunnel going up from the old monks' orchard to the monastery? Well, the monastery happens to be built almost at the top, just below the cross. Which has poked a hole right through God's gut. We only had to squeeze in.'

'And it worked?'

Emma grinned.

'Like God's fire,' she said, to general cheer. 'We just had to consolidate the opening. There are burrows starting right there, much larger than the ones we used in the thighs. We only explored for a little while and got in deeper than ever. It's going to be a breeze.'

I nodded along, acting wise, even though no one was paying attention to me. Mum drained her beer before getting up.

'It will be a breeze once everyone's had a good night's sleep,' she said. 'Shall we?' She held out her hand to me. I was still surprised at the strength she retained in her petite frame, long past forty. I towered over her, but my hand felt flimsy in her grip. She gathered her *mate* and thermos flask, waved to her team, and we left the cathedral before the sun set.

It had been a windy few days. The turbine on the roof whirred and spun furiously, and we could afford to keep the lights on for a little longer than usual. Mum settled on the worn-out sofa with a book. I stared at Dad's pictures, the ghostly outline of the whale resting in the darkness, bones peeking out in places. Even in pre-cataclysm days, Dad had written, people who had managed to record whale falls were few. And yet, the near-elimination of whales and their corpses had come close to destroying sea life as we knew it. Without their gigantic bodies, most of the abyss would have been sterile.

I looked up at Mum.

'Do you think they're really going to find what they're looking for in God's body?' I said.

She sighed.

'No. But why worry? Everybody wants answers. Someone has to be looking.' She closed her book and looked at me, smiling. 'Here's the thing. God had nothing to do with the cataclysm. Heating, storms, plagues, the energy crisis… humans did that. And once everyone was too exhausted to keep ruining the world, the problem started solving itself. God just happened to fall from the sky right about that time. He did make trees grow back faster, I'll give him that. Given the state the planet was in, a giant bag of fertiliser from the heavens was a very welcome gift.'

I did not remember the cataclysm. Everyone agreed that the Earth had started to settle back into a new balance around the year of my birth. Stories of how people used to live before then were both scary and enticing.

I wanted to mention Ilana's words about blasphemy and desecration. The pain on her face when I'd mentioned the cathedral had unsettled me, as puzzling as it was. I found that I had no adequate words to ask Mum about it. The cathedral was what it had always been: a lovely, shaded place with raspberry bushes and mysterious statues. I couldn't see how or why the doctors' presence could disturb believers. After all, not even God's fall from the sky had upset their beliefs – just like Mum had stuck to her serene brand of atheism, and I'd grown up without even wondering if there could be any difference between the huge prone corpse and the mountain that supported it.

Mum rose and put her *mate* gourd on the table without bothering to empty it. It smelled of mornings playing board games with Dad and late afternoons in the cloister. She kissed me on the forehead before walking upstairs.

'Your turn to feed the chickens tomorrow,' she said. 'Don't stay up too late.'

When I showed Ilana the pictures of the whale fall, she gathered the rest of my classmates to look in reverent silence.

'He made this,' she said. I thought she was talking about my dad, and I started to grin, before she turned around and made the sign of the cross, bowing her head to the mountain and the body sprawled on it. Other students nodded, with more or less conviction.

'How will we manage now?' a girl who didn't come often, but whom I knew stayed at the lodgings of the Children of Charity, said. 'What will happen to us if He's dead?'

Suddenly annoyed, I snatched the pictures back.

'We'll manage. We always have. Whatever happened on Earth, humans did it. Don't know why it should be different now.'

Ilana looked at me with a wide, delighted smile.

'Victor is right,' she said, surprising me. 'God wept for our sins, but allowed us to retain the freedom He had given us. And then He gave His son for our redemption, then His own body. Whatever sins we committed, His love for us remains infinite.'

I didn't answer. This was not at all what I had meant, and I looked away, embarrassed, as butterflies materialised in her smile and found their way right into my stomach. I pocketed the pictures, muttering an excuse about my mum being very keen on seeing them all again.

What if she was right? I suddenly thought. Even the most staunchly irreverent scientists agreed that a new bloom had come with God's fall to Earth, and were still trying to figure out why. I thought of the elephant tree, boughs spreading like a cathedral. A gift, from a being so incomprehensible that all certainties had faded when he had crashed on the mountain.

The pictures – Dad's work, and he'd never meant them to prove anything about God's greatness – were stiff in my pocket. I met Ilana's eyes again when I got up. She smiled at me, warmly, fully. I wondered if the look of pure happiness in her eyes came from a truth she knew and I was denied access to.

When I walked back, I stopped by the fig tree. Over a perfectly clear blue sky, its branches unfolded, large curvy leaves swaying. Its flower-fruit were turning from green to a marbled purple, wine-red insides bursting out. I lay a hand against the smooth grey bark. But aside from residual summer warmth, I could feel nothing.

When I reached the cathedral, Mum and her team were just coming back, their clothes still covered in dirt, grinning. Mum squeezed my arm and raised a basket. I couldn't see what was in there, wrapped in plastic, but it was bulkier than usual.

'Hit a vein,' she said, kicking the door open. 'Doctor!'

Uncharacteristically, it took a few seconds for a white-clad assistant to walk up from the bottom of the nave.

'They've all gone to the congress in Marseilles, remember?' she said. 'Good day?'

Mum rolled her eyes.

'*That* congress. The one to which we weren't invited. Of course.' Emma mumbled something, but Kahina grinned.

'They can always feel like fools when they come back from congratulating one another and find out that the big breakthrough happened without them,' she said.

The assistant's eyes went wide.

'What was it? What did you find?'

Kahina laughed and shrugged.

'The usual. Weird lumpy alien matter. Let's run it by Asklepios first. He can tell us it's just a big bag of dirt after all and you can all pop a beer to drown your sorrow.'

They walked into the cloister, me trailing behind them, gazing up at the fresh repairs on the higher points of the arches. I thought of scientists, snakes and ancient spirits, recovering the fallow ground now that not even the pretence of a living god subsisted. I thought of Ilana's words about God's gift of his own body.

Suddenly it felt very important to know what Mum's team had found.

Emma managed to coax the snake out of his slumber, dangling a strip of meat. She took one of the dark lumps out of the basket and held it out. Asklepios slithered forward lazily, tasting the air, forked tongue darting and vibrating.

He reached her hand; she lured him closer to the lump. Mum sighed and shook her head, and began to strip out of her thick overalls. I didn't move.

The snake was close enough to touch the thing. But instead of slithering around to take the meat, he hissed, recoiled and backed away, disappearing down the wall.

Mum and Kahina had grown very quiet. I hadn't made a sound. Emma got up, staring at the brown sample in her hand, and the untouched piece of chicken on her other palm.

'He hasn't reacted like that since...'

'Since we tried to get him to smell figs,' Mum said. 'Girls. We found something.'

A loud cheer erupted. Mum strode towards the computer, lying inactive without the constant whirr of its accumulators. Kahina slapped my back.

'Race you, big boy,' she said, grinning.

I grinned in turn, and we ran to the bikes.

As we pumped on the pedals for all we were worth, the lights on the machine flickered, then grew steadier. I was already short of breath trying to keep up with Kahina's pace. She winked at me and sped up, while Mum cheered both of us on. The screen was now coming to life. Emma had donned gloves, cut one of the lumps in two, then shaved off a veined sliver which she deposited on a gel-filled dish. The doctors were always going on about the priceless, cutting edge machinery they operated while their assistants sweated and huffed on the pedals and their technicians wriggled through the bowels dug into God's body; but for once I felt their excitement instead of annoyance when Emma wired the gel to electrodes and capillaries, and the machine began to hum harder.

The assistant had joined us, standing back, as if shyer now that she found herself alone with the poorly-paid, riotous women who provided the scientists with their vital research materials and hardly received any credit for it. Or perhaps she was surprised that Emma knew how to operate and read the machine. My pace had slackened. Kahina handed me a bottle of water and raced on, indefatigable. Mum and the assistant had started to talk in excited voices, Mum still clutching the basket.

After an eternity, Emma raised a finger. Her face lit up in anticipation. Kahina sat back and slowed down a little. Then Emma froze.

Just when Mum got closer with a quizzical expression, Emma burst into laughter. Kahina and I stopped. Emma was still laughing, tears swelling at the corners of her eyes, pointing at the screen.

'*Tuber melanosporum*,' she said, hiccupping. I looked at Kahina, who sat there with raised eyebrows. 'Truffles,' Emma said. 'We risked our lives for a basket of bloody *truffles*.'

The assistant gaped. Mum stared at the basket, new understanding dawning on her face.

'That's not possible,' Kahina said. 'Have you seen how Asklepios reacted?'

'So what? When was the last time you tried to get a snake to smell a fucking truffle?'

The screen flickered off, but she paid it no mind. She walked away, shaking her head.

'That's it. I give up. We've been all over the place. All we found is rocks and dirt and old roots. And now we know there are truffles growing inside God. Big deal.'

'This is going to be of major interest,' the assistant said. 'In this season, and at this depth...'

'Yeah, yeah. Big leap forward for science, God's filled with mushrooms. But you know what? We're never going to find any alien DNA or whatever it is you want to find. Giant bag of fertiliser is all there is. He's already decayed too badly or there wasn't anything there to begin with. You want me to keep crawling in there? You bloody well better double my pay. Art for art's sake is not my thing.'

All this time, Mum had stayed silent. I got off the bike and came closer. Inside the basket, lumps were piled together, some as small as a marble, some almost the size of an egg.

'Have any of you ever tasted truffles?' she said.

'Course not,' Emma replied. 'I'm not a millionaire.' That seemed to get her out of her sulk. 'If there are people willing to buy these, it won't have been a complete waste of time,' she said.

'Buy these?' Mum stood straight and gave me the basket, which I cradled in my arms, unsure what to do. 'We're not giving these away for *money*. Even if we could sell them for their proper value in town, and we won't. You have no idea, Emma.' She smiled. 'I had truffles once, when I was a child. They taste… Like something you can't even imagine. Leaves. Rocks. Dirt. Blood. Like taking a bite out of our old Earth herself.' The others had fallen silent. They stared at my mother, both surprised and awed by her sudden solemnity.

'These may not be safe to eat,' the assistant ventured.

'Then they shouldn't be safe to gather, should they? And yet here we are.' Mum grinned. 'Ladies, we're all meeting at my house on Sunday. Bring wine. Fruit. All your best. We're going to have a feast fit for the gods.'

Mum talked a lot sometimes, but she never said something she didn't mean. The next day, we got to work, with her giving sharp, excited directions. She churned fresh butter and buried a couple of truffles in it, so they would transmit their fragrance to the yellow fat. She sliced others and marinated them in a jar of olive oil. She sacrificed one of our precious guinea fowls and hung it in the cellar, humming, for the flesh to mellow until the next day. Lastly, she left me with the task of watching the milk that simmered with sugar until it grew thick and golden – Dad's favourite treat, and mine, whenever I missed him.

Cold wind blew from the north the next day, messing up the leaves of the vines that grew around the terrace, still laden with a few maturing grapes. Emma and Kahina joined us, heaping fresh grapes and pears and square apple jellies on the table. Mum greeted them from inside the kitchen, where she was still busy baking bread, and steaming couscous with truffled oil – a combination that drew an outcry from Kahina, until she smelled it, that is. Grinning, I wiped my hands clean of flour and set the table.

When Mum laid fresh slices of bread and butter on the plates and arranged thin slices of the largest truffle on top, we all held our breath. The wind rustled in the pines, and over there, on the preternaturally clear sky, the mountain was cut out like an icon, the gigantic corpse draped over the cliff. I took a small bite, waiting for something momentous to happen.

There was deep silence. Mum's description hadn't done the truffles justice. The flavours that spread on my tongue were unlike anything I'd ever tried; something dark and wild and overpowering, melting and simmering through my entire body. I finished the toast, made myself another, forcing myself to slow down, to savour what I wanted to devour. I looked up to find Mum staring at me, with a happy grin on her face.

'Tell me this wasn't worth it,' she said, and she poured helpings of wine all round.

Emma shook her head, her good humour returned. With the chatter resuming, I arranged the couscous and the guinea fowl on plates, the scent of infused oil rising like wine to my head.

That was when Kahina pushed back her chair, looking in the direction of the mountain. We fell silent.

'Isn't it time we said something for him?' she said. Nobody answered. She smiled, straightened, and took a deep breath. 'You gave us a run, you old bastard,' she said. 'Random rules. Obscure books. I've always thought you must have known it would end up with everyone fighting or making their own lives miserable, and you'd done it on purpose. But you know what? Now I see you there, you don't so much as twitch when we punch your gut open, and I wonder. I wonder if you really meant it. If you really deserved to end up like this.'

She got up, a hand on her heart, located the wine bottle, and poured herself a glass.

'Rest in peace, old fucker,' she said, raising it high. 'No hard feelings.'

And she brought the glass to her lips, swallowed a mouthful, grimaced and put it down.

It would have been just the right sort of moment for Mum and Emma to tease her loudly. Instead they raised their glasses, nodding in silence, and we drank together, a funeral toast for a twenty-years-dead god.

Just as the spell broke and we were going to resume talking, I heard my name called from the road below the house. I craned my neck, and here was Ilana, in walking shoes, coming up with a group of people I recognised from the few times I'd been near the Children's lodgings.

'Are you coming with us, Victor?' she said.

I had entirely forgotten about the outing. Before I could find what to say, she walked up, saw the laden table and covered her mouth.

'I didn't mean to interrupt you, I'm sorry! Good afternoon, madam,' she said, nodding to Mum and smiling. Mum raised an eyebrow and smiled back. 'I told Victor he was welcome to join us on a botanical outing. But only if that doesn't interfere with your day.' She looked at the table, curiously. The smells wafting from the cooling dishes must have been arresting. I grinned.

'Want to try some? It's the best food I've ever had.'

She looked from me to Mum, uncertain, then nodded. Her face lit up when she bit into a piece of buttered toast and sliced truffles.

'This... It's wonderful. What is it?'

'Truffles,' I said.

Her eyes widened and she grinned.

'*Tuber aestivium*. Of course, they're in season! What are you celebrating?'

There was an exchange of looks around the table. Ilana's face went red.

'I'm so indiscreet. Forgive me!'

I drew a chair closer, not knowing what to say, and poured her a glass of wine. She hesitated, and I remembered, too late, about her still, smiling friends waiting below on the gravel road.

She sat down, however, and if she had perceived the same awkwardness as I had, she didn't let it show. She smiled at Mum, exquisitely polite, while the three other women at the table glanced at one another and at me, as if they had no idea what language they should even be speaking to the girl who had just joined us.

I pushed my plate away.

'Don't want to hold you up,' I said. 'Shall we go?'

She rose at once.

'Marvellous idea. Thank you again for sharing your lunch with me, madam. You will have to tell me who you bought these truffles from. Unless it's a secret, of course!' She beamed, and I could swear she sketched a curtsey. Down below, her friends had barely exchanged a couple of words, and had turned to us again with bright smiles. There was something unreal about it all.

Mum gave a wave of her hand, coughing.

'Didn't buy them, exactly,' she said. 'You know.'

Ilana stopped. Her smile faltered.

'How interesting,' she said. 'A gift, then?'

There was a long silence, and I watched with increasing dread as Ilana's blood drained from her face, while her smile hung on, empty and strained like her friends'. Kahina was the first to break into a nervous laugh, as if these few seconds had made disaster unavoidable. Ilana covered her mouth with both hands.

'Oh dear. Oh God.'

I started to speak, fumbling for a justification, but she cut me off.

'You found these… in… in *His* body?'

Mum raised an eyebrow, as if Ilana's reaction merely took her aback. Ilana stared at me, opened her mouth without a sound. Then she turned away and ran back to the road. Before thinking, I ran after her.

'Ilana!'

She stopped and turned towards me. Tears ran down her cheeks and she stared in baffled, disappointed betrayal.

'I didn't mean…' I stammered. 'I didn't know…'

She wiped her eyes.

'You did, Victor. You did know.' She breathed and straightened, as if trying to reassert a dignity I didn't know I had ripped from her. 'I know this is nothing sacred to you. I know you don't believe. And I'm sad for you. Truly, I am. But I've tried not to show it. I've tried to respect you.' She shook her head. 'But you... you didn't even care. You didn't wonder what it would do to me to see His body turned into food, or to eat it without knowing. This is worse than spiting me. You didn't even consider that there could be any respect to show.'

With that she turned away and joined her friends, and I was left on the road, that brief sense of giddy joy I'd felt moments before slipping from my grasp.

I tried my best to behave companionably for the rest of the afternoon. No one was paying much attention to me anyway. Emma made a loud joke about the Children of Charity that sent a roar of laughter across the table. I winced, but didn't think anyone noticed it. The sun was low already when we cleared the table and shared the leftovers.

I stayed on the terrace after that, feeling the chill descend with the first flavours of autumn. I could not get Ilana's expression out of my head. Disrespect or desecration had been the last thing on my mind when I offered her our food. I had wanted to share something of mine, something precious, just like she had tried to share her knowledge and her Sunday walks with me. I had not understood anything.

Mum joined me just after the sun had disappeared. She was smiling; but from her quiet, the way she watched me, I knew she had understood what was wrong.

'You do like that girl, don't you?' she said.

I cringed. Mum might be perceptive, but tact was not usually her priority. I didn't have the courage to walk away just yet, however. I shrugged.

'She's a good teacher. And a friend. I didn't think she would react like that.'

Mum had the grace not to point out my obvious lie. I'd never mentioned any kind of open friendship with Ilana. Really, I knew her very little. And now I would never get closer to her.

'Should I have known?' I said. 'Have I just behaved like an idiot?'

Mum spread out her hands, shaking her head.

'Maybe. Yes. I suppose. Here's the thing, Victor.' I started. I didn't expect her to look so serious all of a sudden. 'She could have known, too. She knows what I do. You haven't been pretending to be a believer, have you?'

I shook my head. From Ilana's previous reactions, it had been very clear that she knew I didn't share her faith.

'But she blamed you all the same for not acting like one,' Mum said. She still looked very grave. 'Please watch out, Victor. These people may be pleasant, but they're fanatics. There's no telling what they can do.'

'They're believers!' I said, immediately ashamed of how my voice had risen.

'No. Kahina's a believer. These people are something else. I'd rather you didn't get too close to them, at least for a little while.'

An instinct told me that I should defend Ilana, at least. Then I thought of her friends, the discomfort I always felt in front of their too-bright smiles. I couldn't answer anything.

'I want to go to Ilana's class tomorrow,' I said after a moment. 'To apologise, at least.'

'I don't think this is a good...'

'Please.'

Mum was silent for a while.

'Fine,' she said. 'Tomorrow. We'll have to discuss this again afterwards, though.' Then she rose and laid her hands flat on the table. 'But tell these people one thing. If they so much as look at you the wrong way, I'll kick up such a hell inside that precious god of theirs he'll smash them down with his fist just to have some peace and quiet.' She swallowed. 'No fanatic is going to touch a hair on my son's head. Make sure you tell Ilana that.'

She squeezed my shoulder and went back inside, and I felt even colder than before.

Ilana was the exact same person when I saw her in class the next day: happy, serene, smiling – though none of her smiles were directed at me. As I watched her pray with renewed fervour amid a group of equally rapt students, my conversation with Mum came back. Mum's job was the most terrifying I had heard of. But her hands on the table had shaken, and my mind kept circling back to that astonishing realisation: I'd never seen her afraid of anything or anyone, before Ilana, my pretty mild-mannered teacher, stopped by our house with her too-polite friends.

Our school day was drawing to a close and I dithered as the first students left. Ilana was already packing her books, and she hadn't so much as glanced my way. My mind raced for something to say, a chance to make amends, to understand what had gone so terribly wrong. For a moment, figuring out how I could undo my stupidity of the previous day was the most important thing in the world.

That lasted until I saw Kahina ride her bike up to us. Until I noticed the streak of blood running down her overall.

I sprang up, heart hammering, desperate denials pounding through my head. When I reached her, I was dizzy with terror, with the certainty of what she was going to say.

Kahina jumped off before the bike had stopped, her chest heaving crazily, and spat on the ground before staggering onward. She wiped sweat and blood off her face, then off her hand, before taking my arm.

'Your mother is trapped in there. There was an explosion.' She swallowed a wheezing breath. 'The Children sabotaged our tunnel. Followed us and blew it up. Emma was already outside, *hamdullah*. She pulled me out. Your mother...'

I closed my eyes, pleading in silence.

'She was alive, last time we could check,' she said. 'But she couldn't get out. Victor, I'm so sorry. We tried to stay. The Children drove us away. Two of us against twelve...'

I realised that I'd forgotten to breathe for a few seconds. I forced my lungs to move again. The Children. I looked at Ilana, desperately hoping that something miraculous would happen and make things right.

Ilana had blanched. She ran to me and Kahina, who ignored her.

'I'm going to the cathedral, tell the doctors what happened,' she continued. 'They'll send a rescue team. We'll try to get her out. If the tunnel hasn't completely collapsed, that is.'

And this time she looked at Ilana, with sad, brutal contempt.

Ilana grabbed my hand.

'I didn't think they'd do something like this, I swear,' she breathed out. 'Victor. I swear I didn't even know they could make explosives. I thought they'd pray for you. I didn't think…'

I yanked my hand back.

'You fucking well didn't, I can see that,' I said, forcing myself to laugh before I burst into tears.

Ilana tried to stop me, but I pushed her away and ran, ran, with Kahina calling after me and then giving up.

I didn't stop running when it started to hurt. I didn't stop running when it became plain to me that I should have followed Kahina, and cried like a baby while she held me in her arms. I stopped running when I hit a rock and fell to the ground, sobbing, and that was when I smelled the scent of honey and alcohol rising from the rotting fruit of the elephant tree.

It towered, ten metres tall and even wider, trunks splitting at its foot like a giant's limbs. I thought of Dad's pictures of the disappearing whale, of the letter Mum and I had penned and sent not two days before, of his relief when he'd get it, knowing we were well, knowing *she* was well – except by that time she might be dead and there would be no way for him to know it before weeks had passed – and for all I knew the exact same thing had happened already and our letter would never arrive because his ship had sunk and I was an orphan and wouldn't know it for days – and I ran to the tree and stumbled, clambered up, embracing the branches, feeling the prickle of their sticky sap on my skin, and I cried and climbed up until the foliage hid me from the world.

It was dark inside the tree, and the branches flexed under my weight, springy yet strong. I went up, and up. Overhead, the canopy stretched, leaves flecked with bright blue and starbursts of sunlight, but all I could see was green, and grey snaking boughs stretching as far as the eye could follow. I embraced the tree, grating my cheek against its bark. Rounded fruit hung at arm's reach, pale green veined with purple, some with a clear drop of nectar emerging between pale pink petals. I touched their skin, mellow, just yielding to the touch. I picked one, and bit into it.

Grainy, tangy sweetness filled my mouth, with the chewy honeyed flavour of the nectar, and I took another bite, then another, heedless of the doctors' warnings or the Children's indignation, I feasted until nothing else existed, nothing but the cathedral of leaves, the full flavours and white sap coating and prickling my tongue, the sky, the air –

– the rocks embedded in my skin and my face pressed into relentless ground

– Ilana's tears when I betrayed her and the tears she had the gall not to shed immediately when she betrayed me

– air in motion, a star radiating heat on my back relentless through summer, colder air, rocks pressed into me the cold of stars and darkness the burning ripping through compressed air falling into the gravity well no way out no way to tear free falling falling *falling…*

– Mum's trapped in there and there's nothing I can do

– creatures prickling crawling on me in me pushing digging growing flowing blossoming sunlight precious sunlight on my leaves little creatures digging prickling inside my fruit shivers and rocks and dirt splitting my face open breaking my insides up – *WHO ARE YOU? What are you doing to me?*

Nothing! I did nothing, what are you doing in my head?

In your head in my body the creature inside me crawling pushing growling pushing out

Mum! Is that her? Are you talking about her? Where is she? Oh God, please. Help her out.

And in a flash I was the earth and the roots and the rocks, and I felt her. Saw her, though it was perfectly dark, was aware of her with every bit of my body as she forced breath in and out, as she made herself feel the rocks around her through a blanket of pain; methodically twisting and prodding them, hoping for one of them to budge. I felt her twisted legs, her hissing breath when pain stabbed her as she attempted to shift, her deep intake of air, eyes closed, and then she pulled her legs from underneath her and screamed my name in a broken howl.

My mind reached out for the rocks, but met nothing, did nothing, only forced useless strength through stony limbs

Get her out!

– millions of creatures water streaming too hot too cold the radiations of stars black holes tearing space apart entropy pulling life apart creatures resisting vanquished still growing still strong pushing through growing leaves

Get her out!

– leaves reaching sunlight benevolent at last and growing unfolding flowing upward upward through sap through leaves wasps on my skin rocks inside moving pain flowing

'GET HER OUT!'

I screamed and dug my hands into the branches until I felt the branches like my own body. I screamed and pushed impotent strength forward, through taut muscles and anguished brain and the vessels in the wood and the roots and water and sap flowing and oozing and ebbing free. I screamed and drowned in void and rocks and swirls of dying stars. I screamed until there was nothing left in the world but falling, and falling, and breaking and reforming and still somehow being, and then I kept screaming.

Then I sat on the ground, sore and cold and bewildered, and when I brushed twigs away from my face and looked up at the tree, the canopy shrank back down, a second of that dream-like sense of displacement quickly replaced by the reality I'd always known: a beautiful, quiet pachyderm of a tree, leaves swaying like huge fans in the wind.

I blinked, tried to hold on to the dream, memories coming back in a dazed trickle. But all I could see was the mountain coming back into focus, the corpse draped over it, and a moment of merging that had somehow left so much unanswered – *Who are you, really? Can you see us? Did you ever care?*

Does it hurt?

There was nothing echoing in my head, except for the blood beating in my temples. There was no blood when I touched my face.

I wondered if I had truly climbed up there, and if I would be able to go back if I wanted. I didn't think so. I could hardly remember the climb itself. Whatever had pulled me up there, drawn that gigantic mind into my own…

Mum.

I got to my feet, swayed, cried out. Then a sound of flying gravel answered.

'Victor?'

I grabbed a branch. It was more flexible than I expected, and it gave way, exposing the road and the figure approaching on her bike.

'Victor! For fuck's sake, boy, I've been looking for you all over the place! Where have you been?'

Kahina raced towards me, jumped off her bike and let it drop in the ditch, then pulled me off the tree and steadied me with both hands. Her face was smeared yellow and wrapped in bandages. Blood was still drying on her clothes.

'Didn't want to go after you when you ran off,' she said, almost as if this warranted an apology. 'You just looked like you needed… well. Time to yourself, or something. But they all gave me hell like never before when I arrived down there, so I went all over the neighbourhood to find you. You'd just vanished.' She shook her head. 'It's lucky I decided to check that tree again just in case. By the Quran, Victor, whatever got into you?'

I looked up. We were standing below the lowest branches, and the ground was sticky with drying fruit. I could still feel the crunch of seed on my tongue. I didn't say anything.

'Do you think you could get behind me on the bike?' she added. 'You're in no state to walk to the cathedral.'

'Cathedral?'

She nodded, grinning.

'They're patching your mum up. She has a couple of broken bones, but she's fine. Tunnel did collapse after all, but not the way we feared. The rocks just tumbled out. We got the police there in time to lock the Children up and retrieve her. She hadn't even passed out. She was crying for you. And for a cup of *mate* with morphine in it.'

I started laughing. My back ached, and my arms were streaked with red welts, tender with the sting of fig sap. I wondered how high I'd really been when I'd fallen, if I only owed my life to the thick boughs that had broken my fall. I got up, feeling nothing more than a few bruises. I winced when I arranged myself on the carrier, but Kahina had already started pedalling, racing down the road towards the cathedral.

I dismounted before she even stopped, and ran inside, until I found the stretcher by the baptistery, carts and drips crammed to the side and nurses bustling around. I threw my arms around Mum and she held me close, made a sound that could have been delight or pain, then held me back at arm's length and frowned.

'What happened to you?'

I wondered if I'd ever truly know – or if the answer was the simple certainty I'd had all along. I'd visited God's dreams, a bewildered chaos that death had not extinguished. I'd felt the Earth against his body, his very substance leaking into the ground, absorbed into roots, ripening into fruit. Somehow, in the dream, I'd reached her. What had happened next, whether I'd managed to push the rocks away or only luck had done that, was anyone's guess.

I was about to speak, when an exasperated exclamation from Kahina interrupted me.

'Don't you have any common decency, girl?'

I turned around, just as the dark outline cutting on the light in the doorway resolved into Ilana's features.

She stopped and bowed her head.

'I just wanted to say how sorry I am. I had no idea they could do such a thing. We all were appalled. We just…'

Kahina slapped her fist into her palm, but Mum put a hand on her elbow, placating her.

'Let her say it if she wants to. She can piss off when she's done.'

Ilana winced at the coldly-delivered humiliation.

'We've tried to ask you to stop before,' she said. 'You all carried on, even though you said you were getting nowhere. You laughed at us. You…'

Kahina wrestled free this time, and strode towards Ilana, who took a step back.

237

'If you think you're going to rub this in our faces...' she began. In two steps, I was wedged between them.

'I ate the figs!' I blurted out.

Everyone fell silent. I heard breaths sucked in, nurses swearing in low voices. Ilana made the sign of the cross. Mum propped herself up.

'What? Why?'

I looked from her to Ilana. I could tell them about the visions, the confusion, the stranded mind that waited, dreaming, in a body that was already merged with our world. I could tell Mum and she'd say she had been right all along, there was nothing useful to be expected from God, as everyone with a bit of sense had always known. I could tell the doctors and they'd say they had always known it, that he was our very first encounter with an alien being. I could tell Ilana and she'd fall to her knees in ecstasy, at this ultimate proof that God was still alive somehow, still here for her.

I shrugged.

'I just did,' I said. 'Nothing happened. I fell from the tree afterwards, though. I don't remember much.'

'That reminds me, I brought you here to have your head checked,' Kahina said. 'Don't you go getting concussions when we're not watching you.'

I nodded, turning my back on Ilana, in hope that she would seize this opportunity to leave without any more fuss. But she only waited until I stepped away, and looked at Mum again.

'What I meant to say is, I was wrong,' she said. 'I should have understood it would end like this. They'd been angry at you for a while. I pretended not to see it and it was my fault. I'm sorry.'

That made even Kahina go silent. As for Mum, she bothered to look at Ilana for the first time.

'You realise that they've been arrested,' she said. 'There will be a trial. For all we know, the Children of Charity will be disbanded.'

'I know. I'll keep teaching, whatever happens.'

And then she turned back at last, and walked back through the door, into the quiet pool of sunlight on the cobblestones. A nurse was already trying to lead me to a chair. I shook my head.

'I'll be right back,' I said, and I ran outside.

I spotted her at last, walking up the street with hunched shoulders.

'Ilana!' I called.

She stopped and looked back, uncertain, as I closed the distance between us. I had not thought of what I was going to say. It seemed that both of us were past apologies at this point, both in need of a fresh start.

'It's okay,' I said.

She smiled, sadly, as if thinking the same thoughts I was having. Good intentions were fine, but there would be no erasing what had just happened, what could have happened to my mother. Trust might come back, in time, but by then it would be far too late for Sunday afternoon walks or friendly conversations on the way home.

Yet we had to try. We didn't know what could be mended, or how; only that the truths that had caused her tears and my dismay and festered until they nearly cost my mother's life had not been erased, and, in another life, they would have hopelessly pulled us apart. But new truths were ours to make, to use in whatever way we wished. God was dead, the old world was destroyed, and as the last rays of the sun bounced off the walls of the cathedral to pool around our feet, I knew that I would never be bound by what had once been normal. The world would grow bountiful again in the dwindling shadow of God's dreaming body, and we would live, and grow, and do better, if we could.

It looked as if Ilana would reply, then realised that even the most careful of words would only hold us firmly to a place we both wanted to leave.

'Will you come to school tomorrow?' she said.

'Course I will.' I smiled in turn. 'I mean, I'll still phase out during prayers and all that stuff. But I still like botany. And books. And I think you're a really good teacher, when you're not talking about God.'

She grinned. It was a beautiful sight, and I took it with gratitude.

'Well.' I bit my lips. 'See you tomorrow?'

'Yes. Thank you, Victor.'

She walked back up the street and soon disappeared among bikes and carts coming home. There were voices, cries of birds and whispers of wind, blissfully alive as the summer ended. Summer was the only thing that was going to end right now.

I went back to the cathedral where the voice of the land, the drone of computers and a myriad little rustles drowned out the voice of God, thinking of the taste of figs on my tongue, and of the many, many years still stretching ahead of me.

On 16th October 2020, a history and geography teacher near Paris was murdered in front of his school. The attacker stated that he had done it in retaliation, after the teacher had, as part of a lesson on recent events, shown his students the infamous caricatures of the Prophet Muhammad that had led to the slaughter of the Charlie Hebdo journalists five years before.

Like many teachers, I was deeply shaken at the thought that we could be murdered for simply doing our job. The direction public debates took in the immediate aftermath of the attack, led in part by far-right voices, was an added layer of pain.

The present lends itself well to despair. It is easy to feel that the world is going mad, and what could be more understandable than the urge to seek simple answers? History has shown that casting blame was always easier than thriving for a real solution, one that might require large-scale adjustments and sacrifices. And as in most difficult times, scapegoating has reared its head, threatening to throw politics into disarray. Enough venom is thrown at migrants, gender theories, the nebulous concept of 'wokeism', environmentalists, even democracy itself to relegate vital concerns into the shadows – climate change and wars and all the misery that goes on unseen in the world.

Apocalypses are not beautiful, or romantic, or solemn. I don't know if we're living in one. What I do know is that fascism, pandemics and climate change are a potent and poisonous cocktail. We need an antidote, and we need it now. Writing this story was my own private antidote to a tiny bit of poison that had seeped into my life. Not to cast blame, not to shout at the sky, not to feel sorry for myself – but to grope in the dark for whatever way forward might remain. To look around for what might still be worth saving and find that, in the end, pretty much everything is, however that might still be done.

As I wrote earlier – I don't have answers, and I don't think I ever will.

But I still have stories.

About the Author

Cécile Cristofari lives in South France, where she teaches English literature and writes stories when her children are asleep. Her work has appeared or is forthcoming in *Interzone, Clarkesworld, ParSec* and elsewhere. She can be found online at: https://staywherepeoplesing.wordpress.com.

ALSO FROM NEWCON PRESS

Polestars 1: Strange Attractors – Jaine Fenn
First full collection from the award-winning author of innovative science fiction and off-kilter fantasy; features her finest short stories, selected by the author, drawn from more than two decades of publication, including the BSFA Award-winning "Liberty Bird", a Hidden Empire story, and a new tale, "Sin of Omission", written specifically for this collection.

Polestars 2: Umbilical – Teika Marija Smits
Debut collection from one of the finest short story writers to emerge on the genre scene in recent years. Her storytelling relies on keen observation of the world and people around her interpreted through the lens of her imagination, dancing between science fiction, realism, and horror.

Polestars 3: The Glasshouse – Emma Coleman
Contemporary tales of rural horror and dark fantasies steeped in folklore from one of genre fiction's best kept secrets. A young divorcee relocates to a quaint rural hamlet but is mystified by the hostility of her neighbours…A man discovers an item in a junkshop that puts him in fear of his life… An impresario dispenses justice while performing as a magician…

Polestars 4: Our Savage Heart – Justina Robson
The first collection in twelve years from one of the UK's most respected and inventive writers of science fiction and fantasy. 100,000 words of high quality fiction, that gathers together the author's finest stories from the past decade, including a brand new piece written especially for this collection.

Polestars 6: Drive or Be Driven – Aliya Whiteley
Eighteen short stories by one of today's most innovative genre writers. Half have been previously published, half are original to this collection, all are related to cars and forms of travel.
"When I read Whiteley's short stories I think of Japanese netsuke – magnificent miniatures, perfect in every detail."
– M.R. Carey

www.ingramcontent.com/pod-product-compliance
Lightning Source LLC
Chambersburg PA
CBHW031219260626
47169CB00007B/2117